Renegade WASP

By Jeff Gordon

MoJuiced—Millsboro, DE
ISBN: 978-0-578-50930-3
Library of Congress Control Number: 2019910881
Available Formats: eBook | Paperback

Cover by Ray Daminger Design (Lewes, DE)

WASP Dedication

Love and thanks to Arlene, Eric, Bob and Carol Renauld, for your belief and encouragement, and to my cat Peaches for keeping me company while I was writing.

In remembrance of the eight young soldiers from our small community who were killed during the Vietnam War, and who are greatly missed.

The traditional standards upon which this country was built and governed down through the years are in danger of losing authority largely because the American upper class, whose White-Anglo-Saxon-Protestant members may still be deferred to and envied because of their privileged status, is no longer honored in the land. For its standards of admission have gradually come to demand the dishonorable treatment of far too many distinguished Americans for it to continue, as a class, to fill its traditional function of moral leadership.
(E. Digby Baltzell, *The Protestant Establishment*)

Prologue
This Is For You, Holly

I received the news about Holly Chase's death shortly after she passed away in 2012. It was an obit from a suburban Chicago newspaper, sent with a note from a friend of her mother, Laura.

Holly was my first girlfriend, and a central character throughout my life. Writing about our time together has become a way to reconnect, and reflect on the events which created such a strong bond between us. Events I would have liked to alter, but now can only report.

Holly died at age 64 of liver disease and left one daughter, Laurel. She had been co-owner of a financial and estate planning business, and, the obit reported, enjoyed "sailing, tennis and the visual arts." Sadly, her death at an early age was not a surprise.

This is both a love story and a life story. It's about how the clay of our character gets shaped, pummeled, teased and transformed by a procession of potters.

Holly would tell you she always knew how to make my clay rise. She had a bold sense of humor. Physically, she'd remind you of the Ally Sheedy character in *The Breakfast Club*. She always smelled like a combination of Old Spice and incense, and as the expression goes, was "sixteen going on forty" when I met her.

She was also, unfortunately, the daughter of David Chase, who came to my potter's wheel with a pound of shit and a twisted heart. He owned the largest estate in Atlantic Villas: my hometown's wealthiest and most exclusive community.

Chase became the ringleader of a group of WASP cronies known locally as "the Four Aces." Think "Old West gang in pinstripes." So much to tell you about those boys.

My hometown is Wampum, a picture-postcard seaside village on Boston's South Shore, partway between Beantown and the Cape. Some folks refer to the area as "the Irish Riviera," which reminds me of my dad's reference to "the lace curtain Irish." But most of Wampum's early wealth was Old Yankee.

If you look at us on a map, we're almost completely round, like a sand dollar. We have one of the most-photographed town commons in America, with its centerpiece churches: Congregational, Unitarian and us Episcopalians, up on a granite ledge, looking down on everyone, especially the Catholics.

Wampum began as a shipbuilding and fishing port and has morphed with the times. As my story begins, the town is enjoying a sudden influx of World War II vets and their Baby Boom offspring. That includes my father Richard Peirce, my mother Elizabeth ("the Princess"), her eccentric mother Harriet ("Hat") and me, Jack, the first of two boys.

My dad is a former Navy man who wants his own boat and a little mooring at the harbor. Other new settlers are rising executives, college professors, medical professionals and the always intriguing "people with money." They come seeking better schools and neighborhoods and, secretly, the status that attaches to their new address.

The rest is dedicated to you, Holly. I'll do my best to get it right.

Let us go then, you and I...

Chapter 1
Blooming Boomer (1947)

On September 27, 1947 I emerged from my mother Elizabeth and dropped headfirst into the Baby Boomer generation—the enormous "pig in the python" postwar population explosion.

I had become a Peirce: a middle class WASP family which now had a cast of four...my father Richard, production manager for a rainwear company; my exhausted but elated mother; her mother, my grandmother Harriet ("Hat") Wadsworth, who secretly wanted a girl; and me, who within minutes would be peeing on everybody.

We were the sons and daughters of parents who grew up poor, thanks to the Stock market crash of 1929 and the years of financial misery that followed.

As if the Great Depression wasn't enough of a character builder, America's sons and daughters had to save the world from a monomaniacal villain and his Axis of evildoers.

Needless to say, postwar parents were seeking a kinder, more peaceful and prosperous world in which to raise their families. As it turned out, many of us would turn their plain vanilla worlds upside down and inside out. We would embrace pagan music, flaunt our long hair, ingest non-prescription drugs, scorn the Vietnam conflict and admire ourselves for choosing "the road not taken."

But back to the cradle...It's 1947. Harry Truman—known as "HST" ("Horse Shit," not "Harry S") to my Republican parents—is President and, looking back, everything is absurdly inexpensive. A new house costs $6650, a new car $1290 and a movie ticket 55 cents. Gasoline is 15 cents a gallon and you can mail a letter for 3 cents. These are all affordable on an average annual income of $2854, which is about what a mediocre major league baseball player now earns for every at-bat.

This is cruel information for parents currently being bled dry by college costs, but in 1947, tuition to Harvard was $420 a year. And back then, collegians would usually leave home after graduation, rather than continuing to run up the tab by relocating to their former seat at the family dinner table.

It's a banner year for the birth of famous people, who can barely wait to "jump the crib." Farrah comes right out of the Fawcett. Doug Henning appears as if by magic. Arnold Schwarzenegger starts pumping his mommy's iron. Bob Weir is Grateful not to be Dead. David Letterman keeps waking up at 11:30pm. Stephen King has vivid nightmares while Hillary Clinton dreams of being president. The Danson family "Cheers" little Ted's arrival. Cheryl Tiegs is a model of good behavior. Elton John, Carlos Santana, Don Henley and David Bowie all "rock the cradle," while Nolan Ryan tosses his ball to Johnny Bench, who passes it to Kareem (born Lew Alcindor) for the dunk.

The Red Sox play their first night game at Fenway Park in June, and of course the Yankees win another World Series. My dad, who bled Red in his Sox every season like the rest of New England, had no way of knowing there would be no World Series banner in Boston until long after his death in 1975. T.S. Eliot was correct: April is the "cruelest month," because for Sox fans it planted hopes that by September were dead on the vine.

On a more positive baseball note, in 1947 Jackie Robinson becomes the first African American to play major league baseball, for Branch Rickey's Brooklyn Dodgers. (Pumpsie

Green was Boston's first black ballplayer, but not until the late fifties, by which time every other team had integrated.)

The world war battlefields are quiet, but ideologies continue to clash. The House UnAmerican Activities Committee opens hearings into alleged Communist activities in Hollywood, and would find the "Hollywood 10" in contempt for refusing to reveal if they or their friends were commies. The UN General Assembly partitions Palestine between the Arabs and Jews, and the day after the decree, Jewish settlements are attacked. An NAACP petition on racism, "An Appeal to the World," is presented to the UN, but fails to inspire a worldwide embrace of diversity.

In the entertainment world, "You Bet Your Life" premieres on ABC Radio, and you can bet your life we Peirces watched Groucho when his show got televised. (TV was the Boomers' "nanny," and we would continue to crave all the electronic stimulation that followed.). On Broadway, Marlon Brando electrified audiences in the premiere of Tennessee Williams' *A Streetcar Named Desire* and created one of modern theatre's most enduring anti-heroes.

***

Meanwhile, my parents are transporting their adorable little bundle back home to Wampum in their Chevy—back to their grey stucco home on Bayberry Road, which at one time had been the servants' quarters to the Colchester estate next door.

We lived less than a mile from my dad's beloved ocean. He had left the Navy to help his ailing father run a barely-breaking-even sporting goods store, but friends often said he should have remained in the service.

3

My mother loved the beach, but had no passion for the sea, or much desire to venture into it. Wampum Beach was her sandbox—a place to play cribbage and catch up with friends during the painfully short summer season.

As an infant, you don't retain an abundance of quality memories. You're just a whining little bundle of pee, poop and saliva, craving food and gnawing on the rug. Later on, you come to realize how many people helped you develop your brain cells and motor skills, but if you're a male you probably don't thank anybody.

I remember the sensory things, like the seductive taste of sugar, the caress of a warm cloth diaper, the smell of fresh baby powder, the sound of my mother's voice after my long cry and the first rays of sunshine on the wallpaper. There's a lot of "alone time" for an infant, so you're grateful to anyone who rescues you from the monotony of the crib.

While much is lost to "infant amnesia," I can still vaguely remember the nocturnal visits of my grandmother "Hat." My mother's mother, she had come to live with my parents after her husband Harold died from dementia-related hypothermia. He was a night watchman who apparently locked himself out of a warehouse on a bitterly cold Boston night, fell asleep outside the door and was found frozen to death the following morning.

Most spouses would have changed the post-mortem details to whitewash the dementia, but not Hat. She actually enjoyed telling horrified listeners the grim story of how "poor Harold was found frozen stiff as a fish stick, and it took the undertaker three days to thaw him out. The keys were right in his coat pocket."

What I remember is the sound of Grammy Hat whispering to me in the middle of the night. She made what seemed like bird sounds and when I awoke she stroked me very gently to

4

keep me from crying. Not every night, but now and then. Apparently she would do this after listening to classical music or a Red Sox night game. She would lift me gently over her head and carry me around the room like Peter Pan. Thus was born an everlasting bond between us: the grey-haired aviatrix and her smiling little projectile.

When Hat didn't show up, I was occasionally visited by a wickedly scary "night terror." It began as a deep voice, summoning me into the upstairs hallway. Suddenly, I would be standing at the top of the steps, staring down into the beckoning darkness. What was it that wanted me? Grandpa Harold, looking for his key? As I was sucked downward I'd start screaming, and usually it was Hat (my mother being a "sound sleeper") who'd come and rescue me.

That's the thing about sleep…You never know what's going to come swimming up from your subconscious.

Our youthful memories are random, and stored in a musty, mental file cabinet. Fortunately, there are black-and-white photo books containing the images our relatives wanted to preserve. Me in my backyard sandbox with a pail and shovel…sitting on my tricycle in a Hopalong Cassidy hat and six-shooter…showing off a pickerel and bluegill that my dad helped me hook. Me with chicken pox at my fifth birthday party, infecting my playmates so they wouldn't be stricken later in life. Getting a haircut from my mom on a Sunday afternoon while she watched Liberace.

The less savory escapades didn't make the scrapbook, like me drinking blue cleaning compound and being rushed to the hospital to get my stomach pumped. No photo of my black eye after a forbidden neighborhood chestnut fight. And no image of the almost-life-sized Thanksgiving turkey I crayoned on my white bedroom wall.

While the photos had their place on the bookshelf, it was TV that introduced us to new companions and experiences. We were the Television Generation, and we rode its magic carpet from cartoons to Tarzan's jungle to Wild West gunfights to creatures from outer space, all in the flick of a dial. It was the beginning of an electronic addiction that continues to dilute our brain tissue.

My favorite TV program as a child was *The Howdy Doody Show*, which spanned the years from my boyhood to adolescence (1947-60). I joined the Peanut Gallery and embraced the zany menagerie of Doodyville characters Buffalo Bob and his staff served up to us: Howdy (with Bob's voice, prerecorded), Clarabell (Bob Keeshan, who later became Captain Kangaroo), Dilly Dally, Chief Thunderthud and the captivating Princess Summerfall Winterspring (who would eventually leave the show to star with Elvis in *Jailhouse Rock*. Under a different name, I assume.)

How appropriate that the villain, Mayor Phineas T. Bluster, was the president of the Bluster National Bank, which held the mortgage to Howdy's hometown. Little did we know how many Bluster-y bankers would cross our paths in years to come.

For me, nostalgia begins with *Howdy Doody*. He was a boyhood buddy whose daily appearance you eagerly awaited. And *Howdy* was <u>our</u> show—not something we had to watch with adults. Disney entertained us at a higher technical level. But my roots were in Doodyland with Howdy's gang and Clarabell's seltzer bottle. Cowabunga!

Howdy notwithstanding, you soon learned that the Big People in the household were in charge. You followed orders. If you misbehaved you got varying levels of physical or verbal abuse. I was seldom disciplined in my early years, and when I was sent to my room for some peccadillo it hardly felt like punishment. I'd just sit in the corner and read one of my Thornton Burgess animal books. Words and pictures; almost as good as gumdrops.

Unless you were one of the few juvenile deviants in town, you ate your vegetables, behaved on the school bus, hung out with the neighborhood kids and "followed the script."

With a few variations, the script for "Growing Up in the Suburbs" included junior membership in your parents' churches, and favorite youth organizations, like Cub Scouts, the community center, the sailing club and Little League. If you were lucky, you avoided piano lessons.

But the girls couldn't escape being groomed for "Life as the Perfect Wife" through ballet or singing lessons, shopping at upscale department stores, proper application of makeup, "attention to domestic duties" and other feminine talents deemed important by the mother.

If you were Holly Chase—my first girlfriend, and clearly a "debutante-to-be"—additional skills would be needed to succeed in the Upper Echelon. You'd need to buy the right labels and look good in them, including clothes with your initials. You'd need to be able to discern vulnerabilities in your female social peers and use them to your advantage.

Athletically, you'd be expected to "hold serve," "sink the five-footer" and "prepare the boat to sail."

In conversation with friends, you'd refer to your spouse by his first and last name. Mrs. Chase, for example, would report that "David Chase is a Scotch drinker," not just "David" or "My husband."

And sadly, you'd do anything to "preserve appearances," even if it meant taking a punch from your drunken husband. "Domestic violence" was something poor people committed. For the Upper Echelon it was implicit in the marriage vows. Any black and blue "badges" were to be carefully concealed and, when necessary, explained with a self-deprecating remark like "I'm always running into things."

All of this would seep in with age and observation. For now, life was mostly fun and games and easy arithmetic. Fishing for flounder off the coast. Eating Ipswich fried clams with tartar sauce. Reading the Landmark series of history books. Beating back a battalion of Nazis down at the beach with polished stone grenades.

Growing up in Wampum. What could be more perfect for a scholarly little white boy?

Chapter 2
Welcome to Wampum (1961)

The year before I entered high school, we had to write a minimum five-page report on the history of Wampum. It was a town tradition, and the winning paper got added to an aging archive of past prize winners at the Wampum Library.

The author got a $50 savings bond from the Wampum Historical Society, presented at a special eighth grade awards assembly by one of the Society's 200-year-old dowagers. Then the writer had to read the report to classmates, who would express their boredom, disdain or jealousy through a variety of ingeniously covert guttural noises.

I was the winner in my eighth grade class, and remember thinking before getting up to read my report that this would be the kiss of death for my high school social life. But my mother—Class Poet in her senior year-- was ecstatic. This was my emergence as a writer, under her tutelage, and she was there in the first row to catch the anticipated bouquets of praise.

The report was archived in my mom's "vault of academic treasures," and is as humorous and embarrassing as the newspaper photo of the dowager and me. But for all its dorkiness, the narrative confirmed that Wampum had been the stage for some fascinating characters and events.

What follows goes way above and beyond the sanitized report I submitted. It will become obvious in later chapters how and why I know this stuff.

Captain John Smith was the first to venture into Wampum, in 1614, sailing into what would become Wampum Harbor and proclaiming the region to be "the paradise of all these parts." In a 1616 map, he would apply the name "New England" to what would eventually become the six-state region.

The next significant date is 1665, when the inevitable "screw the Indians deal" was negotiated with the sachem Wampatuck of the Chickataubut tribe. Lacking any knowledge of property rights, and dazzled by a few shiny tokens, tribal leaders deeded away to the English the land that would become Amity, and later Wampum.

A brief historic footnote: The flag of the Commonwealth of Massachusetts features an Algonquian Indian, presumably acknowledging the bond between Native Americans and the early settlers. The Indian is framed by a blue banner containing the state motto which, translated from Latin, reads: "By the sword we seek peace, but peace only under liberty." As for the colonists' relationship to Native Americans, a more accurate motto would have been: "By the treaty we seek possession, and by the sword we assure it."

Another item of note: The Indian Metacomet, a Massasoit chief living nearby, at first tried to live in harmony with the colonists and adopted the European name of Philip, and later King Philip as the tribal leader. In 1671, the colonial leadership of Plymouth County forced major concessions from him, which included surrendering much of his tribe's ammunition and agreeing to be subject to English law.

Rethinking his mistaken strategy, Metacomet used tribal alliances to coordinate efforts to drive European colonists out of New England. When hostilities broke out in 1675, Metacomet and his followers retreated to nearby swamps. He was fatally shot by a Pocasset Indian who sided with the English, and his head was mounted on a pike outside Fort Plymouth, where it remained for more than two decades. His body was cut into quarters and hung in trees, and his wife and son were sold into slavery.

Interestingly, in the many years since Metacomet's death, numerous places in southeastern Massachusetts have been named after him, including a mountain range, a country club, a regional high school, streets, roads and even a US Navy ship. Not bad for a Renegade Chieftain.

Law and order was strictly maintained in the early days. Whipping posts and stocks were erected to punish the reprobates and heathens.

According to historical records, the miscreants were an odd lot. In addition to petty thieves, destructive drunkards and scam artists, "stock inmates" included adulterers, confessed atheists and many people who simply needed modern pharmaceuticals.

One unfortunate "criminal," way back in the late 1600s, was Abigail Cooper—accused of bearing the child of the town's Congregational minister and then suffocating it out of shame. She was sentenced to two weeks in the stocks but on her third frigid January morning she died of exposure. The mid-winter timing was meant to be harsh, since the murder of a newborn was involved. Abigail's death was almost inevitable unless Providence intervened and ordained warmer weather. It didn't, which to the villagers confirmed her guilt. The minister was allowed to leave town.

(Remember Abigail Cooper. She will return.)

Forging ahead on the historical timeline…In the mid-1700s, Amity began to take shape as a poster child of Anglo-Saxon adaptability to the New World. The First Parish Meeting House was built on Wampum Common (1747) and when the parish converted to Unitarianism in 1824 the Congregationalists built their own church across the street.

11

The Common would eventually become the religious and aesthetic center of the community.

When Amity was subdivided into two towns in 1794, the former Amity-ites considered a number of Biblically-inspired names for their new community. But after careful deliberation they decided on "Wampum" because it "combines commerce with cultural heritage."

Many years later, when aerial photography became popular, it was discovered that Wampum was remarkably close to circular in shape when you followed the boundaries. Town natives commented that it looked like a sand dollar, and that "Wampum" had certainly been the perfect and prescient choice for a name.

After the War of 1812, the town began to capitalize on its oceanfront location through shipbuilding and mackerel fishing. The Protestant Work Ethic was shifting into a higher gear, with the construction of new homes near the village, fishing vessels launched into the Atlantic, farming on the outskirts and concerted efforts to "plant seeds of knowledge and virtue" in young minds.

One of Wampum's early Significant Events was a nautical disaster. On October 7, 1849, an Irish "famine ship" ran aground about a mile offshore. On that deadly night, 99 passengers and crew perished in storm-battered seas; only 23 reached shore safely. The deceased who washed ashore in Wampum were buried in a mass grave.

Despite the tragic loss of life, the incident became a dark comic metaphor for Irish-Yankee relations in the mid-nineteenth century. The Irish predicted that local farmers would plant potatoes on the mass grave, as a "memorial" to the victims" and "so they wouldn't waste good farmland." For their part, the Yankee townfolk snickered that survivors had been offered passage back to Ireland on the lifeboat *Homesick*, along with a few heads of cabbage and a fishing pole.

This was only the beginning. A century later, ethnic animosity had intensified as the formerly oppressed Irish ("No Irish Need Apply") established a political stronghold in South Boston. Growing up in a WASP household, I heard almost nightly diatribes against Irish politicians, "lace curtain Irish," Irish Catholic "Papists" and of course the Kennedys: "Honey Fitz," Joe, Rose, and "the whole rotten bunch of kids and their corrupt, spoiled friends." More later.

Shortly after the shipwreck, a majestic beacon was built on the ledge where the ship had run afoul. It prevented any further maritime disasters and became a quaint, locally-marketed "must see" for tourists.

By the end of the 1800s, Wampum was transforming into a summer playground for the wealthy. They socialized at hunt club breakfasts and horse shows, played croquet at lawn parties, cruised on steam-powered yachts and danced at private formal fundraisers. Extravagantly-built villas and English country homes began to pop up, especially on North Wampum properties with ocean views. The privileged had discovered a perfect place to congregate—far enough away from lower class "hoi polloi" but close enough to access Boston's arts, culture and commerce.

One Yankee native—a local historian—described this chapter in the town's history as "the period when Wampum went feudal...when the 'codfish aristocracy' built their estates and the rest of us became their serfs." It continued that way for many years, through the tumultuous world wars, the Great Depression, and the gradual redistribution of wealth from those "born privileged" to those driven to succeed.

Not all those "driven to succeed" were welcome, however. Joe and Rose Kennedy tried to infiltrate the mostly-WASP "ruling elite," but were blackballed for membership at the Wampum Golf Club. They had to continue south to Hyannis Port to build their castle. (Many years later, JFK would win Massachusetts handily in the 1960 presidential election, but lost Wampum to Nixon by several hundred votes.)

The feudal metaphor works well for Wampum from the 1880s to the mid-twentieth century. Not a British but a Yankee aristocracy, with ultimate allegiance to the welfare of the town, but with clear-cut neighborhood boundaries. North Wampum was wealthy WASPs; South Wampum was farmers, lobster fishermen and blue collar workers; Central Wampum was the Common, now surrounded by local government and commerce. East and West were in the early stages of development, awaiting the "Wampumania Boom" of the fifties and sixties.

And the Peirces rode in on this high tide of newcomers, like shells and seaglass. It was our turn in an evolutionary procession that began with microbes, sea creatures, Indians, explorers, pilgrims, drowned Irishmen, wealthy merchants and now urban expatriates.

***

So as I began by saying, Wampum has been the stage for a fascinating series of events. ...The lights come up over the Atlantic, at the point where Greater Boston Harbor ends and Massachusetts Bay begins. The townfolk shuffle themselves to their appointed places—the women applying makeup, the men guzzling coffee, and both donning their white and blue collars.

We're not *Our Town*, although Thornton Wilder once performed nearby as the Stage Manager in a summer stock production of his famous play. We're more like "town

14

pageant meets soap opera." And I would argue that Wampum itself is a character as well as the setting... but you can decide.

It's about two weeks after my presentation of the prize-winning paper. As the day begins, my mother has bugled her daily wake-up call ("It's time to rise and shine"), and I'm stumbling into the bathroom to shave the few random hairs on my upper lip. There's a report on the radio that has caught her attention, and I hear her respond with surprise and dismay.

"There was a kidnaping yesterday at the A&P out on Route 4. A woman was putting her groceries in the trunk and when she got in the car her little daughter was gone." (This is before child safety seats.) "She said there were no other cars nearby and she didn't see anyone on foot. Dear God, what a tragedy!"

The story dominated the local, regional and eventually national media for weeks. Theories and opinions were expressed by law enforcement, media-recruited crime experts, family, friends and even psychics. In the end, every clue ran dry. The kidnaper was never captured. Jennifer Quarry, the cute little blonde daughter, was never found. The mother, who had continued to plead in vain for Jennifer's return, died a few years later in a head-on collision with a tree that most assumed wasn't an accident.

I went off to school that day, confident that at age 13 I wasn't "high risk" for kidnapping.

Welcome to Wampum, where these things never happen.

Chapter 3
Hat-echisms

My grandmother "Hat" Wadsworth was the least grammy-ish woman I have ever met in my years of meeting grammies. She was the anti-grammy, who played the role "against type" in what could have been her own smash hit sitcom called "Lock Grammy in the Basement."

She was my mother's mother, and the mother-daughter resemblance was striking, except for their height. My mother Liz was a conventional five feet four; Hat was almost six feet. (Not surprisingly, she claimed to be the illegitimate child of circus performers.) Neither mother nor daughter had an ounce of fat ("borderline skeletal" in Hat's words); both had long, elegant fingers (Hat: "Your mother had perfect hands for the piano, but no patience for practice."); and both had Jane Wyman-ish (the mother on TV's *Father Knows Best*) good looks.

Temperamentally, they seemed like polar opposites, but in retrospect perhaps not so much. The Great Depression and the war toughened them up and "straightened their backbones." Hat emerged as a wisecracking realist, my mother as a middle class WASP romantic. Mom was the Princess who didn't quite get the prince; Hat, the court jester, reminded her that life seldom ends "happily ever after."

Born in 1890, she had lived what many would call, but she would dispute, a "hard life." Her father was a drunkard who deserted Hat and her mother at the turn of the century to seek his fortune "in the gin trade." Hat, an industrious girl, worked at a bakery to help support her mother and graduated from

Medford High School (near Boston) with honors. She put herself through secretarial school—the only business career path then available to a woman—and worked successfully for many years at John Hancock Insurance.

While continuing to support and care for her ailing mother, Hat married the tragically-destined Harold in 1914 and they produced their only child, Elizabeth, in 1916. Harold was a "blue collar guy" who did "fixer upper" tasks, never made much money, but at least didn't abandon the household. This short bio is courtesy of my mother, because Hat never talked about her life. "She has very broad shoulders," my mother would say. "Few people know it, but that woman has endured the trials of Job."

These life experiences might well have produced a cynical sourpuss, but Hat was anything but. She was, in fact—as I later described her in my college application essay—"a bright spirit, who supported me in everything I attempted. She never behaved like an 'old lady' with limited patience for young people. Every day was an adventure, and she relished it. Best of all, she made us laugh, all the time...even my brother Frankie, who almost never laughs. She would take Yankee expressions or Biblical passages and give them her own hilarious twist. We called them 'Hat-echisms'. (OK...My mom helped me out with this. I wasn't mature enough yet to describe anyone as a "bright spirit." But I wrote a decent first draft.)

Not surprisingly, Hat was reluctant to come and live with my parents after Harold's death. She would tell my mother, "Why in God's name do you want an old bag of bones like me living under your roof? Talk about 'three's company'!" Or she would refer to her own experience as a care provider: "There were nights when your grandmother would be having a

17

coughing fit and I'd be thinking 'Sweet Jesus, do me a favor and take one of us!'"

But she finally acquiesced, largely because I had just been born and she could justify her role as "Nanny to the Little Prince." No one knew then, of course, that it would be the care and kindness she provided for my brother Frankie that held the family together and preserved some sanity for my confused and distressed parents. Being nanny to me was angel food cake compared to Frankie.

The thing about granny Hat was that she always appeared at just the right time. Our German shepherd puppy would poop on the floor and she'd clean it up with the flick of a wrist and a funny remark like "That's what puppies do...They do Doo Doo." Frankie would have a tantrum, throw his blocks around the room and Hat would come in and say, "Frankie...What's my little artist doing? Practicing to be an actor? We need to teach you some Shakespeare." Then she'd get down on the floor and help him build a fort with the blocks. Or she'd catch the smell of my mom's burning hamburger and rescue the meal by adding cheese.

My dad would often chuckle about my mother's cooking, but Hat would always come to her defense, just as my mom was getting irritated. "It's my fault. Blame it on me. I let her write poetry rather than develop her culinary skills." Hat would step in and cook dinner when she noticed her daughter looking tired or stressed. On those occasions, my father would lavishly praise the meal as my mother rolled her eyes. Hat would deflect the compliment by saying something like, "Liz does it better than I do. I'm just giving her the night off for good behavior."

It was at the family dinner table that I began to notice the gender imbalance in domestic duties. The women went to the market, prepared and served the food, put away the leftovers and washed the dishes. My father drank a glass of wine or two, enjoyed his meal and left the room without having to leave a tip. While mom and Hat occasionally joked in private about being the "Mother and Daughter Maid Service," they never complained in his company. And it wasn't like they lounged around and ate Hershey Bars all day. Both worked part-time. Mom did payroll for a local engineering company and Hat, remarkably, worked six hours a day at the post office, sorting mail. Hey, this was the "exclusive little village of Wampum," and the cost of being middle class was starting to go up.

Hat became a "Sunday surrogate" for my mom, a Congregationalist who found my dad's Episcopalianism a little too rich for her blood. Dad was a proud "Anglican Catholic," who considered every other Protestant denomination pitiably lowbrow. So on Sunday mornings it was dad, Hat (who always wore gloves) and me (whom dad had groomed as an acolyte) who were spiritually cleansed, while my mom cleaned the house. She joined us occasionally, "when the Holy Spirit moves me."

St. Matthews Episcopal was an austere granite Gothic structure, built on top of a stone ledge in the center of town. Like the shipwreck beacon, "Saint Matt's" was a tourist attraction. Its 57-bronze-bell carillon concerts attracted music lovers from far and wide. The carillon was a gift from Rosalind Sterling, a Wampum icon and daughter of an original owner of *The Wall Street Journal*. Hat described her as "a woman guaranteed admission not only to Heaven but to Heaven's board of directors."

My father reveled in every trapping of the Saint Matthews experience: the blonde wives with their preppily-attired children; the moment before the processional when the organ music swelled from diminuendo to crescendo and the congregation rose obediently; the talented and well-rehearsed choir, with its several paid soloists; the delicious fragrance of the incense; the beautifully-written Communion service, with its elegant prayers; the body and blood of Jesus, so fleeting to the taste but so fortifying. All this was, for my father, a deeply transcendent experience. He was in absolutely the right place with absolutely the right people, and he literally floated out of St. Matts, with the blessing of Father Noble a final cherry on his Sunday sundae.

While Hat was careful not to say anything to diminish my father's good mood, her experience was altogether different. What my father viewed as magnificent pomp, she saw as pompous. At some point during the day—usually while my father and I were watching pro football—Hat would take my mother out for a smoke and amuse her with observations about parishioners she deemed to be sanctimonious phonies.

"God, what's with Martha Craven?"...(Puff, puff)..."You could smell her perfume down in Duxbury!" (which was several towns south of us)..."And she was showing enough cleavage to get a free drink in the combat zone" (a well-known Boston red light district)...(Puff, puff)..."I know her husband's out of town most of the time, but the next thing you know she'll be taking an ad in the church bulletin: "Looking for a partner to read Scripture together"...(Puff, puff)..."BYOB, and I don't mean Bible!"

By this time, my mother is in hysterics, because this confirmed everything she believed about St. Matts churchgoers. And because Hat is hilarious, with that deadpan delivery of hers. The woman was gifted.

Here's a church-related anecdote that still makes me laugh out loud. My parents frequently hosted bridge parties. Bridge was very big "back in the day," before electronic entertainment made everybody a High-Def zombie. On this particular evening, Father Noble and his wife Sybil were among the guests. I was upstairs doing homework and at one point took a potty break.

About thirty seconds later, Hat appears in the open doorway of the bathroom and says indignantly, "What are you <u>doing</u> up here, peeing like a cow on the rocks!...The <u>minister</u> and his <u>wife</u> are downstairs!" I confess I was embarrassed about leaving the door open. But where Hat came up with "peeing like a cow on the rocks" I will never know.

There were two subjects about which Hat was especially vocal: New England winters and annoying behaviors. She had an impressive arsenal of Yankee expressions and self-diagnosed maladies she could apply to both.

Hat was an outdoor person: a gardener, a walker, a naturalist, an adventurer. Winter thwarted all of her favorite activities, and she took it very personally. She divided the year into two parts: the "season of light and life" (spring and summer) and "the season of dark and death" (usually beginning in late October, with the loss of late afternoon daylight, and continuing until she felt the temperature was "finally warm enough to bring the polar bears out of hibernation.") My mother claimed that Hat's seasonal metaphors "made me a poet. I came to see everything as growing in the light and dying in the darkness."

In the dead of winter, when she felt totally incarcerated by the weather, Hat would complain that "It's cold enough to freeze two dry rags together." When we got one of our famous Nor'easters, she'd say, "The wind is so strong it's blowing straight up and down." When the winter began to drag on interminably she'd gripe, "We have two seasons up here: winter and the Fourth of July." (Popular expression now, but not back then.) When spring finally made an appearance, Hat

21

would announce, "You can take off your top three layers of clothes. It's actually tolerable out there."

Winter aside, Hat's favorite subject was the peculiarities and eccentricities of human behavior, beginning with mine. When I didn't want to get out of bed on a school day, she'd tell my mother I had "blanket fever." If I left the dirty dishes lying around after dinner, she'd accuse me of being "allergic to dishwater." A few years later, when she knew I had a thicker skin, Hat would nail me for avoiding my chores. ("Jack, you're moving slower than a toad in a tar bucket!") When I'd try to explain why I didn't rake the leaves or trim the hedge, Hat would say in a mock-sympathetic tone: "It's OK, Jackie. I understand. You're not feeling well. You probably have water on the butt." That became a long-time joke with us. Whenever anyone was trying to fake it, we'd nod to each other and whisper "Water on the butt."

But Hat's sharpest salvos, by far, were aimed at the snobbish and pretentious, and there was a sizeable herd of them in Wampum. "I can spot a bluenose a mile away," she would exclaim. "They're the ones with the snotty handkerchiefs!" So, I came to learn, it wasn't just the cultural divide between the WASPs and the lace curtain Irish. It was the financial and social divide between the "salt of the earth" old Yankee stock and the upper-class aristocrats Oliver Wendell Holmes labeled "Boston Brahmins."

The bluenoses were guilty of believing that "their poop doesn't smell," and Hat had a long list of them, including several ministers and their wives (although not ours), the town librarian, most of the members of the Garden Club, all of the members of the "Hysterical (Historical) Society," and a very significant percentage of the North Wampum population, some of whose names will be revealed later. You could be wealthy and not a bluenose, but you had to have a sense of humor about yourself or some other redeeming virtue, like collecting scrimshaw or being kind to Frankie.

Grammy Hat will be with us for the entire narrative, so you'll hear more of her Hat-echisms. Let me share one more memorable moment.

During my first year on the Wampum cross country team, I got "the runs" during a race and had to finish with a hefty load of crap in my shorts. The visual was embarrassing enough, but the stench was worse than a bad chemistry experiment. I didn't want to say anything to my family, but I had to confess this mortifying experience to someone. I decided Hat would be less judgmental than my parents, and so shared my tale of woe in a voice quivering with shame.

When I finished, Hat put her arm around my shoulder and gave me a reassuring squeeze. "I know how terrible you must feel, but I want you to know how proud I am. You finished the race. You didn't run away and hide. That took real moxie (meaning "gumption") on your part."

She paused for a moment and then uttered these words of wisdom: "Listen…At some point in our lives, and usually many points, we all end up with poop in our pants. We can't avoid it."

It was my first epiphany.

You now have a "hot clue" as to how I became a Renegade WASP.

Chapter 4
Mud WASP

Before I continue with the story of my life as a young WASP, a little background on the origin of our species.

As I'll explain in a later chapter, I began writing a column for "non-traditional print media" in the early seventies, to generate some income and write editorials that were "outside the box." You won't be surprised to learn my *nom de plume* was *Renegade WASP*.

The "*RW*" columns gave me a voice and a readership, for which I'm grateful. They also inspire (present tense, because I'm still writing them) readership responses ranging from empathy to antipathy.

I'm going to drop in my first two *RW* columns—written in 1972--which were published in six metro weeklies in four New England states, and for which I was paid nothing. They're about the derivation of the acronym WASP by its creator E. Digby Baltzell, a gifted sociologist and University of Pennsylvania professor. I attempt to draw a parallel between WASPs and wasp insects, and to identify my place in the wasp "lowerarchy."

I will drop some "RW" segments into the narrative from time to time, and have included five of my favorites at the end.

***

Renegade WASP: The Buzz Begins

No doubt you're familiar with the acronym WASP: White

Anglo-Saxon Protestant.

It was popularized by E. Digby Baltzell, an eminent sociologist, author and professor at the University of Pennsylvania. His 1964 book **The Protestant Establishment: Aristocracy and Caste in America**—with chapters on "Caste and the Corporation," "Aristocracy on the Campus" and "The Club"—explores the gradual loss of moral authority among America's upper class elite.

This loss of authority, Baltzell declared, was the result of "anti-Semitism and ethnic prejudice" that made the WASP aristocracy reluctant to integrate The Club. While he seemed a model of WASPy decorum, biking daily from Rittenhouse Square to the Penn campus in his tweed jacket and bow tie, he had been deeply affected by his experience as a World War II naval aviator. He came to recognize that while social stratification was inevitable, the highest socioeconomic levels needed to be accessible by merit, not by birth...to Jews and minorities, not just WASPs. Baltzell's book has helped me—a middle class WASP Baby Boomer—understand my ancestral roots. And of course, there's the humorous connection between the human and insect species.

Wasps are parasites, and many of the 100,000 species are predatory. They provision their nests with insects and spiders (welfare applicants? illegal immigrants?) killed as food for their young. The wasp queen wanabees eat the eggs of their rivals, not unlike WASP trophy wives.

Yellow jackets are considered the "common wasp," and can sting repeatedly and painfully (think old guys in yellow blazers re-telling bad jokes at the bar). I most closely identify with the mud wasp, which is less aggressive and lives in humbler surroundings. We mud wasps have a different take on life, which I'll be sharing with you in the weeks to come.

Politically, socially, financially, philosophically…we fly to the beat of a different hummer.

Perhaps like you, I'm a Child of the Sixties, entering that incredibly transformative decade at age 13 and exiting at 23. Entering while watching a black-and-white TV western and exiting after *Midnight Cowboy*. Entering a sexual "wannabe" and exiting with the question *"Who do I wannabee?"* Consider all the cultural ingredients that "seasoned our broth" as young adults. Some of us became carnivores, some herbivores (or herbinhalers), some family-centric, some self-centric and, yes, some ec-centric.

Me, I became a Renegade WASP. Next week: *What's that?*

***

WASPville

Last week I introduced myself as a Renegade WASP. What is this odd species?

In the insect realm, it's a "solitary wasp" which prefers living in the mud to life in the Big Hive. In human terms, it's a WASP who can't afford an expensive home and lacks the wardrobe to masquerade as a preppie at "madras pants parties."

In WASPville, the privileged WASPs may actually mix with the solitary WASPs for a few years. Then their parents send them away to "prep" at exclusive hives scattered throughout New England and other select locations. While there, they learn how to protect their nest and preserve the social hierarchy. But in my hometown—my "fly zone"—the mud-dle class WASPs live in much nicer mud than most.

Beachfront property or not, we feel fortunate to buzz around in our posh little seaside community, bounded on the east by the vast Atlantic and on all other sides by those who wish they lived here. My parents blew in with the new colony of "stucco building" Anglo Saxons as well as other industrious immigrants like the White Collar Commuter ants and the Lace Curtain Irish moths. Everybody scrimped and saved to move their families closer to the Coastal-Dwelling Big Hivers.

The new colony served on planning commissions, volunteered for town committees and managed the scout troops and Little League teams. They made sure the roads got repaired, the sewage treated, the new schools built and the rules enforced.

They admired and preserved Old WASPville's ship-building heritage, dutifully drove their children to the library and tried to appreciate the arts, even if they preferred TV and sports.

The WASPville I grew up in had its religious, political and cultural differences, and socio-economic neighborhood boundaries. But there was always an overarching civic pride and commitment that brought us together.

By the time I finished college, things had changed. Remember those social studies reports we had to write about a country's imports and exports, like bananas, coffee, hemp and non-precious metals? WASPville's imports were becoming civically unengaged social climbers and expensive home furnishings; exports were Boston-bound commuters and disenchanted, overcharged summer tourists.

So these are a few of the environmental factors that shaped this Renegade WASP. It may not remind you of your hometown, but I would observe that anywhere there's mud nests and Big Hives you've got a breeding ground for social stratification.

Next week: Selected memories of a WASP childhood. I "Triple Dog Dare You" not to miss it.

***

Perhaps you wouldn't have paid me for those first two columns either. But I think the *Renegade WASP* masthead intrigued a few readers who were looking for something other than advice on cooking, etiquette or bridge. Based on the fan letters I received back then, a lot of folks view themselves as members of an un-WASPy underclass. So I clearly tapped into the anti-establishment mood of the times, although that wasn't my intent. I was really trying to understand the behavior of the "uber WASPs," and their membership criteria. For that purpose, Wampum was the ideal locale.

Let me introduce you to a pair of Wampum residents: Carson Trueblood, an "Uber WASP" and John Wheeler, a "mud WASP." Carson is a partner in a Boston law firm; John owns Wheeler Hardware. While neither survived the end of the twentieth century, as characters in my narrative they are both alive and well. They are good men, and worthy of respect. I single them out because they perfectly represented their respective species.

Carson lived in Atlantic Villas, the most exclusive community in North Wampum. My dad knew him from St. Matthews, where he was president of the vestry, a respected position. While not a handsome man, he was an impeccable dresser, possessed a firm handshake and was aggressively social.

A Yale graduate, Carson--as Hat would say, and in fact did--"married pretty rather than smart." His wife Crystal was a stunning blonde and, in my mother's estimation, "the perfect

28

hostess." Carson and Crystal had two children, Spencer and Margaret ("Meg"), both of whom attended prep school and, hopefully, would "marry well" — that is, within the "Uber circle." Carson was "in his element" at St. Matt's. Episcopalian is highest in the Protestant hierarchy, and so tends to attract the well-to-do Christians and filter out the plainer folk, who become Methodists or, God forbid, Unitarians (whom my father views as "a half step above agnostics").

John Wheeler was a fourth-generation Wampumite, from a family of merchants. To many in the community, he was "Mr. Wampum": president of the Rotary, Boy Scout troop leader, Little League umpire and pillar of the Congregational church. He took over Wheeler Hardware when his dad died, and it became the favorite town meeting place. You always ran into friends and neighbors at Wheeler's, and if they didn't have what you needed in stock, they'd get it for you within 48 hours, guaranteed. John won a Silver Star at Iwo Jima, but never talked about his war experience except to say "I was one of the lucky ones." His wife Cindy, John's high school sweetheart, was a nurse at the high school and also worked at old Doctor Reeves' office. Their son Richard ("Rick") — the only child John and Cindy were able to have-- idolized his dad and wanted above all else to be a Marine. I "played soldiers" with a number of kids, but nobody ever played like Rick Wheeler. He had the most elaborate battle gear anyone had ever seen, and his battlefields covered half the town.

I'm not sure how well Carson and John knew each other as kids, except for an occasional greeting at the hardware store. They certainly didn't attend the same parties. Carson played tennis and golf. John played baseball and football with Rick and went fishing whenever he could get away from the store. But Spencer and Rick would later cross paths in combat duty, and I will share their remarkable story later.

Looking back at this chapter in my life, it seems like Wampum's brief interval of peace and harmony. The townspeople seemed happy to settle into a niche, based largely on their political and religious affiliations and the childrens' social connections. You might covet a neighbor's yacht or country club membership, but you shared two important things in common: citizenship in this exceptional little community, and your caucasianism.

Be assured this isn't just another story about wealthy villains and hard-working middle class heroes. Caring and generous individuals commingled with the selfish and self-serving in every neighborhood and even every family. It wasn't a money thing; it was mostly a "good breeding" thing. But when good breeding didn't overcome dark impulses, it was something else. It was/is faulty wiring or chemical imbalances or soul-crushing experiences or an overwhelming desire to conquer others. Or all of the above. Or none of the above. I'm still trying to figure it out.

Let's get back to Wampum, where all of these forces and factors are at work on a minute-by-minute basis.

Chapter 5
The Neighborhood (1961)

It's a balmy late spring day. Let's go out the front door and I'll introduce you to the neighborhood.

Hat and my mother are both avid and competitive gardeners, so you'll notice the abundance of flowers and bushes. Hat has the front half of our long, slender property and my mother the back (and better) half. They are delighted for each other when a new front or back plant blooms, but there is constant one-upsmanship in terms of their birthing new flora and fauna.

My mother favors marigolds, begonias and petunias. Hat prefers hydrangeas, rhododendrons and sunflowers. She has just succeeded with black-eyed Susans, which she calls "the official flower of Wampum" (a reference to domestic violence, I find out later). My mother counters with impatiens, which goads Hat to try knockout rosebushes, which fail, to my mother's immense (but unspoken) relief. Meanwhile, nature, in the thicket behind the back fence, has its own "wild cards": tiger lilies, Queen Anne's lace, New England aster and garden phlox. It's like Horticulture Gone Wild. Hat explains, "It's our post-menopausal outlet," which I never understand and never ask about.

Across the lane from our "dueling flowers" is the Colchester estate, home of Charles and Aurora and their children Trevor, Andrea and Susannah, all attending "top shelf" prep schools (St. Paul's, Rosemary Hall and Ethel Walker). As I mentioned earlier, our house was at one time the servants' quarters for the estate, which includes a tennis court, dog kennels, a goldfish pool and a main house with twenty-six rooms, including a billiard area.

Charles is CEO of Colchester Elite Safari Rifles, "the choice of the world's leading hunters." His estate is like a gun museum, and the walls of every room are adorned with the heads of animals Charles has "murdered" (my dad's word, not Hat's) all around the world: lions, tigers, moose, grizzlies, elk, zebra, a grizzly, a snow leopard and too many others to mention. My dad says it would only be sport if the animals could shoot back, and "they're not shooting back, or even running away, with a baseball-sized hole in their head."

Since Massachusetts has no such exotic species nearby, Charles has to be satisfied with shooting coot and other ocean birds. He heads out at dawn on Saturdays and takes his four retrievers to fetch the kill. While he's away, his wife Aurora-- an exotically attractive woman with long, dark hair— entertains herself by gardening, sewing her own clothes and making ornate pottery objects that sell for hundreds of dollars each at upscale stores in Boston. She donates all profits to environmental charities. She and Charles met at the University of Colorado and married before graduating. It's rumored that she is an American Indian, or at least descended from Indians, but of course in 1961 there's no way to Google her ancestry online.

Trevor is an ace tennis player and gives me lessons on the family court when he's around. Andrea and Susannah are accomplished riders and sailors. I'm grateful that none of them treats me like "the white trash from the servants' quarters." Perhaps their parents lectured them about "putting on airs around those less fortunate" or they may just be non-judgmental kids. On their winter holidays we occasionally go sledding ("belly bumping" in Yankee-speak) down their long, steeply-pitched driveway and Mrs. Colchester always invites me in afterward for hot chocolate and cookies.

My parents are cordial with the Colchesters, although of course not on their guest list for summer lawn parties. Trevor occasionally, with his father's blessing, invites me on a coot-shooting trip, but my father demands I politely decline. I think he's afraid I'll get addicted to killing things.

The Colchesters and we Peirces live on a private lane, set back from the main road, with stone pillars and walls bordering our properties. There are two other large homes in the immediate neighborhood. The Campbells and their winter residents the Goldmans occupy "Camp Campbell," so named because in the summer there's a constant influx of Kitty's ballet and vocal students. "Cap" (short for Captain) Campbell is a history professor and track and field coach at the Naval Academy. He becomes my first mentor.

The Campbells are only with us for three months a year. At the end of August they give the keys to the Goldmans and head back to Annapolis. David Goldman is an Associate Professor of Mathematics at Harvard and his wife Sylvia is a published poet and social activist. Their son Alan is one of my neighborhood buddies. By the time we part company in ninth grade there isn't a single board game or "build it yourself" we haven't tackled. Alan can build anything, usually without directions. He deserves 99% of the credit for any Tinker Toy, Lincoln Log or Erector Set creation we produced, but he always gave me credit for my meager assistance.

The Goldmans were my first introduction to Judaism. As mentioned, Wampum's religious population is overwhelmingly Protestant and Catholic, with the 5% "Other" being mostly atheists and agnostics. Dad classifies the Goldmans as "reform Jews." I am always amused at how quickly people want to determine whether you're a member of their religious "club." Catholics want to know immediately if you're "of the faith." If not, I guess you're not a Premium Label Christian—just a discount brand.

Next door to the Campbells, although not quite "nextdoor neighbors," are the Burkes. According to my parents, the Campbells and Burkes had a property dispute and the genteel Cap had been thwarted in his efforts to resolve the dispute amicably with Colin Burke, a hothead and heavy drinker. Colin eventually left town, having pocketed the family funds and pawned his wife Rosemary's jewelry. She then became sole support of son Charlie, my age, and a spacious Colonial home on an expensive street. Fortunately, Rosemary ("Rose" to most) had recently completed certification as a real estate appraiser, having perhaps sensed that Colin would become more of a financial anchor than a sail. Starting, in her words, "with incredible fear of failure and a single business suit" she eventually went on to become the most successful realtor in the region, and was perfectly positioned for the Wampum real estate boom.

Charlie Burke, who would later become a Wampum High football star, was one of my best buddies. He loved outdoor games and had a vivid imagination, which could transform any landscape into the site of a medieval battlefield, a Viking warrior beach landing, or a Martian invasion. When it got cold, he was the first to test the ice to see if it was thick enough to support a hockey game. If so, he'd light a fire in a pit he built and kids would magically appear with their skates and gear.

Despite his aversion to Catholicism, my dad embraced all kids, and virtually adopted Charlie when his father left town. We took Charlie to the beach, on fishing trips, to Red Sox games, and had him over for dinner about five nights a week so his mom could focus on building her business. My mother and Hat doted on him and said he looked like "a young Tyrone Power," the movie star.

Rose Burke, who as a Catholic and recently-abandoned spouse had her own issues with "Yankee snobs" and men in general, always raved about my father and his influence on Charlie. She would gush, "I can't begin to thank you for your kindness to Charlie. You've become like a father to him, and you have your own family to support." Then she'd usually tear up and add something like, "I'm doing my best but I'm not the mother I should be." Dad would always shrug off her compliment and tell her, "You're in a really tough situation. He knows that. We all do."

So that's the immediate neighborhood, in a nutshell. Not many people, but it's the suburbs and there's more space between families. I didn't include the Kerouacs, because we didn't know them socially. Mr. Kerouac, a salesman, was always "on the road," according to his kids Jamie and Jake, who were usually on the other team from Charlie and me. Priscilla Plath was a quiet, studious girl with pigtails who would occasionally join us for a whiffle ball game on the Colchesters' front lawn. Her parents were "Boston people" who chose city culture over suburban recreation.

Our neck of the woods was sort of the gateway to North Wampum. Bayberry Road twisted its way up the street to where the "real money" was. Interestingly, Charles Colchester had a cool disdain for the "yacht club crowd," as he called them. He might have viewed them as poor prospects for safari rifles, or perhaps felt a slight chill from people who likely viewed him as "nouveau riche" or "a half-educated westerner." One night, after a couple of drinks, he told my dad he'd like to take some sharpshooters up to Atlantic Villas "and thin the herd of a few of their conceited assholes." I heard dad complain to my mother, "I fought to make the world free for gun freaks. Terrific."

Before we end this little walk, I want to circle back to Cap Campbell. (Yes, I had a "Hat" and a "Cap" for all kinds of weather.) If I were casting his part, it would be the face of Spencer Tracy and the temperament of Jimmy Stewart. Cap had heard from my parents that I was a sports fan and wanted to see how much I knew.

A typical meeting with Cap took place in his barnlike garage, always filled with diverse items. There were Kitty's old dance shoes and music stands; Cap's golf clubs and baseball memorabilia; and daughter Nancy's saddles and riding equipment. Nancy almost made the US Equestrian team in 1968 before "going hippie" with a bizarre eccentric who we all suspected was sponging off her. (Hat called him a "wallet-sucking bottom feeder," which convulsed my parents.)

I got my first kiss from Nancy, but not the kind you read about in romance novels. She was a robust young woman— two years older than me—with an unusually strong upper body and would occasionally wrestle me down in the grass and pin my arms. One day, when she had me in the pin position, she blurted out "You'd better watch out who you're messing with!" and, abruptly, kissed me on the mouth. From then on, she'd taunt me by saying "If you don't behave, I'll kiss you again."

Nancy notwithstanding, I'd drop in on Cap about once a week, after dinner. He'd ask me a question or two about sports—usually the Red Sox—to test my knowledge, and was always impressed with my correct answers. He was, I came to learn, well connected with the Red Sox organization and, through his network of sports contacts, was able to identify talented collegiate players, a few of whom ended up in the

Sox farm system. I will never forget the gift Cap left for me on my twelfth birthday. It was a baseball bat that Ted Williams had used in spring training. With it was a card: "Happy 12th to my favorite Bundle of Information."

I'll save a few other Cap anecdotes, since we didn't officially part company until years later. He was a "Gentleman WASP" of the first magnitude: a Boston "blue blood" with a ton of humanity and not an ounce of pretension. My modest accomplishments in cross country and track owed much to his interest in my development and his training suggestions. Thanks to him, I am still running today and enjoying the health benefits of having sweated off most of the calories that my sweet tooth has dumped into my gut over the years.

It's 1961: the beginning of the most culturally turbulent decade in twentieth century America. The Russians detonate a 50-megaton H-bomb, but we don't hear it in Wampum. A battalion of anti-Castro paramilitaries is slaughtered at the Bay of Pigs, while we launch our sailboats down here on the South Shore. *West Side Story* is a smash hit on Broadway, although few in our town have ever seen a Latino, and gang violence only happens in Boston's bad neighborhoods.

Today there's a sweet smell of lilacs in the neighborhood, and nature awakens in all of its young male creatures— especially us teenagers--the urge to pollinate.

Chapter 6
The Underwear Drawer

Now that we've completed our walk through the neighborhood, I'll give you a brief tour of our home here off Bayberry Road. The outside is gray stucco, which I always thought was a homely material, but agree is perfect for a "mud WASP" family.

There's a two-car garage, occupied by a VW Beetle (for dad's commute) and a '57 Chevy Bel Air, for my mother's errands. Over the garage is an attic, containing all the sentimental family heirlooms that will never again see the light of day. It smells like the inside of a damp sneaker up there, and all I can find are old photos buried in cardboard boxes and my mother's diaries, which are disappointingly mundane to a teenage boy.

Behind the garage is a strip of grass, a concrete patio and a flower garden. This is my mother's favorite spot. She is a sun worshiper and craves the tanning rays, which replace winter's pastiness. She is happiest with an iced coffee, a copy of *Life* magazine and a half hour alone with her thoughts.

My dad doesn't tan well and prefers the cramped stone cellar where he keeps tools he uses only when necessary and putters with our stamp collection. We have looked in vain for valuable stamps in mint condition, but it seems a hobby for well-connected collectors with way more time and money than we have.

You enter the living room through the screen door, which never fully closes, and a wooden door, which tries its best to fend off months of damp, cold winds. The piano is to the immediate right; it has as many nicks as keys. My mother is the better pianist, but seldom plays; my dad has a repertoire of about three songs, which he performs with gusto, but not finesse. The top of the piano gets more use, as a repository for mail and framed family photos. The area between the piano legs is wide enough to be a goal for tennis ball hockey, which we sometimes play on rainy days when no adults are around.

The living room furniture is eclectic, with a red Naugahyde chair, two wingbacks (my favorites for reading) and a blue cloth sofa where our Belgian shepherd Baron sleeps. He is a purebred watchdog, but is overzealous about chasing cars and has paid the price. Acutely arthritic, he can barely jump up on his blanketed sofa bed, which makes us all wince.

There is a stereo next to the sofa which plays the music of the forties for my parents ("now THAT'S Music") and the electric guitar stuff I listen to—always too loud and "raucous." My mother relents from time to time and praises the vocalists who aren't backed up by "barnyard animals" (Hat, of course). But there would never be another Sinatra or Bing Crosby. The room's "piece de resistance" is a lovely oriental rug, but it has recently fallen victim to Baron's weak bladder.

The most underrated feature of our living room—especially to those who judge a room by its expensive decor—was the library. My parents and Hat had collected a Whitman's sampler of wonderful books—acclaimed classics, popular novels, comedic gems, collections of poetry, ancient and modern history, atlases and almanacs…all great reads. "A good library is a poor man's vacation ticket" according to Hat, and it's just as well because as far as I know she never got out of New England.

The kitchen is "Fifties functional," with a breakfast bar that serves as the family dinner table for every meal except Easter,

Thanksgiving and Christmas. That means the dining room becomes a project room for my mother and a torture chamber when it comes time for her to review, edit and type my term papers. During all my years as a resident of the Peirce Household, I don't remember a single kitchen renovation, not even a new refrigerator. We middle class WASPs "made do."

The rec room, with its shiny red tile floor, is the main congregating spot for the male family members. Hat seldom invades our space. She believes television caters to those who lack the imagination to entertain themselves, but doesn't broadcast this opinion. My mother watches an occasional episode of *Ozzie and Harriet* or *Father Knows Best*, but is usually busy in the kitchen.

We males are happy to be transported anywhere beyond Wampum, especially to the Wild West and its "thrilling days of yesteryear." We ride along with a cavalcade of cowboys: the Lone Ranger and Tonto (Jay Silverheels as the only Indian "good guy" I can remember), Roy Rogers and Dale Evans (remember the lyrics to "Happy Trails"?), Hopalong Cassidy (ever meet anybody else named Hopalong?), Matt Dillon, Wyatt Earp, Paladin, Brett and Bart Maverick, The Rifleman, The Cartwrights, Cheyenne Bodie...and that's just our Top Ten. (No wonder we ended up with a nation of gun-toting zealots.)

There's also a ping pong table, but often no ping pong balls because Baron likes to chew on them and we don't remember to buy replacements. Too bad, because I'm just starting to challenge my dad at pong. He has a wicked reverse spin backhand serve that he unleashes when I'm within a couple of points. The dart board doesn't get much use because the darts have become defective and don't stick in the board. Last year, in a rage because he was beating me, I threw a dart at my brother Frankie and it stuck in his head. I haven't played since.

There are fourteen carpeted stairs on the way to the second floor. They are perfectly spaced for our Slinky, which has slinked its way down twelve of the fourteen. At the top of the steps, to the right, is Hat's room. It is always impeccably clean, and seldom occupied, since Hat strongly prefers the outdoors. (Her argument: "I have the rest of eternity to spend inside.") Her room is as "Yankee simple" as they come, with a single bed, a cedar chest, an oak bureau and a small desk for writing thank you notes. The top of the bureau is crowded with family photos, which she rotates seasonally. She thoughtfully includes photos of my dad's parents, although they have been dead for years.

I have outgrown indoor Hide and Seek, but at one time we would include Hat's room in our hiding places. Frankie's favorite spot was under the bed, which included the extra camouflage of a long quilt. I would hide in the closet, and always be surprised at the small cache of clothes hanging there—barely enough to conceal me. I would secretly refer to Hat as "The Good Witch" because her dresses were all long and dark, like Halloween costumes.

At the end of the hall was the bathroom—a high traffic area since it had to service three males and two females. My dad was a notorious bathroom hog. When nature called, he always had a long conversation. After a half hour he would emerge with a favorite book, leaving behind a "low tide from Hell" aroma (my description, not Hat's. She felt he deserved his time "on the throne" because he supported us.) In the evening, my mother had top priority and my dad never preceded her before bedtime. My bathroom time increased as my facial hair began to sprout and I was forced into hand-to-face combat with my zits. Frankie had to be threatened into

41

hygiene on a daily basis. Hat never spent more than two minutes in the "powder room." I once heard her scoff to herself: "Cosmetics are a waste of money on this face."

I have the corner room to the right of the bathroom, with views of the front and backyards. My prize possession is a GE desk radio, which connects me to the worlds of sports and music. It is a great time to be a Boston Celtics fan and to listen to their operatic play-by-play announcer Johnny Most, whose vocal range is deep bass to high falsetto. When describing the exceptional talents of a Russell, Cousy or Sam Jones he is in the upper register; he is equally passionate, in his gravelly lower tones, about describing an opponent's foul as a "mugging." To a young fan he is the perfect, partisan "home towner," elevating Celtic games into mythic skirmishes against savage barbarians.

The radio music tried its best to seduce me away from homework and into a realm of romance where it was cool to break the rules, sneak out of the house and meet a mystery girl for a kiss in the moonlight. All those sixties songs, digging their neural channels into our pleasure centers, chord by chord, lyric by lyric. ("Don't know much about science books. Don't know much about French I took. But I do know that I love you. And I know that if you loved me, too...What a wonderful world it would be.")

My mother seemed satisfied with the minimal disorder of my room. It was acceptable for a male, in her mind. All I did to pass muster was shove everything into the bottom drawer once or twice a week. Frankie's room, on the other hand, was a "rat's nest" which daily seemed to mutate into a more chaotic mound of rubble. No amount of parental pleading, scolding or even insulting could induce Frankie to better manage his mega-mess. He was listening to other voices.

My parents' bedroom was up a step to the left of the bathroom. Unlike Hat, my mother had a fairly extensive and colorful wardrobe for each season. She had managed to usurp about ninety percent of a spacious closet, forcing my dad to make do with a lean wardrobe. There was a well-stocked makeup area in the corner, and I would always startle my mother if I came in while she was sitting there. In the numerous youthful photos of my mother scattered around the house, makeup accentuated her youth and good looks. Now, it could only conceal her age, and that depressed her.

In the opposite corner was my dad's dresser, and in its second drawer—his underwear drawer—was a small, covert collection of adult novels. I would sneak into the drawer when dad was at work and my mother and Hat were elsewhere. My favorites were the Mickey Spillanes, with detective Mike Hammer. Each book had several three-to-four-page sexual encounters with various "gorgeous tomatos," easily seduced by Hammer's verbal foreplay. After skimming through a Spillane a few times, I would know exactly where to locate the orgasm and avoid wasting time on the foreplay. And just when I started to get bored with one of the books, a new arrival would replace it.

There were many volumes of literature in the Peirce library, but I always thought of my dad's underwear drawer as "the erection section"…my paperback sex primers.

So that's our house, minus a few nooks and crannies. It's not Atlantic Villas, by a long shot. But for my parents it's a big step up from their humble beginnings. A tennis court fifty yards from the front door, for God's sake, even if it wasn't theirs. Two beaches within a mile.

For most of my youth, 264 Bayberry Road was, despite being cramped, a haven of light, life and good spirits …but that was about to change.

Chapter 7
"Frankie-Stein" (1963)

My brother was named after my dad's brother Frank, who had died in childbirth. Five years my junior, he was a fair-complected redhead, whose temperament, my parents believed, was probably related to his hair color, as in "bad-tempered redhead."

This was the first of many erroneous attempts to explain Frankie's odd behaviors. As a baby, he cried and screamed relentlessly, day and night. He was an exasperatingly finicky eater—rejecting all varieties of baby foods and often hurling the contents into the face of his feeder. He resisted potty training so stubbornly that he actually wore a diaper to kindergarten, and had to be bribed with candy before he'd stop wetting his bed.

The village physician, Dr. Hayes, assured my mother that "Frank is just going through a phase and will grow out of it." So much for diagnostics in the 50's. In truth, it was a phase Frank would grow *into*, like a dark labyrinth with no discernable exits for him or his caregivers.

The odd behaviors were at first a mild source of amusement for us, since Dr. Hayes had promised a return to normalcy was right around the corner. Frankie would jump up and down in place, seemingly delighted by simple stimulants like rain or a conversation in another room. He would carefully organize objects on the top of his dresser, and if you moved one he would return it to its original position immediately. He would also hide cookies and crackers behind the sofa or under his bed so he could sneak food between meals.

Despite my mother's best efforts to import playmates, Frankie's only companion was our dog Baron. A typically loyal and vigilant shepherd, Baron accompanied Frankie everywhere—usually to small and large bodies of water, where my brother would bounce back and forth for hours. When around, Hat would sometimes follow at a distance to observe his behavior. She was careful not to frighten my mother, but it was clear from her descriptions of Frankie's activities that his behavior was highly eccentric.

He couldn't, and then wouldn't, ride a bicycle—a skill which might have helped connect him to playmates. In fact, during his entire life, his legs were his only means of transport. In adulthood, he became legendary for his long-distance walking, and was observed in every neighborhood of Wampum, striding along with his head down and his legs churning.

In school, he was soon assigned to a small caste of aberrants labeled "Slow Learners," before the less offensive "Special Ed" came into vogue. It was a highly heterogeneous mix that included the mentally retarded, whatever they called the ADDs and ADHDs, autistics, physically handicapped, the criminally ill-behaved and the "as yet undiagnosed," which included Frankie. Frankie would remain incorrectly diagnosed for all but the last five years of his life.

But to call Frankie a "Slow Learner" was to ignore his enormous talent for retaining information that fascinated him. He knew the names and seasonal locations of every constellation visible over Wampum. He "sponged up" everything he could find about lighthouses, hurricanes, flesh-eating dinosaurs and poisonous snakes. He literally devoured the data. Having finished reading, he would gnaw on the edges of his reference materials. I remember that the "C" edition of our *Compton's Pictured Encyclopedia*, which contained the segment on constellations, looked like it had been attacked by paper-eating termites. So too with many books in the Peirces' "edible library."

Every year of Frankie's young life, his mental health issues would flare up a notch or two and his temper tantrums would become a little more volatile. He hated to lose at games, so we would have to manipulate the results in his favor. If not, he'd fling the playing cards across the room or overturn the board game and all its loose paraphernalia. He became a very good candlepin bowler, but on a bad day would get so frustrated he'd toss the ball at the pin-setting machine. Occasionally, a neighbor would mention to my parents they had seen Frankie throwing rocks at Baron, who suffered the abuse without flinching.

My father, who claimed that Frankie's affliction was inherited from his side of the family, did everything possible to keep Frankie's behavioral train "on the tracks." He had been a model dad in supporting my youth activities: coaching my minor league and Little League teams; teaching me Morse code and knot tying as Boy Scout Troop Master; instructing me, as acolyte supervisor, on the fine points of leading the procession as the crucifer. I was always the obedient and dutiful student, respectful of adult authority as you were taught to be in a conservative Republican household.

Not so with Frankie. In no way could Frankie be considered a "team player." Baseball definitely wasn't his game. He had trouble throwing the ball and once he'd been plunked on the chin a couple of times, he was done with the game for good. Cub Scouts and Boy Scouts were too regimented for him. He was always losing parts of his uniform and getting publicly reprimanded. He was too young as a Cub to rebel, but he flamed out before reaching First Class in Boy Scouts. As for the acolytes, my dad was smart enough not to train him as a crucifer. He carried a taper (long candle) for a couple of years and only had one disaster I can remember, which actually made him a temporary hero to the other acolytes.

On that particular Sunday, we had the monthly visit from our only paid choir member, the mezzo soprano Miss Biegel (she pronounced it "bygul" but we acolytes said "beagle" because she looked like one). She was, admittedly, a talented singer, and made our volunteer choir sound almost professional...and yes, there were always more parishioners in attendance on her particular (third of the month) Sunday. But she wanted to be treated like Maria Callas, and woe be the professionally untrained soprano who tried to ascend to her vocal heights. Miss Biegel would fix upon her would-be competitor a look of such scorn that even those of us in the rear pews could feel the chill. So while she was well paid for her guest appearances, she was not well liked by the choir members.

During the processional, Frankie got distracted and his taper somehow managed to make contact with Miss Beigel's choir vestment. It wasn't intentional, because he had no idea about the choral politics. But by the time the choir reached the front of the church, Miss Biegel was clearly smoking, and it took Bill Wheelwright, arms flailing, to extinguish her. (Later he whispered to my dad that he and the other choir members believed Frankie "became an instrument of God.") Apparently, Miss Biegel felt "professionally humiliated" by the incident and didn't return to Saint Matthews for several months. It was the high point of Frankie's youth.

The sad truth is that, in the fifties and early sixties, the diagnostic tools for mental illness were primitive. I guess that statement can be challenged; after all, I'm an English major who took one college course in Abnormal Psychology. Maybe there was a clinic somewhere in Switzerland that could diagnose and successfully treat every behavioral oddity. But the answer to the riddle of Frankie…the path out of his mental maze…the directions that would perfectly align his behavioral Rubik's Cube…were not available to my parents or the professionals to whom they were referred.

I remember there was one ray of hope: the Bright Path School in Pennsylvania. An educator friend recommended my parents take a look at it, and from what little they could find — again, no internet—it began to seem like The Answer. Their brochure promised "compassionate care from highly-skilled teachers and consultants in a supportive environment" free from judgmental peers and indifferent public school administrators. Bingo, right? But somehow Fate always dealt Frankie the bottom cards. Following what seemed to my parents like a superficial series of tests, Frankie was deemed "too hostile and aggressive" for admission.

My parents returned from their trip devastated, and spent weeks second guessing what they could have done to change the decision. Hat once again hit the nail on the head when she suggested they should have promised a big gift to the Bright Path endowment fund. But unfortunately that wasn't an option.

They had been so close to a humane solution. So close to being able to lead Normal Lives. Just one "Yes" away from a household free from stale cookies hidden under the furniture, free from volumes of books that looked like beaver food, from the daily succession of disruptive behaviors that were gnawing away at our nervous systems.

But instead they got the deadly clang of a "No," like the slamming of a jail cell door. And it was a Life Sentence. Suddenly, all the air had drained out of my parents' Hope Balloon. They had brought an aberrant into the pristine little duchy of Wampum and he was destined to be an outcast.

***

It didn't dawn on me until years later that this was the point at which my parents' lives began to unravel. The occasional glass of wine became a nightly glass, followed by another and eventually even another. The once occasional marital arguments became more frequent, the volume increasingly louder and the tone more shrill. The noose was tightening.

As JFK was fond of saying in those days: "Let me make one thing perfectly clear..." Let me be perfectly clear that I had very little empathy or compassion for Frankie. He was a major embarrassment. And Wampum was a small town, with no patience for deviance from the norm—at least public deviance. The sight of a tall, strapping redhead stalking around became increasingly unnerving for Wampum folk, especially the elderly. And there I was, guilty by association: "Brother of the Village Idiot."

I did everything I could to ignore Frankie and my familial connection with him and to keep him away from my friends. When I hit high school, I blamed Frankie for my social failures, assuming that it was the fear of his mental illness that alienated attractive girls, and not, as was really the case, my own awkwardness. I remember the toxic inquiry of a nasty little neighborhood girl on Halloween: "Hey Frankie-Stein, wanna go Trick or Treating tonight?" Welcome to Wampum: "We'll Act Nice If You'll Act Normal."

Frankie will be with us for the rest of the story, but I'll share with you the diagnosis my parents finally received from the esteemed Holy Redeemer Hospital in Boston, when Frankie was twelve: Paranoid Schizophrenic. Okay. A terrible form of mental illness but at least the beast was out of the cave, so to speak. Only problem was, it was the wrong diagnosis. So for the next forty-three years he took the wrong medication, making him increasingly belligerent and, if you'll excuse a technical term, "crazy."

It may surprise you that I have quite a few positive memories of Frankie from the early days.

He was a pretty decent "play buddy" when no one else was around. After considerable coaching, he could catch a football in stride (although couldn't throw it back very well); could smack a tennis ball over the tennis court fence behind me (but couldn't pitch very accurately); could always hide-and-seek in surprising locations; and was excellent at darts. I told you about the afternoon when, in annoyance, I threw a dart at him and it briefly stuck in his head. I worried for years that I might have aggravated his mental illness.

Socializing was torture for him. He could blend into group activities like sledding, skating and outdoor games, but "one-on-ones" never worked out. He would usually end up at his favorite little creek tossing stones for (or at) Baron, oblivious to the playmate, who would eventually wander home.

When my friends came over, I would often catch a glimpse of Frankie hopping up and down around the corner, animated I guess by the chance to overhear our "onstage" conversations. It occurred to me that he almost looked like Howdy Doody with invisible strings: fate's marionette.

Chapter 8
Run One (1963)

My friend Brian Farrell introduced me to running during my freshman year in high school. His dad and mine were business colleagues at Golden Sportswear (owned by garment industry bigwig and employee abuser Irving Smallberg), and the Farrells had recently relocated to Wampum. Brian was a year ahead of me and, already a promising track athlete, convinced me to try his sport. I had been a mediocre baseball and basketball player and so was a willing convert to a sport that rewarded sweat and effort over hand-eye coordination.

My internship began with cross country, and I staggered through the summer of '61 getting in shape for the first meet in September, while Brian glided along beside me. He had an immediate impact on a team that had often been ridiculed by the football players as "nerds afraid of getting hit." We certainly weren't your classic jocks. In cross country, the skinnier you were the better. At the top of a long hill, you needed to forge ahead, not collapse in a heap. I spent the year at the back of the pack, but was satisfied with gradual improvement and the hope of winning a varsity letter. Brian always finished in the top three, and inspired the rest of us to fight off Burning Lung Syndrome. Wampum actually won three meets, as opposed to none the year before.

I soon grew to love the training. It was so easy to lace on my running shoes, do a few warmups and head off, with or without Brian, along the ocean or into town. I bought a stopwatch, so I could time the duration and speed of my workouts. I learned little tricks, like leaning into a hill to help

51

my forward momentum and "speed up/slow down" when I was getting tired. I tried to manage the fatigue and not fight it like a drowning man. I knew when it would creep in and how it would eventually settle on my tongue, tasting like sweat, stale oxygen and blood.

One of my favorite courses took me on a five-mile jaunt through some of the most beautiful sections of Wampum. I always enjoyed running it around dusk, when I could almost blend into the landscape. I'd start out on Bayberry Road, which took me past our skating pond and out to Dickinson Drive, the ocean road, where I'd bear right. This led me up a long gradual incline to a cluster of stately homes, mostly Tudor, with probably the best vantage points in town. This was the "quiet money" in Wampum—the folks who didn't want to trumpet their wealth like their neighbors a mile to the west in Atlantic Villas, but who knew it was they who had the better views. The Dickinsonians really lived below the radar, and in retrospect I can't remember ever seeing a single occupant out for a walk or riding a bike. The realtors in town claimed these homes never went on the market; they were all sold privately by the owners, to others who craved living in secluded opulence.

From there it was downhill to the Wampum Private Beach, reserved exclusively for residents with stickers. Trespassers got a $25 ticket instructing them to pay at the police station before they left town or their license would be suspended after 30 days. And, by God, by virtue of a cozy relationship with the Massachusetts Department of Motor Vehicles, the penalty was enforced, despite the scofflaws' curses and vows never to return. That's how Wampum keeps unescorted out-of-towners from defiling its shores.

Beyond the beach were more "feudal manors," set well back from the road and hidden by dense foliage. You had to look very carefully to find their driveways—the message being "If you don't know where to find us, you don't belong here." None of my friends lived in the neighborhood, so I assumed any children were prep schoolers. Once again, beautifully-crafted homes with unobscured views of the cobalt-colored Atlantic. You imagine the Indians out there a long time ago, freezing their asses off trying to catch cod and flounder in cold, choppy waters.

Then it was across Longfellow Bridge, which actually was a very "short fellow" of about thirty yards. Beneath the bridge were rapids created by a strong flow of water from the Atlantic to Marsh Harbor, a safe haven for birds, spawning fish and young boaters. It was here that Morgan Shrike, whom I'll formally introduce later, tossed a surly teenaged alien off the bridge and nearly killed him. The kid swallowed more sea water than he had drunk beer and was lucky to make it to shore. Shrike told the Wampum police chief he had been assaulted while out for a walk. The "inside story" had him flagging down a car playing loud music—obviously a punk joyrider—and ordering the driver to get his junkheap out of town and never come back. When the degenerate badmouthed him, Shrike pulled him out of the car, slapped him around and gave him the "heave ho." The chief ordered the waterlogged delinquent to leave town, and Shrike became a town hero for months.

Although Shrike was tall and solidly built, he had a medical condition that kept him out of combat during the war. Apparently, he now viewed himself as a Banisher of Unsavory Invaders. The word was "Don't mess with Morgan."

Not far from the bridge was a right onto Walden Way, which led past Marsh Harbor toward Wampum Common.

This had been a sparsely populated area until the Fifties, when upper middle class commuters to Boston—a little wealthier than my parents—started building what were then affordable homes, especially with help from the G.I. Bill. Here there were more signs of life, including driveway basketball, hockey sticks slapping tennis balls off the garage door, upstairs radios playing Del Shannon and Connie Francis. At the intersection of Walden and the Common, near the historical landmarks I mentioned earlier, was the brown clapboard home of my first girlfriend, whom I met at a sixth grade spin-the-bottle birthday party and who remains the best late-night phone whisperer in my mental rolodex.

Walden gave way to Mayflower Passage, the oddest name for a town's "Main Street" I've ever heard. (Hat scoffed: "The spinsters from the Hysterical Society must have come up with that one.") Anyway, it was a hard starboard onto Mayflower and a long uphill climb past high trees and hedges to a more traditional middle class neighborhood with Colonials and Cape Cods. "Traditional middle class" is relative, of course; ten miles west, this would have been the wealthy part of town. These Wampumites were actually neighbors in the real sense who said "Good morning!" and helped each other shovel snow or drive a missed-the-bus student to school.

Further down Mayflower was the Little League ballpark—not exactly a "field of glory" for me. My dad loved baseball, drilled me patiently in the basics, and coached our Dodger team, but there was no Ted Williams in my swing. More like Tennessee Williams. Years later, I still go to games. The kids are bigger; there are now a couple of brave girls playing; and the parents are less hostile…either better medicated or less lubricated.

Smaller, well-manicured homes to my left and right. Congregationalists, Methodists, town council members, local businesspeople, veterans, mostly Republicans. Folks who attend the town meetings and volunteer at the Wampum Christmas Festival on the Common.

Easy to romanticize these Wampum neighborhoods in my youth, but as I aged they became less Currier and Ives and more John Cheever. A few on this street are struggling to pay their bills and don't want the neighbors to know. Some are trapped in bad marriages. Others hate every newcomer who dilutes the native bloodstream. *Forest Ave*

About a mile past the ballpark I go right on Hawthorne Hollow, a woodsy stretch being aggressively sliced into two acre lots by doctors, dentists, lawyers, and a Whitman's Sampler of Boston area arrivals who are right on the cusp of affluence. They will wait for their land to appreciate and then hope to ascend to Atlantic Villas.

I don't know the kids on "The Hollow." Many of them are preppies whose parents are exporting them to one of those WASP hives I mentioned. You can get into an Ivy League school as a high-performing Wampum High grad, but "Hollow" parents prefer the cachet of prep school.

The early arrivals to The Hollow have created a template for the second phasers to follow. You need at least a hundred yard driveway to get you away from street noises and rubbernecking weekend gawkers. Glass and wood are *de rigueur* and a front yard metal sculpture confirms your aesthetic credentials. It's a tough stretch for us runners, with a lot of little ups and downs, and no shoulders to protect you from fast-moving foreign cars. You do see the occasional trim-looking couple in khakis or corduroys working in the yard or garden--always oblivious to your presence.

Especially in the fall, the smell of the woods always lifts me temporarily above my labored breathing and muscle fatigue. It's a robust cologne of burnt leaves, salt sea air, drying cement and just a trace of auto exhaust, which continues to invigorate me after decades. The smell of nature commingling with civilization.

At the end of The Hollow is a dramatically steep hill with a history of violence. In the mid-Fifties, a carload of drunken teens went plummeting over the hill, crashed through the thin white fence at the bottom and dropped ten feet onto the rocks. Only one of five survived, as a paraplegic. Numerous daredevil sledders and bicyclists, heedless of warnings, have broken bones there, and runners have slipped on ice and had nasty falls. Finally, on a vote of 4 to 3, the town selectmen approved placement of a "Steep Hill Ahead" sign. Further mayhem almost certainly awaits. On a dry day I trot down very slowly; on a wet day I avoid Hollow Hill completely.

Today I jog down to the right and rejoin Dickinson Drive about a mile above where I started. This is the filet mignon of Wampum real estate. Many of the immense Victorians along Upper Dickinson were built in the early 1900s by merchants and financial magnates. Over the years, their horse stables and other eccentric appendages have been replaced by tennis courts and lavish flower gardens.

A lot of the Old Money went bankrupt during the Great Depression, and others who kept their wealth intact decided to head West. Wampum's New Money is more focused on getting a "social return." Dickinsonians invite their business colleagues and the "upwardly striving" to come and gush at the ocean view. Drinking is obligatory. This is the pre-cannabis era, so there is no other social vice except the occasional act of adultery.

There are several acres of prime, undeveloped land across the street from Atlantic Villas, which are being eyed for purchase so no upstart developer can "steal the Villas' ocean views." It will eventually become the Upper Dickinson

56

Environmental Center, under the jurisdiction of a Villas-governed nonprofit board that could care less about the environment.

On this day, I am about to pass the Chase estate, the centerpiece of Atlantic Villas. There is a wide expanse of impeccably trimmed lawn and up to the left a tennis court, with two female players. The younger one catches my eye and I decide, uncharacteristically, to stop and watch. They play gracefully, attempting to keep the ball in play rather than win the point. I have seen them before in town, but through the fog of fatigue I can't remember where. The older woman—I assume her mother—is trim and tanned and avoids the backhand. The younger hits harder but also more erratically, and laughs at her mistakes. After a minute of distant spectating, I start running again.

I'm less than a mile from home, although financially I'm in another zip code. Up on the right is cummings circle (not capitalized to prove they're nonconformists): a cluster of architecturally eccentric homes which include two on stilts (Hat says to protect them from the Big Tsunami) and an actual tree house occasionally featured in upscale magazines.

Further along, on the left, is Rabbit Run, the Siamese twin of the other Dickinson Drive enclave I mentioned at the beginning of my jaunt. It's a little cluster of Tudor and Terra Cotta people who allow themselves two hours with *The Times* on Sunday morning and spend the rest of the week bulked up on vitamins and pharmaceuticals. There's actually a "Bunny" Riordan living in Rabbit Run and we wonder if she changed her name after moving in.

One last landmark to mention: the new "Serenity Shore," which used to be St. Mary's Villa, a retreat for nuns. I remember seeing the nuns at their little rocky beach cavorting in their Victorian black-and-white bathing attire. My dad called them "the penguins." Apparently the Catholic Church got a better real estate deal and decided to move St. Mary's to the North Shore, much to the nuns' chagrin. The Villa was quickly converted into an upscale health care facility, one of whose residents would have an indelible influence on my life.

It's back on to Bayberry for a few hundred yards. I accelerate and pretend that the two stone pillars at the end of our lane are the finish line of the Boston Marathon. The girl on the tennis court? I suddenly remember I have seen her in church.

Chapter 9
Chase-ing Romance (1964)

"The girl" was Holly Chase. I didn't recognize her because she was already "prepping" at Miss Cabot's School in a neighboring town. After my accidental sighting, however, she began to appear more often, like a new character in a movie. (I mentioned earlier she resembled the actress Ally Sheedy, but in every way was her own unique personality.) She and her tennis partner mother (Laura) occupied a front pew at St. Matthews and I found myself starting to look for her. She was very pretty and wore timeless "WASP chic" fashions from the family cedar chest. When I led the recessional as crucifer, we would make eye contact and I was always the first to look away.

My parents would normally never have socialized with the Chases—being "out of their league"—but they met at a St. Matthews reception and struck up a conversation. My dad and David Chase shared Navy stories, although Chase had "remained stateside" during the war. My mother and Laura Chase discussed the Kennedys—both secretly admired JFK— and Laura apparently hinted that Holly had noticed me.

My mother tends to get chatty after a glass of wine, and apparently complained that we had a woodchuck who was eating her flowers. David overheard and mentioned he could "help out" --a pledge my mother quickly forgot. But being a romantic, she was excited to share the "Holly Chase thinks you're cute" tidbit with me. I, of course, reacted nonchalantly but was secretly thrilled. I had been spending more time in my dad's soft porn drawer, imagining Holly's face on the bodies of the paperback playmates.

About a week later, on a Saturday morning, we heard a loud popping sound in the backyard. Two minutes later there was a robust knock at the front door. My mother answered — my dad was camping with a Boy Scout troop — and there was David Chase, dressed in camouflage gear. I had never met him, and I remember that he spoke in the most authoritative adult voice I had ever heard.

"Good morning! I just took care of your woodchuck problem. Sorry if I woke you up but they're early feeders. I knew this would be the best time."

My mother was an animal lover and cried during *Bambi*, so I knew this would be tough for her, especially since she, in Chase's mind, had ordered the execution. Somehow maintaining a stiff upper lip, she invited Chase in for a cup of coffee, but he declined, explaining he was on his way to hunt ducks.

"If you have any other pest problems, give me a call. Just about anything could come out of that marsh area."

I remember thinking that he looked like an executive in a hunting costume.

"Thank you, David. It was very…*thoughtful* of you to help us out. Please give Laura my best."

Chase smiled and departed quickly, having completed his first task of the day. He drove off in a pickup truck — not a typical "second car" for a Villas resident.

I told my mother I'd bury the woodchuck, and noticed she was starting to tear up.

"Thank you…I feel so sorry for that poor animal. I can't bear to see it. I wish I'd never opened my mouth. I had no idea he'd come over and shoot him. The *poor thing!*"

60

As it turned out, the bullet had pierced the woodchuck, taking its life with it, and exited through the back fence. I wrapped the body in an old tarp and buried it in the woods, as quickly as I could. All I can remember is the feeling of "dead weight" and the relief that, surprisingly, there was very little blood.

Later, Hat commented that she felt Chase had "way overstepped his bounds," no matter what mother had said to him at the church event.

"He should have phoned, and you would have told him there's no way you want a rifle being discharged on your property. That's criminal trespass, if you ask me!"

Of course, she was trying to diminish her daughter's guilt. In truth, her sympathies were closer to the garden they had planted than the woodchuck who was devouring it. The next day, her true colors were flying again.

"If I told David Chase that Martha Sterling (a local nemesis) was coming over in the early morning and cutting our flowers, do you think he'd shoot *her??*"

That got a subdued laugh from my mother, and the dark cloud passed over.

When my dad found out about the incident he was incensed, and deeply annoyed that he hadn't been home, but my mother convinced him to drop it. He just scoffed, "Another Gungho Gun Guy running amok. We could have used him on Iwo Jima."

***

Now that the Peirces and Chases were "joined by blood," Holly and I seemed destined to orbit each other more closely. There were numerous opportunities for young daters to explore their mutual attractions, although they were intended

61

to match you up with someone in your own "socioeconomic sandbox." The Catholics had CYO dances. The few Jews had shared activities at Passover. The wealthy WASPs had Yacht Club socials. The rest of us had basement parties that our parents reluctantly agreed to host after stripping the party area of any furnishings worth more than $10.

Holly invited me to go sailing on her Catboat, a 12-foot day sailer named *Pegasus,* with cedar planking and a single navy blue mainsail. It was a cute little craft and virtually unsinkable—built by the Beetle family of New Bedford, who would provide Caroline Kennedy with her first sailboat. My only nautical experience was on my dad's 20-foot inboard (the *Side Boy*), with a crank engine and the lingering aroma of dead fish.

Pegasus was like a spirited pony, eager to inhale a gust of wind and carry you away. At first, Holly was amused at my lack of sailing experience, apparently assuming that all Wampum children were given sailing as well as swimming lessons by the local Red Cross. However, she praised my ability to "find the wind" and stay on course. After several outings, she decided I had progressed sufficiently to earn the role of First Mate and join her for one of the weekly races outside Wampum harbor.

We finished second out of twelve in our first race, on a calm Saturday in early June. I was impressed with Holly's ability to break out of the pack and remain ahead of everybody except Betsy Warren and her brother Thatcher, who attended Exeter and already had the look and pedigree of a future America's Cup skipper. Betsy, a Miss Cabot's classmate of Holly's, was content to let her brother master the course while she chainsmoked and moved languidly around the boat. This irritated the competitive Holly, who had mild contempt for both of the Warrens.

"That little bitch isn't doing a damned thing. It's a wonder she's not painting her nails. Except she'd need another hand for the cigarette. Her brother thinks he's god's gift to the yacht club. He only got into Exeter because his father went there."

As for me, she managed to move me around the boat without hitting me with the mainsail or dumping me overboard.

"You're doing great. If you weighed a little more, we'd probably be leading. Weight usually helps, although fatso Barnes usually finishes last...I wish I could block the Warrens' wind, but Captain Poophead is too far out front."

We raced on four Saturdays that summer and actually won the fourth because "Captain Poophead" was in Paris. I was given a little more responsibility each time and learned enough that I was able to hold the lead in the home stretch of our win. Sailing was a natural high for me: the acceleration when your mainsail caught the wind just right; the shimmer of the sun on the water; the "clean sheet" smell of the ocean breeze; the camaraderie of the sailors; and the comedic commentary of my sailing partner. Holly had an impressive, instinctive talent as "Navigator in Chief," but never took the race too seriously and always acknowledged my contribution, however minimal. And she would occasionally zap me with a remark like: *"You know the great thing about this boat if you're a parent? There's no below deck, so you don't have to worry about birth control."*

There was more than enough chemistry to keep our budding relationship accelerating ahead. I was firmly on second base and had no immediate urge to go any further. My father liked Holly, especially because she was Episcopalian, and was happy to chauffeur us to movies and a weekly dancing class that included instruction in all the ballroom maneuvers we'd never use and ample opportunity for us to sneak away and make out.

Mrs. Chase drove us to a Wampum Yacht Club dance in July. All the preppies were home from their regionally competent or nationally prestigious New England schools. The boys' uniforms were khaki shorts or chinos, Izod golf shirts or long sleeve pinstripes for those with skinny arms, and Topsider moccasins. The girls wore pastel skirts and blouses from Talbots, headquartered in nearby Hingham.

I remember the music was perfect for a warm starry night on the harbor: Connie Francis' ode to heartbreak, "Everybody's Somebody's Fool"; Chubby Checker's "The Twist," with the girls gyrating sexily and the boys stiff as boards; Johnny Burnette's bouncy teen love ballad "You're Sixteen" ("Ooo, You come on like a dream, peaches and cream, lips like strawberry wine"); early Motown from the Shirelles ("Will You Love Me Tomorrow"); the plaintive "I'm Sorry" from Brenda Lee; everybody singing along and laughing with "Alley Oop" from the Hollywood Argyles; the inevitable Elvis ("Stuck On You"), with the boys trying haplessly to imitate the Great Gyrator; "Runaway," the latest from hit machine Del Shannon; "Travelin' Man" from TV heartthrob Ricky Nelson; last summer's out-of-nowhere smash hit, "Itsy Bitsy, Teeny Weeny, Yellow Polka Dot Bikini" from Brian Hyland; and one of the great "We're gonna slow things down" numbers, "Save the Last Dance for Me" by The Drifters.

By this time, most of the partygoers had drifted out to the dock for a cigarette or a sip of booze from a stolen flask. I was mildly surprised to see Holly light up but it was then an epidemic, especially with teenagers, whose parents were oblivious to the lung cancer perils. We knew most of the teens from our catboat races, and the girls were talking about their summer jobs. Several were summer baby-sitting for families on Martha's Vineyard and Nantucket--a popular choice for preppy girls desiring maximum beach time and minimal "heavy lifting." Also popular with WASP parents, because it removed the potential for mother/adolescent daughter conflict, stationed the girls with the "right people" in the right ambience and planted a maternal seed that would hopefully flower in rich soil.

Before leaving, we got a surprise boat ride around the harbor from lobsterman "Freddy" (short for Federico) Fernandes, on the trip home from checking his lobster pots. Freddy made extra money by booking weekend fishing trips, and my dad and I had been out with him several times. He looked like a cross between Anthony Quinn and Robert Shaw, and was a highly-respected "man of the sea" and village personality.

"Hey Jack…How did you end up over hea on the Right Side of the hahba?"

"Easy…I got invited by a Yacht Club member."

"You folks wanna take a short ride? It's a beautiful night."

We jumped aboard and I introduced Holly to Freddy. He was familiar with David Chase's 40-foot yacht *Bull Market* ("That's the best-looking boat in the fleet!")

Holly was curious about lobster fishing, and Freddy was happy to provide an intro.

"Few people know this, but lobsta used to be called 'poor man's food'. Back in the 1800s they were so plentiful you could catch them from shoah with your baya hands. Now it's a little tuffa; you need a boat, traps and buoy mahkuz. Mine are blue and white—the Wampum High cullas."

Throughout Freddy's little lecture I was steering his boat around the "hahba," trying not to collide with any high-priced

65

sailing or power yachts. (*"If you hit anything, Jack, make shoea it's small and ugly."*)

"*So I'm just coming back from checking my traps,*" he continued. "*Nomally my nephew Franny ("Francesco") crews with me, but he's bahtending at the country club. On the way out we bait the traps with salted herring that we put in these mesh bags with the drawstring. Two traps get attached to each buoy, and we drop them at a depth of about fawty to a hundred feet. The bricks are what weigh them down so they sink. The trap has a kitchen, hea, and a parla, hea…see? The lobsta entas the kitchen, where the bait is tied. When it tries to escape, it goes into the parla. These small vents hea allow the smalla lobstas to escape, but the larja ones get stuck.*"

Holly asks how big a keepable lobster needs to be.

"*Heas a keepa. It needs to be 3 and three-eighths to 5 inches from hea on the body to hea. You don't want to bring back any undasized lobstas cuz that's the day the Coast Gahd will be checking and they'll hit you with a fine. Then they'll staht stopping you moa often. On a bad day we'll throw back three kwatuz of the catch. We put a band on the keepas and drop them over hea in the holding tank. Now one otha thing: if you catch a female lobsta that's carrying eggs, called "berrying," you hafta cut a V in her tail fin and throw 'er back.*"

I got us back to the dock without incident, and we thanked Freddy for the lobster lesson.

"*My pleasah! Wave if you see me out on the watta.*" Freddy never missed a Wampum football game. His nephew and crew member Franny Santos was a source of great pride: an All Conference lineman who was destined to become the family's first college graduate.

***

Holly and I discovered we had something unique in common: brothers who were highly eccentric and way outside the mainstream of normalcy. She had met Frankie on a couple of occasions and was unusually sympathetic compared to my other friends, who were at best amused. It turned out she had a brother "Benjy," a year younger than Frankie, who was severely autistic and attended a "special school" in Newport.

Despite pleas from Laura, David Chase apparently wanted to keep Benjy as far away from home as possible. He would be spending the summer at a "special camp" in New Hampshire, managed by the "special school" and attended by many of its current students. Holly informed me that when Benjy very occasionally visited the family home in Wampum, her father would arrange to be out of town. The mere sight of his mentally impaired offspring apparently repulsed him. Laura Chase visited Benjy monthly, but was never accompanied by her husband.

One day Holly showed me Benjy's artwork, which was unusually dramatic for a child his age. He painted seascapes in vivid blues and oranges, but his oceans were turbulent and there were often characters in conflict. I remember one where a man was strangling a woman in the surf while people sat nearby on beach towels paying no attention. I could barely draw cartoon characters at that age. Like Frankie with his ability to retain very detailed information, Benjy had a gift. But unfortunately, both Frankie's and Benjy's gifts were concealed beneath layers of behavioral barbed wire.

Holly was unusually protective of Benjy—certainly compared to my indifferent treatment of Frankie. She praised his intelligence and creativity and resented her father and others treating him as an outcast. From what I remember of Benjy's room, it was devoid of any childhood joy. There were no posters on the wall, no toys on the floor, no sports equipment or memorabilia anywhere. His art and art supplies were concealed in a mahogany box under the bed.

67

I didn't see much of Holly for the rest of the summer. She was vacationing with her parents in Nantucket and I was getting my introduction to the "working world" at Golden Sportswear, my dad's employer in Dorchester, outside Boston. The drudgery of summering in a warehouse was partially offset by the joy of receiving and spending my first paycheck and interacting with a loveable crew of blue collar "lifers." When Meyer The Manager (whose son was a math major at Harvard) wasn't patrolling the floor, the lifers and I would amuse ourselves by playing hide-and-seek and other games which proved 1) that we were children at heart and 2) that we weren't the slaves of management. I, of course, had the extra pressure of not getting caught goofing off since it would embarrass my dad.

Looking back, I realize that the sailboat races were at one end of the WASP spectrum and the factory floor at the other. While the Uber WASPs socially navigated among the yachtsmen, we were meant to follow behind in a dinghy.

But social caste-ing aside, it was a pretty enjoyable time of life. I was doing well at school, getting better at a sport I enjoyed, dating an attractive girl, growing up in an elegant seashore community. Everything but my zits, and occasionally Frankie, seemed All Good.

***

Holly wanted to see me before school started, and decided to sneak me over on a mid-August Friday, when her parents would conveniently be out to dinner with friends.

It was a cinematically stunning evening, with a pale red communion wafer moon that transformed the briny Atlantic into a champagne carpet.

I had learned a shortcut through the woods to The Villas and was there in fifteen minutes.

Holly met me at the front door with an intoxicating aura of perfume. We kissed in a new way that was more adventurous.

We drank the remainder of an open bottle of wine and Holly told me how much she had missed me, especially when she heard the songs from the yacht club dance.

I remember being nervous and talkative, and that it was Holly who finally led me upstairs to her room and turned out the light.

She guided my hand under her skirt and I felt an odd combination of arousal and anxiety. *What now?*

"Let's get under the covers."

We stroked each other, and I discovered the delicious moist spot that Mickey Spillane had prepared me for. *What next?*

"That's as far as I can go tonight without getting us in trouble."

I thought *Thank God* and then wondered if that made me a wimp.

"I hope you don't think I'm a cock teaser…I just wanted us to be a little more than kissers."

"Not at all."

"The good girls' sex manual says not to go past third base until you're eighteen."

"Can I borrow your copy?"

We talked and fooled around for a couple of hours and then Holly suggested I sneak out to avoid any embarrassing parental confrontations.

As I was leaving, I heard a distressed voice in the direction of my exit route, which crossed behind the Chase's screened porch.

"*How in God's name did this happen, David. <u>How</u>?*" Laura Chase sounded hysterical.

"The headmaster said there was a late day swim. Benjy and a group of kids were playing water tag behind a big wooden raft. There was a counselor with them, but apparently he got distracted. One of the kids started yelling for Benjy. The counselor dove in but couldn't find him for a couple of minutes. They did everything they could to revive him, but by the time they got him to the hospital it was too late." David Chase's account of this tragic story sounded like a network news broadcaster—solemn, regretful but composed.

"*How does a counselor of special needs children get <u>distracted</u>? My son was <u>drowning</u>. Oh my <u>God!</u>*"

"I told him we wanted a complete investigation. He said the police were contacted and are on the scene questioning everyone who was there."

"*I wanted Benjy home this summer, David. I wanted him <u>home</u>. He was away for a whole year. He should have been <u>right</u> <u>here</u>, where I could have watched out for him.*" She was sobbing.

"I'm sorry, Laura. I'll do everything I can to make sure we get answers."

After a long pause: "*I'm going up to get him. I don't want him lying alone in a strange hospital. You stay here with Holly and tell her what happened in the morning.*" Laura left the porch abruptly, followed shortly by David.

I bolted off through the woods as if I were being chased by Benjy's ghost. I realized I was running faster and faster, and had no idea why. About two minutes from my house I tripped over a tree root and fell headlong, striking my face against a rock and splitting my lip open. At home, I noticed I had blood on my shirt, and washed off as much as I could to keep my mother from asking questions.

As expected, Holly called me the next morning and was inconsolable. I could only tell her over and over how sorry, how very sorry, I was.

Chapter 10
"A Moral Compass"

After Benjy's death, Holly and her mother wore very dark veils of sadness. Following a private family funeral, they left town for two weeks to visit Laura's sister in Virginia, and when they returned, Holly was back in school. My parents wisely advised me to give Holly "space and time to process her grief" and I complied as well as a lovestruck adolescent could manage.

I remember a conversation with the as-usually-too-candid Hat in which she suggested that Holly might for a while associate me with the bad memory of the incident. She wasn't aware, of course, that we had more than an old-fashioned date. I had mentioned nothing except my bloody fall. There hadn't been much "community chatter" about the accident, according to my mother. Townspeople didn't know Benjy. He was just the "poor disturbed child" who drowned by accident, and his memory was soon buried.

I had a couple of after-dinner chats with Cap Campbell before he returned to Annapolis. Cap had become my honorary running coach. He was, I had discovered, the Naval Academy's cross country and track coach and was pleased to share his extensive knowledge with me. This included tips about warming up; recommended workouts for cross country and my track event, the 880; improving leg strength and stamina; and even race strategy ("Shadow your main competitor until the last hundred fifty and then accelerate past him to the finish line.").

Cap asked me to write to him occasionally and share my competitive results, which I did until graduation. He always responded immediately with welcome words of encouragement and tidbits about running. I could tell he was amused by the detailed accounts of my races, which got even longer as my results got better.

Cap had heard about Benjy Chase's death—probably from my mother—and offered his condolences, knowing that I was dating Benjy's sister.

"Jack, I'm sorry to hear about Benjy Chase. That was a tragic way to die."

"Thanks, Cap. Yes it was. Holly, my girlfriend, is very upset. She and her mom left town after the funeral."

"I don't know the family. Beth (Cap's wife) has met Laura Chase and says she's a good person…a strong woman."

"She and Holly are very close. They spend a lot of time together."

"There can be guilt as well as grief in these situations, Jack. Sometimes the best thing we can do is just listen. How is the father?"

"Holly doesn't feel he's grieving in the same way as her mother. She says he seems detached."

"He may not feel comfortable expressing his feelings. Men tend to have a problem with that. But I hope he and his wife can find a way to grieve together rather than apart. It's a heartbreaking loss for a parent. I can't imagine how devastated I would feel."

I CAN imagine, I remember thinking. *And it's not the way David Chase is responding.*

In mid-September, Holly called to tell me that her parents were transferring her from Miss Cabot's to Berkshire Academy in the western part of the state. They felt she "wasn't being challenged" at Miss Cabot's, and that living at home was "distracting her from her studies."

73

While unhappy, Holly seemed resigned to the decision and had apparently discussed it at length with her mother. She assured me we'd be able to get together during vacations and the summer, and wasn't interested in dating other guys. I told her the news was a shock and her absence would leave a big hole in my life, or something like that. I did pull it together enough to wish her luck and tell her I felt the same way about dating.

She was packed up and deported in a few days. I got letters from her almost every week, and continued pledges of fidelity, but this was long before cell phones and the opportunity for almost minute-by-minute communications. In those days there was one pay phone, several floors away, and a long line of homesick girls. All part of the paternal plan.

This didn't torpedo my relationship with Holly, but certainly blew it off course. Now there was a wide moat and a high castle wall to keep us apart, like in all the old stories of forbidden love.

***

High school in the Sixties: Chino pants and white socks...crew cuts and a dab of BrylCream...the humiliation of pimples...the humbling sight of your body in the locker room mirror...the frustrating insolubility of advanced math...the feeble attempts to impress girls...standing outside the campfire of the In Crowd...Four years of strict regimentation to toughen you up for life as an adult...But here and there a few pleasant yearbook memories: a couple of writing awards; most of my track and cross country competitions; and another unforgettable mentor, my English teacher Earnest ("Ernie") Gardiner.

If you loved to read and write, like I did, "Ernie" was your guy. He made the written word come alive. He'd select favorite passages, assign you one of the characters, and you'd be up in front of the class as if you were on stage. At a certain point he'd stop you and ask about your character, like what you (Hamlet) mean by "slings and arrows of outrageous fortune." It didn't seem possible, but we believed he had memorized *Hamlet*. He knew all the speeches and scenes without ever looking at the text.

His favorite literary theme was the "moral compass." It was the set of values that impacted a character's actions and ultimately determined his or her destiny. "True north" represents the right moral course to guide a character to a desired goal or outcome. Lady Macbeth steers Macbeth away from true north by suggesting he murder the king rather than wait his turn. Iago convinces Othello that Desdemona is an adulteress, although her love is actually true north, and his jealousy destroys them both. Huck Finn finds true north while traveling south on the Mississippi and experiencing the differences between decent people and deceivers.

Ernie would eventually become chair of the Wampum High English department and remained a mentor, friend, bridge partner and occasional contributor to my newspaper. He had wanted to teach at the college level but succumbed to Wampum's charms and "settled in." While I was at Wampum High he "promoted me" to Honors English—based on a humorous essay I had written for the school newspaper—encouraged me to enter several of my creative pieces in a national scholastic writing contest (two of which were winners), and wrote a glowing college recommendation that probably got me accepted at several schools that were "close calls."

Ernie had about ten thousand books, and at any one time about eight thousand were loaned out to Wampum students. He would hand one of his dog-eared volumes to a student with a comment like "The author of this book wrote it for <u>you</u>. It will change your life." Years later, students who were Wampum expatriates would come back and tell him how much his "loaners" had meant to them. Dickens, Hemingway, Baldwin, Salinger, Steinbeck, Twain, Joyce Carol Oates, Vonnegut, Dr. Seuss, whoever. Students of all abilities would rave about Ernie "opening doors" they had never thought of entering.

Ernie introduced me to two New England Johns: Cheever and Updike, and a ton of dramatists, among them Eugene O'Neill, Arthur Miller, Tennessee Williams, and Edward Albee. Being the dedicated Gardiner he was, he planted seeds that nourished your intellect. Cheever and Updike were masters of language who probed the psyches of suburban males, like the ones I was growing up with. The playwrights captured the poetry and pathos of characters in conflict and put it on stage, to remind us that we're all characters in a daily drama.

I became an English major because of Ernie, and more importantly, a Renegade WASP...trying to find and steer toward true north and often veering off course.

***

I graduated from high school in 1965, and I share one thing in common with my fellow Baby Boomers who graduated at that time: the shock and horror of the JFK assassination on November 22, 1963.

Born and raised in Massachusetts, educated at Harvard, courageous skipper of PT109, author of *Profiles in Courage*, US

76

Senator, husband of the lovely and sophisticated "Jackie," and for thirty-five months probably America's most charismatic President, JFK was "one of us" to Wampum folks, whether Democrat or Republican. His Hyannis Port home was not much more than an hour south of us on the Cape. As Walter Cronkite delivered the terrible news in a voice choked with grief, we all sat in stunned silence. After a few seconds, there were stifled sobs from a few girls who could shed the tears we boys couldn't.

In 1988, on the 25th anniversary of that terrible November day, I wrote a *Renegade WASP* column titled "Pondering JFK," which concluded as follows:

"So now, 25 years later, there are memorials everywhere bearing JFK's name and reminding us of his impact—on our national Center for the Arts and our Space Center, a major airport, hundreds of schools, buildings, roads and monuments throughout the world. His picture remains on the wall in millions of homes—his extramarital affairs either denied or forgiven.

JFK's inaugural address inspired our generation as no other president has done. But today, in our forties, we seem preoccupied with our own ambitions and responsibilities. We don't ask what we can do for our country; we ask what government can do to lower our taxes.

'If a free society cannot help the many who are poor', JFK warned 'it cannot save the few who are rich.' But twenty-five years later, there are more poor people than ever, and few crusaders dedicated to educating and employing them.

Jackie's pink dress, stained with blood from the bullet that assassinated her husband, didn't motivate us to pass sensible gun control laws. We insist on our Constitutional right to bear arms, although the Second Amendment is about maintaining an armed militia, not arming every citizen with a weapon of war.

So what is it that endures, twenty-five years after the death of Camelot? I believe it's the call to action that infused JFK's inaugural address and so many of his speeches. The torch that he passed to a new generation has taken us to the moon and beyond, mobilized us to volunteer for just causes, and accelerated the civil rights movement.

After 25 years, we can acknowledge JFK's moral flaws, and our own. But his passionate words and thoughts continue to challenge us to engage our better selves."

***

How is a moral compass like a real compass? I'm not a student of science, but I know that the magnetic North Pole is not the same as "true north," the geographic North Pole. It's about 1,000 miles south of true north, in Canada. Finding Ernie Gardiner's moral "true north" is just as elusive. Lots of forces are influencing that needle: DNA, parents, hormones, personal influencers to name a few.

I doubted that David Chase had a moral compass. But I feared whatever compass he had was steering him in my direction, on a collision course.

Chapter 11
Olympia

I can't close the book on high school without devoting a chapter to a very important influence on my life: Olympia Jefferson. Olympia and Holly Chase came along almost simultaneously, and I still wonder how I managed to juggle my relationships with them. Perhaps it's because one (Holly) was romantic and the other (Olympia) was intellectual, but there's more to it than that.

Near the end of my junior year of high school, Ernie Gardiner mentioned he had been contacted by an interesting woman: a new resident at the Serenity Shore health facility I mentioned at the end of "Run One." Her name was Olympia Jefferson, and she was taking a leave of absence from her faculty position at Boston University to recuperate from heart surgery. She had called the high school because she was interested in hiring a student part time to drive her to local spots of interest and also to "discuss works of fiction by African American writers, as preparation for the student's possible major in English at the college level."

I wasn't overly excited about the reading part of the job, which prompted Ernie to scold me for my lack of intellectual curiosity and ambition. "This is a great opportunity for you. It's a chance to study with a college professor WHO IS PAYING YOU to read great books. It's like an Advanced Placement tutorial. I thought of you first, but I'm sure the next person I approach will jump at the chance."

I asked Ernie for a night to think about it and discuss it with my parents. I already had a summer job at my dad's company and wasn't crazy about chauffeuring an ailing academic who wanted to talk my ear off about literature. And I had no idea that my "Holly thing" was going to blossom faster than an orchid in high heat.

My parents, of course, were highly enthusiastic about the offer. "You should be flattered that Mr. Gardiner offered you this chance!" said my mother, always attentive to Intellectual Development Opportunities for her Jack. My dad was enthused about my earning money, which he assumed would lower his tab for my college education. And since he was a BU grad, he was proud that I'd be working with a teacher from his alma mater. Both of them knew within seconds that Olympia Jefferson was an African American, although that hadn't occurred to me despite the focus on black literature.

I reluctantly agreed to meet with Ernie and Olympia at the high school in late May to "discuss her terms." While I had seen black women on TV, I had never met one in person. My first impression of Olympia was "dramatic and dignified." She was a large woman with piercing brown eyes and jet black shoulder length hair, which eventually would morph into an Afro cut.

I remember being somewhat intimidated in Olympia's presence, although she was gracious and never interrogated me. She mostly asked me about school, what books I enjoyed and what I hoped to do after high school. At one point she asked about my driving, and I told her I had learned on a '57 VW bug "cement mixer." She flashed a wide smile and said "That's quite an image!" I had never seen so many flawless white teeth. Then she took me completely by surprise by asking "Would you be embarrassed to be seen driving a Negro woman around Wampum?" I replied: "I'm a little embarrassed to drive anyone around in that car, except my friends." That seemed to be an icebreaker. She let out a deep throaty laugh, like two notes from a saxophone, which will always be My Favorite Laugh.

Olympia then told us about herself, her parents, her love for literature, her dream of writing a biography about W.E.B. DuBois, and her decision to take a leave of absence from teaching to recuperate from surgery in a "serene environment." She assured me that I would not need to drive her too far afield; perhaps a few trips back to Boston but not during the commuter rush. She offered me $25 for two weekly visits, plus 10 cents a mile, which Ernie thought was "very generous." I accepted and we agreed on a starting date a week later. Ernie told her to give him a call if I didn't keep up with my weekly reading assignments. "Jack is a very lucky guy. We white kids don't grow up reading Negro writers. It just isn't assigned and not considered part of the curriculum. But I've started putting a Baldwin or a Richard Wright on my summer reading list."

"Good for you! Don't forget Ralph Ellison and Lorraine Hansberry," Olympia remarked. "She just passed away from cancer, bless her heart."

To borrow the title of the well-known Alfred Uhry play, I spent the next two summers ('64 and '65) *Driving Miss Olympia*. We visited every library, book store, historical landmark, fashion and jewelry boutique and ice cream parlor in a twenty mile radius, and she introduced me to the educated person's "must see" Boston highlights, and made me take notes.

Faneuil Hall hosted impassioned speakers like Samuel Adams, abolitionists like William Lloyd Garrison and suffragettes like Susan B. Anthony. The Old South Meeting House was where 5,000 Sons of Liberty met in 1773 before marching down to Boston Harbor, boarding a British merchant ship and staging a surprise (Boston Tea) party. We ate clam chowder (pronounced "chowda" in Beantown) at the Union Oyster House, where Daniel Webster himself consumed their oysters; we browsed through the Old Corner Bookstore, which had published the original works of Hawthorne, Longfellow, Emerson and Thoreau; attended free Shakespeare on Boston Common, the country's oldest public green; rode a Swan Boat in the Public Garden; and visited the African Meeting House, built by black artisans as the First African Baptist Church in 1806, and where William Lloyd Garrison founded the New England Anti-Slavery Society.

On the rides home from these places, Olympia would make me describe what I had seen, enjoyed and learned. If she found my description unimaginative, she'd make me "use better words" or "put some icing on the cake" or "wake me up; I'm falling asleep." She was always teaching. To her, every object, every location, every person had a story, and it was your responsibility as a "man of letters" to learn the story, tell it to others and become wiser in the process.

Then there was the literature, and the history behind it. Olympia baptized me, holding my head under water and then bringing me up for breath long enough to make sure I understood what I was reading. When she was satisfied I did, she thrust another book in my hands and plunged me back under. Nineteenth century slave narratives. Booker T. Washington. The Harlem Renaissance. Langston Hughes. Zora Neale Hurston. *Native Son. Invisible Man. Black Boy.* Gwendolyn Brooks. *A Raisin in the Sun.*

We'd be driving and she'd start talking about Sojourner Truth and how, with help, she composed *The Narrative of Sojourner Truth* even though she never learned to read or write; counseled President Lincoln; helped women slaves escape from the South; and desegregated streetcars in Washington DC. Or she'd tell me about the book she hoped to write about Massachusetts-born W.E.B. DuBois, who was the first black to earn a doctorate from Harvard and was a co-founder of the NAACP. Author of *The Souls of Black Folk*, he believed that racial integration was the key to democratic equality. I could tell he was Olympia's hero, because she was always quoting him.

My favorite was James Baldwin, which seemed to please Olympia and perhaps confirmed that I was worthy of her private tutorials. We had long talks about Baldwin's life and works. In her opinion, Baldwin's writings contained the themes that were central to black writing: slavery, spirituality, racism, self-discovery and the dream of social equality.

The world of John Grimes in *Go Tell It on the Mountain* (Harlem) was as different from mine as Jupiter and Mercury. Still, wherever you go to church—Baldwin was a Pentecostal preacher; I was a suburban altar boy—you come to realize the wide gap between prayer book Christianity and the self-centeredness of the average Christian. The older I get, the more that gap seems to widen.

I continued to read Baldwin during my twenties, and still re-read him now. Fascinating man. Passionate civil rights champion. Friend of most of the major African American leaders and writers of his time. And yet an outsider, who expatriated to Paris because America was too narrow-minded for a gay, outspoken black man. To a young white man beginning to "kick the tires" of my WASP identity, Baldwin was a powerful voice in the pulpit. He was a Renegade Black.

Olympia Jefferson was much more professorial than political, but a South Boston political figure named Louise Day Hicks became a focal point for her ire. The daughter of a lawyer and influential judge, Hicks was elected to the Boston School Committee as a reform candidate, but became an outspoken opponent of court-ordered busing of students to inner city schools. Thirteen of those schools were 90% black and looked more like jails than educational facilities. Hicks — whom the columnist Stewart Alsop once called "Joe McCarthy dressed up as Polyanna" — tapped into the "Southie"-centric racial animosity that surrounded the anti-busing issue and later almost got elected mayor of Boston. But during the days I spent with Olympia, Louise Day Hicks was becoming a hot and polarizing news story. Olympia opened up to me about it during one of our walks together.

"Jack, forgive me for this. I'm a tutor. I should be nonpartisan. But this Louise Day Hicks campaign against busing makes me livid. She tricked the voters into thinking she was a reformer and then put on a white hood. Now she's the patron saint of South Boston racists, who don't want their little Patricks and Mary Magdalenes getting bused to underfunded ghetto schools."

"I thought busing was ordered by the court?"

"She's doing everything she can to prevent it except lie down in front of the buses, which is probably her next step. There's a lot of ways to be subversive, especially if you're well connected...Sick outs...Bus safety inspections...She'll probably file a series of appeals to the court order and get backing from her father's legal cronies."

"What do you think President Kennedy would have done if he were still alive?"

"He would have had his brother Teddy look into it, and maybe he could have persuaded her to back off. But you never know what skeletons are in the closet. Did the Kennedys and the Hickses socialize...or was there political animosity over Joe Kennedy's ambitions for Jack? We'll never know. JFK was a pragmatic idealist about things, including race."

"What would James Baldwin say about this?"

"He'd say it's another example of how we fail to live up to the ideals of our founders. All men are not created equal, and we're

becoming less equal all the time. And he'd say 'Watch out, because the anger is coming to a boil, and we need to fear the consequences'."

***

This was my racial sensitivity training in the Sixties: a few good books by black writers and tutoring from a warm, articulate and socially engaged black professor. Olympia's poor health prevented her from returning to the classroom, but she continued at BU as a diversity recruitment officer and consultant. She remained a friend and mentor until her too early death in 1992. I contribute annually to the Olympia Jefferson Scholarship Fund, established by the university in her honor.

As for the anti-busing battles in Boston, I wrote about them frequently as a small town newspaper editor. The Racial Imbalance Act of 1965 was just the first salvo in an extended conflict that raged throughout the Seventies and Eighties, not in Selma or Montgomery, but in our own Boston backyard. A man was injured by a flag-wielding assailant, and in retaliation another man was dragged from his car and beaten to death. Working class families protested loudly and children refused to get on the buses. Court appeals were litigated and adjudicated by people from outside the city whose children attended private schools, which only aggravated the sense of injustice. Whites fled to the suburbs, since most of the racially imbalanced schools were in Boston. Public school enrollments declined.

When the smoke finally cleared, the victors appeared to be suburban populations, parochial schools and all those remunerated for their efforts during the crisis. The vanquished included poor city public schools, students caught

85

in the crossfire and especially constructive and respectful dialogue (i.e., "good will toward men").

None of this ruffled any feathers in Wampum, since no one was planning to bus black kids to our faraway white campus. Eventually, we volunteered to accept some diverse faces, just to confirm our commitment to civil rights. But with real estate prices climbing there was little concern that the families of minority students could afford to relocate here.

Chapter 12
BA...Bachelor of Artifice (1965-69)

Back to the other woman in my life...

Holly's banishment to Berkshire Academy—four hours away in Massachusetts traffic—had the desired effect of keeping us apart. Add to that my summer "Olympia duty" and Holly's child care on Martha's Vineyard and we might as well have been a priest and a nun.

We kept in touch by phone (frequently busy at her end, there being only one in the dorm) and mushy letters, but there's no substitute for human touch, especially for adolescents. My two trips to "The Academy" were in retrospect hilarious attempts to navigate a minefield of romantic obstacles, including nosy dorm supervisors, libidinally clueless roommates, an overly illuminated campus, and a balky old VW that barely got me there and back. I rode home with pine needles in my crotch, but it was OK. We were still not ready for sex and it gave us something to laugh about years later.

Our senior year in high school was crammed with all the rituals of preparation for college life. Our secret plan was to apply to schools in the same proximity. Holly was perfect for Smith or Mount Holyoke. I was academically qualified for one of the small men's colleges, with the help of glowing letters from Ernie Gardiner, Olympia and Captain Campbell.

Just a few months before graduation, our plan was "on course," rounding the final buoy. We had even managed to spend a secret, amorous night together while I was interviewing in Holly's new neighborhood. She had been accepted at Smith on early decision and I was waiting to hear from four colleges, all within a ninety minute drive of the Smith campus. Holly was completing a senior project and preparing for the New England prep school sailing regatta. I was putting the finishing touches on the Wampum HS yearbook and training for the state small school 880 race— hoping to break two minutes.

As it turned out, David Chase fired a torpedo into the bow of our *Good Ship Lollipop* and sank us.

We were too naïve to realize that if he didn't want us becoming high school sweethearts in Wampum, he wouldn't let us become college sweethearts either. Holly had been careful not to discuss my application plans with her father, and whatever she told her mother would, she was sure, be kept confidential. But we forgot about the families' Saint Matthews connection, and the possibility of my mother proudly sharing the news of her son's acceptance at Trinity College in Hartford. Which, unfortunately, she did in late April, to David Chase. Chase, who knew damned well that Trinity was a mere "hour and change" south of Smith, was profuse in his congratulations to my mother.

Within twenty-four hours, Chase informed Holly that she needed to pursue her degree in another part of the country, where she could "experience a different culture." And oh yes, he knew a dean at Stanford—"a terrific, top notch school...every bit as good as the Ivy League"—who could guarantee her admission, given her excellent record. He would buy her a convertible so she could enjoy the beautiful weather and pay to have *Pegasus* sent across country. It was shameless bribery, but Holly knew she wouldn't be allowed to refuse, unless she chose to wait on tables and attend community college.

So it became, for us, "the sad summer of '65." I took the Martha's Vineyard ferry from Woods Hole a couple of times and we watched a few sunrises on Katama Beach, but the impending East Coast/West Coast divide was as untraverseable as a trip to the moon. We imagined a hundred scenarios that could liberate us but they all required more money or impulsiveness than either of us could muster. As independent as we imagined ourselves to be, we were pawns of a plantation system that segregated the Haves from the Have Nots. And David Chase was Massa.

I remember a brief but satisfying exchange with Chase after my last service as crucifer at Saint Matthews before summer break. I noticed him sitting alone in a rear pew as I led the choir out during the recessional. He had an expression that I couldn't describe at the time, but today would call "benign contempt." A few minutes later, he was waiting in the rear parking lot as I exited.

"Holly tells me you've been accepted at Trinity. I want to congratulate you. That's a fine school."

I shook his extended hand very firmly and briefly.

"Thanks, Mr. Chase. I've also been accepted at Pomona College in California, so I've got a decision to make. They're a Top Ten small college nationally, and they have an excellent English program."

Actually I hadn't applied to Pomona, but had spent a few desperate hours researching California schools. If California were a baseball stadium, Claremont would be in the "nose bleed" section, but it was close enough to Stanford, in Palo Alto, to give Chase some serious *agita*. I wanted him to spend a few nights stewing at the thought of Holly and me sailing in San Francisco Bay on the boat he had paid dearly to ship west. I imagined him trying to bribe the Pomona admissions director to withdraw my acceptance.

"Well, whichever school you attend will be lucky to get you. Good luck!"

He turned and left as briskly as he did the day he shot the woodchuck in our yard. Superbly trained corporate animal that he was, he never blinked in wishing me good luck. But I knew that when he found out I was bullshitting him, the war was on, and he would deliver the next kick to the balls.

***

As Holly and I prepared for college in Connecticut and California, friends whispered their concerns that long distance consumes relationships like Japanese beetles eat flowers.

True as that turned out to be, we both landed in what turned out to be the right places. Holly escaped her father's tyranny and transplanted to a northern California climate rich in culture and diversity. I was able to leave an increasingly unhappy household and get absorbed into a delightful community of "creative brothers."

Hartford, an "Insurance Capital" and onetime home of Mark Twain, was a comfortably-sized New England city surrounded by well-heeled suburbs. Trinity—then still an all-male enclave—was nestled in a classic, pastoral campus surrounded by an iron fence. Along with Amherst, Williams and Wesleyan, we were part of a consortium of small, selective colleges throughout New England and upstate New York which would produce the next generation of Corporate Executives, Community Leaders and a few Well-Educated Slackers.

I attended Trinity from 1965 to 1969—during the most turbulent period of American history in my lifetime to date. While I matriculated in serenity, fires were burning around the country and the world. Martin Luther King Jr. and 2600 others were arrested in Selma for protesting discriminatory voting laws. Deadly race riots in Watts, Detroit, Newark and Birmingham. The assassinations of Dr. King and Bobby Kennedy in April and June of 1968. Violent antiwar protests at the Democratic National Convention in Chicago. The 1969 Stonewall riot in New York City--the beginning of the gay rights movement.

Freshman year was a painful adjustment for a provincial public school kid. The "preppies" were more familiar with dorm life and better trained to schmooze with their professors. The required science and math courses were inscrutable to a "left brainer" like me, and left me with scratches, bruises and grades of "low C" or worse. In cross country and track, I was right alongside the competition until the last few hundred yards, and usually behind at the finish.

But my toughest adversary turned out to be Time Management. I would always put off my term reports and papers until the last minute, and then hyper-caffeinate myself to survive one or several "all nighters." I once had to pull four consecutive all nighters, during which one of my roommate's dates pointed at me one-finger-typing in the corner and said "What's THAT?" After finishing, I turned in the history paper, returned to my dorm room and fell into a non-medically-induced coma from Thursday afternoon until Saturday morning.

My freshman grades were mostly dismal, and provoked justifiable rebukes from my parents about their return on investment. I was majoring in "Road Trips to Women's Colleges" and minoring in "Non-Assigned Reading." I advanced rapidly in "Social Development," but it didn't show up on the transcript.

If I had continued on this path, I would have graduated "summa cum lousy," but thanks to a summer pep talk from

Ernie Gardiner ("You needed a year to break out of your shell; now flap your wings and get going!") I took a better attitude back to campus. I climbed up to Bs first semester and was allowed to pledge a fraternity. I accepted a bid from "The Kappas," a diverse group of creative individuals who truly became "brothers" during our time together. We were not the football frat or the rich boys club or the Dean's List Role Models or the Drunk Around the Clock crew. We were rowers and fencers, poets and philosophers, motorcyclists and tinkerers, and lovers of the bizarre and eccentric.

At the time, Theatre of the Absurd was the "in thing," with its nonsensical dialogue and characters caught in bizarre situations. Prominent TOA works included Beckett's *Waiting for Godot*, Albee's *Zoo Story*, Ionesco's *The Bald Soprano* and Pinter's *The Homecoming*. The eccentric plots and characters seemed to mirror the absurdity of the times, especially Vietnam and the Sixties counterculture. We Kappas would often engage in absurdist dialogues until the wee hours of the morning in the frat kitchen area. A slice would sound something like this:

"Brother Boyd, what brings you to our circle from the nether regions?"

"My hunger, my boredom and your company, in that order."

"Well, now that you're in the company of your intellectual superiors, you'd better not be boring."(The italics include everyone other than Brother Boyd.)

"Oh <u>please</u>...I have mold in my refrigerator that's intellectually superior to you." (Boyd gets coffee and joins the group.)

"We're inventing a new game called, "Femme Fatales." You give the first name and a clue, and the group guesses the last name. Has to be a girl. So 'Anna the big hugger' is 'Anna Conda'"

"I got one. Ginger who had a nervous breakdown."

(Silence) *"Ginger....ails?"*

"Not bad, but I was thinking of Ginger Snaps."

"Terry who talks too much."

(Silence) "Oh come on. Nothing from the Intellectual Giants? How about Teri-Yaki? Yaki as in *Yak, Yak* on the phone?"

"It's not brilliant, Boyd...but we won't throw you out. Here's a better one: Barb, a girl you can get hung up on."

"Um. Bar...barbiturate"

"You're trying too hard. Hung up on what? Barb <u>wire</u>."

"It's <u>barbed</u> wire, not barb wire."

"See, that's your problem, Boyd. You're so focused on the petty stuff, you miss the right answers."

And on and on it would go, until the wee hours of the morning. Were some of us stoned? You be the judge.

Let me try one on you, the reader. We'll pick a "Femme Fatale" in honor of Holly: "Holly who pawns her watch?"

***

Holly and I had "released each other" during the summer between our freshman and sophomore years. It just wasn't possible to maintain anything except a "pen pal" relationship. So I was surprised to hear from her during Christmas break. Her mother had insisted David Chase send her a round trip plane ticket, and she called me a couple of days after Christmas. My mother—a Holly lover from the outset— eagerly handed me the receiver, her face aglow.

"Hi it's me...Do me a favor and take this in another room."

I went up to my room and closed the door. "Hi. What's up? I'm surprised you called."

93

"I need to talk to you. It's not about the breakup. It's about some very serious shit and I don't know who else to discuss it with. Can you meet me?"

"Sure. Where?"

"It has to be a private place. Do you know the little beach on the dead end street off Dickinson, just past Longfellow Bridge?"

It was an occasional make out spot, but not during the winter months.

"Yup. That should be private enough."

"OK. I'll meet you there in an hour. Please don't tell anyone. It's absolutely that serious."

An hour later, she was sitting in my car in the pitch dark. She had lit a cigarette, and was dropping the ashes in a coffee cup.

"Jack, I had a visit from someone during Thanksgiving break. I don't know how in God's name he found me. (Her voice was quivering.) He's a senior at Choate and was visiting his dad in San Francisco, who had just had a stroke. (She stopped to gather herself.) This guy--his name is Peter—was one of Benjy's camp counselors the summer he drowned. He says it wasn't an accident, Jack. *It wasn't an accident!* The swimming counselor told him that the headmaster, Bannon, sent him on an errand and said he'd watch the swimmers for 15 minutes. When the kid came back, Benjy had drowned. This bastard Bannon told him he'd cover for him with the cops. Then a few days later he bribed him with a thousand dollars for the emotional suffering and promised to get him into an Ivy League school. And you know what school he went to? Dartmouth. *Dartmouth. My father's alma mater.*"

At this point, Holly began to sob and I held her for several minutes.

"Holly, how could that have happened? The police were all over it for weeks. Your father hired a lawyer to make sure all the evidence was gathered and investigated."

"They all know each other, Jack. The cops and Bannon. It could have been a cover-up. The camp brings a lot of money into that community. The cops may be in his back pocket."

"So you think Bannon wandered off or got distracted and then had to cover his ass?"

"Or was the counselor off smoking a joint somewhere. Jesus. My head aches and I haven't been able to sleep more than a half hour at a time for weeks!"

"Did he give you the counselor's name?"

"No. The cops have it but the kid's father is a prominent doctor and he also got a lawyer. Their story was that the kid had diarrhea, had to leave the area and couldn't find anyone to cover for him. Bannon had to fire him, but no charges were filed."

"Could your father's lawyer track him down and get a confession?"

"I don't know. I just think it's a 'done deal'. It's all dead and buried now. The freaky little disabled kid swallowed some water while somebody wasn't looking and life goes on for the normal."

"What does your father think?"

"I haven't told my father, or my mother. I don't want to put my mother through any more anguish. My father...Why haven't I told my father, Jack?"

"I think because you're afraid he may be part of a cover up."

"And why would he cover up the death of his own son?"

"Because he was ashamed of him."

"Now you know why my life has been a living hell. Because whatever happened has been sealed up. Nobody's guilty. Everybody walks away. Except Benjy...and me."

95

We just sat there for a long time. Holly was completely drained. Finally, she opened my car door and stepped out.

"Thank you, Jack. I couldn't talk to anyone else."

I called the next few days but never reached Holly, and when someone finally answered it was her mother.

"It's good to hear your voice, Jack. Holly said she saw you and you looked great. She just left this morning and said if you called she'd be in touch."

Actually, she wouldn't be in touch for another six years.

***

My college years passed very quickly. I'd grade the overall experience a "B+"--a major comeback from freshman year. I became a more discriminating reader and a less pedantic writer. I dabbled in the business world: a part-time job with an insurance company leading to summer work in Boston. I ran cross country and track, without distinction, but scored a few points for the teams. I sang second tenor with the glee club and especially enjoyed the joint concerts at women's colleges. And I learned to play bridge, which pleased my parents and led to a lifelong expenditure of thousands of hours which could have been spent more productively.

The high point of my baccalaureate experience was social and the low point was what I'd call "social conscience."

As I shared briefly, my non-traditional fraternity experience was a joy. It was like swimming in a tank with many varieties of tropical fish. We "frat dwellers" lived on the moldy side of sleaziness—especially our bathrooms, which resembled the inside of a used condom. Our girlfriends or dates either accepted the slum motif or never came back. We were satisfied with semi-clean plates and eating utensils, a rusty coffee machine, mostly insect-free food and—our piece de resistance—a well-stocked and furnished bar area. If that wasn't good enough, the hell with you; you belonged at a more mainstream establishment.

Sexually, it was the most active environment we likely would ever encounter. It was a pre-marital buffet before the post-marital TV dinner. These were the years when you were an Old Maid if you weren't married by 25, so the coeds were expanding their sexual resumes before their seduction of Mr. Right.

Young men like me were under the false impression that we were introducing female ingenues to the Wonderful World of Sex. In truth, the ingenues were way ahead of us. They were surprised and delighted when they found someone who knew what he was doing, which of course "included me," although it probably didn't. They were prepared to deal with all kinds of erectile dysfunction, and to coax our sometimes deflated "Mr. Happies" into doing something that could please them.

My goal was an orgasm at around two minutes; that was sexual success according to my frat buddies. My foreplay was what it took to get a girl hot; there was no seductive finesse in my playbook. I seldom deviated from the missionary position, to give my partner a more erotic sensation. If I got my rocks off, I was blissfully satisfied, and certainly, in my mind, that was enough for both of us, especially if my partner "faked it," which most did. The facts of life are passed along clumsily from male to male but ideally should be communicated by an aunt or a female doctor. As if that's going to happen, right?

But while the sex itself was less exhilarating than it might have been, my liaisons with the opposite sex were memorable. The gender role I played most successfully in college was "liberator." I spent the night in a girls dorm at Vassar, which earned my bedmate the admiration of her dorm sisters and a badge of honor as a Violator of The Curfew. I smoked joints in a dorm at Mount Holyoke, which led to heavy "f word"-laced dialogues about lecherous and condescending professors. I had a threesome with roommates at Connecticut College, one of whom later confessed the experience made her realize she was a lesbian. I dated a black girl at Smith, which satisfied our mutual curiosities about interracial sex. For three years, college was a Whitman's Sampler of Erotic Adventures. Sadly, I didn't mature much beyond the mindset that young women were conquests, not potential partners. I was too busy posturing as a Sensitive Male and "Liberator in Waiting."

Nor did I risk my personal safety protesting racial discrimination or US military engagement in Vietnam. I watched television coverage of race riots and read a few anti-racist best sellers. I engaged in passionate late-night diatribes against the stupidity and absurdity of the war effort. But I never occupied a building, never risked bodily harm or arrest or even dared to be incarcerated.

My urges were hormonal, not ideological...self-gratifying, not self-sacrificing.

I wrote an article for the college newspaper called "Oversleeping the Revolution," but was afraid to submit it for fear of being judged harshly by my more activist classmates. I kept a handwritten copy though, and will share an excerpt here because it may speak for other armchair idealists like me:

There are blood stains in the streets following this apocalyptic year of 1968. Protesters in jail for confronting the Establishment. Freshly-dug graves for civil rights champions Dr. Martin Luther King and Senator Robert Kennedy, the latest casualty of the Kennedy family. Rows of coffins returning in transport planes from Vietnam with the remains of American soldiers.

I, however, have no blood on my clothing or grime on my hands. I have survived without cuts or bruises by oversleeping the revolution. When the alarm went off to remind me it was time to

98

assert myself and 'take arms against a sea of troubles' I simply
turned it off and went back to sleep. Perhaps tomorrow."

I graduated into the Real World in June of 1969, the year that reminded us of a famous sex act. A "2S" medical deferment spared me from the rice paddies of Vietnam, but I had done nothing to prepare for a career. I could apply for a public school teaching position through a "TEP" (Temporary Emergency Permit) despite not having any education credits. So I signed up with a placement agency and started sending my credentials to schools with English teacher openings for undrafted candidates.

"You're about to become a product and you need to learn how to sell yourself" would have been helpful advice, but career counseling wasn't a strength of small college English departments back then. They had handled my Basic Training and it was now my job to venture out, dazzle the world and contribute annually in ever increasing amounts to the alumni fund.

My English instructor and adviser, Dana Hollis, provided a welcome perspective on graduate school: "I know a lot of your fellow English majors are planning to get a masters or doctorate. I'd give that some serious thought. Three or four years from now the field is going to be more glutted than it is now. You'll be one of a hundred applicants to teach freshman English at Podunk. How about looking for a job in the private sector, like publishing or communications or public relations? Even teaching at the secondary level. You can earn some money and start considering your options. To be perfectly honest, that's what I wish I'd done now that I can look back."

Without his advice, I probably would have taken the "default option" and gone to grad school. It would have been the wrong choice. I needed to get out of the library and start making my way down Career Street.

p.s. "Holly who pawned her watch?" *Holly Hawks/hollyhocks.*

Chapter 13
The Wampum Totem (1970-72)

As the Apollo astronauts prepared to land on the surface of the moon in the summer of '69, I was preparing letters and resumes in hopes of finding a landing spot outside my college campus.

I had spent my senior year avoiding any effort to plan a career. It seemed futile given the likely prospect of military service in Vietnam. That seemed even more inevitable when my birthday was the thirteenth number chosen in the '69 military draft lottery. But as it turned out I was spared by my own neurology.

During my junior and senior years, I had begun to experience sharp pains on the right side of my face, brought on by triggers like brushing my teeth, shampooing my hair or even a strong breeze. A famous neurologist at Boston's Lahey Clinic identified my affliction as "trigeminal neuralgia," aka ticdoloreux. It was caused by friction between nerves and blood vessels and, based on the doctor's letter to the draft board, was enough to bump me from a 1A to a 2S draft status. Over the years, I'd have numerous injections and finally an operation to stop the spasms. (Dick whose face is contorted by pain? Dick Doloreux!)

With my combat boots filled by another unlucky draftee, I was able to start looking for a job. At the time, given the public school teacher shortage, I could teach under a Temporary Emergency Permit (TEP) with no teaching credits, as long as I took education courses in the summer. I was offered a high school English position at New Britain HS outside Hartford, where I was a mere three years older than the seniors. More than twenty of New Britain's non-college-bound seniors were sent to Vietnam that year. They didn't have the exotic health issues or other escape routes available to me.

I taught for two years and saved every penny I could pinch. A math teacher and I split the rent on a little cottage on a lake and, amazingly, I was able to save almost half of my $6500 first year salary. I found I enjoyed the classroom and the interaction with young people, who were willing to be seduced by literature if you breathed some life into the characters and situations. I was big on dramatic readings and would assign fictional characters to class members as a way of getting them to talk about themselves. Every now and then they would blow me away, as when I asked them to write their own variations on the Romeo and Juliet balcony scene. There would always be that quiet boy or girl who'd "take the stage" in front of the class and surprise everyone with their comedic talents. (This theatrical "playing it forward" is all thanks to you, Ernie Gardiner.)

My very first class was "10D," which the all-male students told me stood for "10 Dummies." They were the blue collar workers of the future: mechanically gifted but grammatically oblivious. They struggled to write two coherent sentences. To them, a term paper was three paragraphs and no punctuation. For nine years they had been passed along as virtual "uneducables." Their English teachers would try to pry open their prefrontal lobes and spoon in some culture, but 10D resisted it like brussel sprouts.

They loved to talk, though, and especially argue, so I got them reading editorials and writing talking points about various topics like Vietnam, freedom of speech and what's wrong with education. Because they were hunters and fishers,

102

they were willing to read a few of Hemingway's Nick Adams stories and *The Old Man and the Sea.* They liked Holden Caulfield in *The Catcher in the Rye* and wrote about what they thought he would become in adulthood. Two paragraphs max. Their favorite was *Of Mice and Men* because they knew a mentally disabled man like Lenny who had shot and killed himself while hunting, and some thought it had been a suicide.

As you might guess, 10D was my favorite class. I enjoyed the honors classes, of course, but 10D had a refreshingly stubborn integrity. If they didn't like something--poetry, for instance--they'd complain "Nobody talks like this" or "If it doesn't rhyme, it's not poetry, right?" If they discovered a personal connection, though, they could stay engaged for an entire class period, which I viewed as a home run. Other rewards were seeing the 10Ds reading non-assigned books in study hall. Gotcha, buddy!

The challenge for me wasn't the students, it was the teachers. Or at least most of them, who seemed to deeply resent their students and complained bitterly about them in the Teachers Lounge. I didn't have the education credits they had accumulated, but my gut told me you needed to try to like these young folks, who were no more juvenile deviants than we were at their age. Some of the teachers had taught their current students' parents, and would verbally savage the entire family, as if to suggest that the mother or father should have been neutered—not allowed to produce any more ignoramuses.

There were also diatribes about how the new generation of teachers didn't know how to teach grammar or "business English." Who, me? I wasn't supposed to personalize this, I guess. "TEP," in their minds, must have meant Temporarily Employed Pretender. "We're not here to be friends with the students, Mr. Moustache," they insinuated. "We're the drill sergeants who prepare them to obey the grammar book or perish in the employment office."

OK, I admit I was a different breed of cat. I was more an English "marketer," trying to sell the beauty of the language and the joy of a story well told. As for grammar, I snuck up on the 10Ds from behind. I would give them examples of poor writing and everybody who could identify an error in usage got one point. First guy to 25 got a large bag of M&Ms. Stuff like that. Probably not a Recommended Classroom Procedure.

After my first two months, I stopped going to the Teachers Lounge. That was a signal to the "lifers" that I had defected to the dark side and should be viewed with extreme suspicion. I was probably smoking dope with the delinquents. Luckily, I found a few kindred spirits who also avoided the Lounge Lizards and we met in an abandoned supply room, which we called the "Palace Without Malice."

So it went for two years, at which time I had developed a plan of escape and stashed away enough acorns to partially fund a "sabbatical." During the summer of '71 I was able to visit London, Paris and Rome for less than a thousand bucks, which would be my only trip abroad for the next 20 years.

Then I returned home to Wampum to try something I knew was a mile over my head.

***

Recalling the advice of Professor Hollis to consider alternatives to teaching college English, I developed a plan to start a community newspaper, based in Wampum—the theatre equivalent of writing a play, performing it in your garage and then assuming you could take it to Broadway. It was an optimist's pipe dream, unless your last name was Rockefeller or Hearst.

The plan included my moving back home, since I had to hoard every dollar to start the paper. The home front had been destabilized by my four-year departure and Frankie's unnerving temperament. It was now a wasp's nest tyrannized by a crazy dweller who kept biting the other inhabitants. Hat had aged drastically while trying to keep the peace. I think she secretly wanted to die and ascend from earthly hell to a calmer place.

I did what I could to combat the daily traumas. I took Frankie to candlepin bowling twice a week. I went on walks with Hat. I insisted that my parents accompany me to the movies or some other local entertainment on the weekends. The rest of the time I was learning about newspapers, mostly by working as a general factotum (wonderful word meaning "a person with many diverse activities") at the *Quincy Constitution,* the closest newspaper to Wampum. I set type, wrote obituaries and sports reports, took photographs and occasionally swept the floors. It was great preparation for becoming the *Constitution*'s future competitor.

Meanwhile, I started searching for possible locations for my Wampum newspaper. I had a name —*The Wampum Totem*— which made it seem real and achievable in my optimistic moments. I particularly liked "Totem," because of the link to Wampum's Indian heritage and the totem pole's depiction of historical and cultural incidents.

So it seemed providential when I saw a sign in Wheeler's Hardware about the second floor being available for rent. I asked John Wheeler to show me the space, and, John being John, he wanted to know why. I trusted him with my plan for *The Wampum Totem* but made him swear he'd only tell his wife and they would keep the secret. I knew he could be trusted. I asked him about the rent and he quoted a price I couldn't afford, but we agreed to keep talking. John was Downtown Wampum's biggest advocate, and I could see a bulb go on when he considered a newspaper being published in his building.

Somehow the Peirces survived the holidays of '71 and I continued my apprenticeship while reading every book and article I could find about starting a newspaper. I had slightly over $5,000 in savings, but wasn't adding to that amount. My "allowance" at the *Constitution* was just enough to cover living expenses. I summoned the courage to ask John Wheeler about becoming a part owner of the *Totem*, but being a frugal and savvy Yankee he smiled and declined "for now." He did offer to make improvements to the second floor as soon as the rent checks started coming in.

My dad offered financial support, but I thanked him for the free rent and food and told him to save his money for Frankie. My parents didn't have much in the bank, but they had invested wisely in moving to Wampum, and would be rewarded a few years later when their modest home sold for five times its 1954 purchase price. Meanwhile, Frankie was working part time for my dad at Golden Sportswear, although his attitude and behavior wouldn't have been tolerated by anyone else. I'm sure my dad relished the two days a week he didn't have to commute with his hyperactive, improperly medicated son.

Winter finally melted into spring of '72 and I felt like I had shared my *Totem* secret with a dangerously large segment of our little village. My Wampum "inner circle" was cheerfully supportive and offered good advice and ideas for further networking. I had leads on possible staffers, potential advertisers, printers and paper suppliers, discounted furniture and equipment, lawyers and accountants. I kept increasing my budget to accommodate all the people and purchases I hadn't anticipated. Perhaps it was time to go back to Hartford and seek a stable career in insurance. (I had also forgotten to budget for insurance.)

Then, one day in April, about a week after a very discouraging visit to a local bank, I got an unexpected call from Holly. She was in town to visit her mother and had heard the rumor about my starting a newspaper. She wanted to talk about it and suggested we get together for lunch at the Chowder Bowl, the local watering hole for townies. I was eager to catch up, but will readily confess that my pilot light still burned for Holly. Seeing her again stirred a mix of memories and emotions. She had let her hair grow longer and was prettier than ever.

"So listen, I'll tell you everything that's been happening since you dumped me—just kidding!—but you go first. What's this about a newspaper? I think it's a great idea!"

I told Holly the whole story, including my getting shot down by the bank.

"If you had the money, could you make it work? Are there enough advertisers? Will people read another newspaper?"

I explained that there was a new mall being built in Hanover, one being planned in Hingham and strip malls popping up on the commuter routes to Boston. The stores need to reach the upscale customers on the South Shore and the South Shore folks want to read about themselves and their children and see their photos in the paper. We understand these communities better than the *Constitution*, which is more focused on Boston, and we have some well-educated married women who can write and edit and photograph and sell ads for a modest fee.

Holly was much more interested in talking about the paper than about herself, but she shared that she had just completed

107

her bachelors in Sociology at Stanford, having dropped out at the end of her sophomore year for "lack of motivation." She was working in the Oakland area for a community development organization, where she specialized in health and human services for the poor. It didn't pay much, but she had her father's subsidy, so could live outside the slums. Her mother wanted out of Wampum and was hoping to convince David that she needed to move in with Holly and help her "transition to professional life." Then she just wouldn't return home. But it was tricky. If Chase wised up to her deceit he'd turn off the money spigot for both of them.

I asked: "Our last conversation, six years ago...Did you find out anything more about Benjy's death?"

"No. I couldn't get confirmation of anything. The camp counselor who came to see me never returned my calls. Benjy's school wouldn't give me the name of the swim counselor who went to Dartmouth. They said it was an invasion of privacy. I even asked my father for help but he swore that all the questions had been asked and acceptable answers given. All the doors are triple locked. But I'm never giving up. Something's going to float out of the black hole eventually, and I'll be there."

I wanted to ask Holly about her social life, but couldn't. I don't understand why, but I felt like she didn't want me to ask. She could have asked about MY social life and I would have been happy to tell her I doubted if I'd ever meet someone I cared about as much as her. But she didn't ask, so I assumed she had moved on emotionally.

Two days later, Holly called me with some startling news.

"My mother wants to invest ten thousand dollars in your newspaper. No interest, and you can pay her back later."

"How?" That's the only word that came to my mind.

"She gets an annual allowance for putting up with him, and it seems to get bigger every year. He doesn't ask how she spends it."

"All I can say is, it's an unbelievably generous offer. I'm happy to sign anything she'd like that confirms the agreement."

"She trusts you, and I don't think she wants any paper he could discover while rummaging through her stuff. Not that he'd ever do that, of course."

Combined with my savings, the loan gave me enough working capital to launch the *Totem*. Enough for six months rent, a web press, second-hand furniture, basic signage and a handful of minimum wage jobs negotiated by handshake.

The next twelve months were a roller coaster of highs and lows, with ingenuity and insane work hours just barely overcoming the brute forces that conspire against small business success. These included "the competition" undercutting our ad rates; nasty winter weather that thwarted our distribution system; and quality control issues until we replaced our first print partner.

Fortunately, every time it looked like our *Totem* was going to fall over or blow away, some Good Spirit interceded on our behalf. In fact, community goodwill was the key to our success. After they'd seen a few issues, townspeople decided that having a Wampum-based paper was the logical next step in our evolution as a Premiere Community.

Not surprisingly, the *Totem* was all over South Shore sports, politics, social life, education and local issues. But we also profiled talented businesspeople and accomplished artists whose achievements were often "below the radar" of city-focused papers. We had round-table discussions with religious leaders about secular and non-secular topics. We interviewed local historians about the unique character of their communities and demographic changes that had taken place over time. We asked school superintendents about their priorities and challenges. We conducted "Totem Polls" on a quarterly basis, with topics ranging from current events to "Which new stores for the Shore?" to "What happens after death?"

It's a wonderful feeling when your little wave of popularity starts to grow. People toss you compliments at the supermarket checkout line or the dentist's office or the town beach. The enthusiasm of our readers kept the adrenaline flowing. I remember the comment of one citizen whose point of view we had defended in opposition to a town council member: "You know what I told him? The *Totem* has you by the scrotum!"

The investment we made in building relationships—with all kinds of people at all levels—was the difference between the paper's succeeding and failing. Those relationships came together like threads in a spider web (I never kill spiders) to form a community network that would support us no matter who ended up in the web.

By the end of '72, we had enough new advertisers to grow our tabloid from eight to sixteen pages. Holly had returned to Oakland, but I mailed her every copy. I've always considered Holly and her mother Laura my Founding Angels, who arrived in the nick of time to transform the *Totem* "from concept to content."

What an incredible time to be in the newspaper business. Woodward and Bernstein were beginning to track evidence that connected the Watergate burglary to Nixon's White House. By doing so, they affirmed the power of the press to get behind the curtains of deceit and expose corruption at the highest levels. Vietnam War correspondents increasingly questioned the rationale of Washington's strategy against the backdrop of Saigon political instability and the savage stalemate on the battlefields.

Here we were in the affluent suburb of Wampum—seemingly immune from global turmoil—but in fact our own little microcosm of darkness and light. And I'd get to be its chronicler.

Chapter 14
The Four Aces

I've mentioned Wampum's Atlantic Villas on several occasions. "The Villas" was developed in the mid-Fifties by Byron Bentley, whose vision was to create a community that rivaled the Newport Cliff Walk estates. Bentley was a master marketer who knew that his vision would stir memories in his preppy WASP clients of family visits to Doris Duke's "Rough Point," the Vanderbilts' "Breakers" and the lavish 70-room "Rosecliff," featured in the Hollywood film of *The Great Gatsby*. He had less acreage than the Cliff mansions, and his homes were several city blocks from the ocean, but if you owned a property in the Villas you were as close to the Dukes and Vanderbilts as you could get with a name like yours, that didn't smack of the Boston Cabots or Lowells.

Bentley, who had made his early money building sturdy homes in the suburbs for returning GIs, sculpted two "bookmark" stately mansions at either end of his property, which he called "Whitecaps" and "Captain's Watch." He decorated them lavishly, but tastefully, with mahogany, stained glass and New England antiques. He then scheduled open houses with area realtors and promised them an extra 5% bonus on their commission for the first ten homes sold at the Villas. When the bookmark mansions were sold within two weeks—to a Boston restauranteur and the eccentric widow of a Gillette executive—the Villas was mobbed by well-to-dos eager to drop anchor near the edge of the Atlantic, facing The Old Country.

Among the early "lords of the castles," as they came to be called by townspeople, were four men who would bond socially and athletically. They would share a passion for tennis, and would monopolize the Wampum Country Club singles and doubles championships for over a decade. They would become sponsors of charitable community events. And they would share a deep-seated but well-concealed contempt for anyone they viewed as "the competition."

The men were David Chase (wife Laura and children Holly and "Benjy"), Oliver Hawk (wife Trudy), Stan Kestrel (wife Bunny and daughter Kristin) and Morgan Shrike (wife Muffy). Their nickname, "The Four Aces," was a tribute to their skills on the tennis court, where they dominated from the service line—serving aces—and overwhelmed ("aced") their competitors.

You've met Holly's parents, the Chases. David is employed by Monarch Financial and is rising so rapidly in the company that he is assumed to be the next CEO. In today's parlance, he is an "Alpha Male," but "Dark Alpha Male" is more accurate. Think of the Polo label with the rider carrying a sword rather than a mallet. He dominates Hawk, Kestrel and Shrike, although they don't acknowledge this to themselves or their wives. At work, he's the one everyone around the conference table defers to, and whose opinion you'd better not challenge unless you'll be OK with a transfer when he takes charge.

Chase was thought to be a "self-made man," but Laura and Holly, over time, provided a different perspective. Chase's father had inherited the family insurance company, but a combination of his poor health and indifferent work ethic left the company on the verge of bankruptcy. At that point, Chase's mother asserted herself and took control. She taught herself the insurance business and began to compile a network before "networking" had even been discussed as a business tactic. Long story short: she transformed an imminent failure into one of the most successful woman-run businesses in the northeast. Laura described her mother-in-law as "the most charming and ruthless woman I ever met and ever hope to meet, may she rest in peace." (She passed away from a stroke in the late fifties.)

"Celeste Chase verbally abused her husband into an early grave and then proceeded to manipulate David, her only child, in every way possible," according to Laura. "She taught him how to seduce others into helping achieve his goals, and to always maintain The Upper Hand. I thought of her as the Wicked Witch in *Snow White*—always ready to offer some rival a poisoned apple. One of those rivals was me, so I never accepted any fruit from her," she said with a chuckle.

"But I'll say this for her..." Laura continued. "She fought tooth and nail to push David up the social ladder, even when it meant depriving herself. Best prep school, best clothes, best social contacts and admission to Dartmouth, an Ivy League school. She positioned him for success in what she knew was still a Man's World, and made sure there were successful—by her standards—role models to teach him 'the ropes'."

Oliver Hawk (Hawk Luxury Motors) owns an automobile dealership in a neighboring town, at the epicenter of wealth on the South Shore. His wife Trudy is the prototype "trophy wife" for the Villas. Always exquisitely coiffed and made up, dressed a little more provocatively than the other wives, and an aggressive party girl who can drink most of the men under the table and never slur her words. She was starving for excitement and recognition in her old neighborhood, but is thriving in this new soil. Eventually, if you want the perfect chairwoman for your nonprofit event, you'll ask Trudy Hawk, and she'll carry it off with flair and panache. The Hawks are childless; Trudy didn't want the stretch marks.

Stan Kestrel, son of a dentist, is a highly successful plastic surgeon ("Finishing Touches Surgical Associates"). He was born Jewish, but has repudiated all vestiges of Jewish faith and identity, and hopes we assume he's a WASP, like his wife Bunny. Their daughter Kristin, like Holly, attends Miss Cabot's School, and the Kestrels hope she will adopt a preppy persona. Bunny is a bit more intellectually curious than Trudy; she subscribes to *Vanity Fair*, while Trudy seems content with *Cosmo*. Bunny and Stan are a formidable mixed doubles team and will own that trophy at the country club for as long as they choose to compete. Stan's clients include show biz stars, whose names he won't share with us common folk, and the wives of high-ranking corporate execs, trying to keep the wrinkles to a minimum and fend off any seductive young competitors.

The foursome is completed by Morgan and Muffy Shrike. Morgan runs an exclusive import/export business (Shrike Global Imports) catering to those who like to fill the rooms of their estates with expensive objects and then replace them every five to ten years. I introduced Morgan very briefly in chapter eight as the guy who threw an out-of-town troublemaker off the Longfellow Bridge—almost drowning him—and got away with it. This would have made his father, the late Marine Colonel Harlan ("The Hammer") Shrike, very proud had he not passed away years earlier following a life of excess and verbal violence. Morgan had found his late father extremely difficult to please, especially after passing up the Marines for service in the Coast Guard, which The Hammer referred to as "the Presidential yacht club."

Byron Bentley found a way to squeeze thirty-six "mini mansions" into the Villas, and installed a gated entrance—the first such security device in the region. He incented Villas-neighborhood landowners by offering them the opportunity to be "incorporated" into his community. They sold him their land and he offered free upgrades to their properties and other services; in return, he could build a few additional mega-homes within his exclusive acreage. Win/Win.

By the late Sixties, Bentley had soured on The Villas and sold his properties to The Villas Ownership Group. There were rumors he was having an affair with a Villas wife; or that he was secretly bankrupt, which was very far from the truth; or that he had found a great location for Villas II near Hyannis Port, on the Cape. None of the above. He had confided with someone I consider a trusted source that "I sold my homes to the most obnoxious bastards and bitches on the Eastern seaboard, and I never want to see them again. If I had a gigantic tractor, I'd shove them all into the Atlantic and piss on their heads." Or something like that. He apparently took his fortune and bought a sprawling ranch in Montana, where he lived happily ever after, free from the arrogance of the *nouveau riche*.

The Villas Ownership Group then created a seven-member committee, four of whose members were? Yes, "The Four Aces." The Committee—with the aid of their resident lawyers--drew up a contract of rules and regulations which discouraged any expressions of resident nonconformity and made allegiance to the safety and security of the Villas paramount. In effect, it became its own fiefdom (or duchy, if you'd prefer). Some of the less doctrinaire Villas residents would joke publicly about "The Compact," but you needed to be careful what you said. If you were perceived as a malcontent inside The Villas, you might suffer "Empty Mailbox Syndrome" the next time cocktail invites were issued.

We "Outer Villas" folk were invited inside the security gate twice during the year for charitable events. For $50. a couple we could board a little trolley bus and visit as many

116

"Villastates" as we wished during their May Open House to benefit the Wampum Little League. The teams and townspeople competed on a broad expanse of lawn in a wide variety of games like egg toss, baseball throw (the challenge—"Reach the Atlantic!"—was never met) and potato sack races. Prizes galore for all ages from trendy shops not often patronized by the winners. And a hefty sum for the Little Leaguers, very few of whom lived on the premises.

This event was eclipsed by the Villas' Christmas celebration, a fundraiser for the Wampum Historical Society. For this one, you judged each property's external Christmas decorations and the winning homeowners were acknowledged prominently in the *Totem* once we were up and publishing in '72. As you might imagine, the displays of lights were lavish, and the embarrassment of finishing outside the communal "Top Five" was enough to keep residents shelling out larger and larger sums to secure the talents of the most creative exterior designers.

All in the Christmas spirit, of course. For a mere $15 a head—which increased $5 annually—we fortunate attendees got hot chocolate, dozens of varieties of cookies and candies and the effusive goodwill of the Vill-ians who, most of us felt, were staging this annual event not out of charitable largesse but out of guilt for their inequitable share of good fortune. But hey, it's not like the Wampum villagers were eating sardines for Christmas dinner. For all but a very few of us, there were plenty of presents under the tree.

Growing up, I honestly never felt the sin of "Envy of the Affluent." There was a reason for wherever we were on the socioeconomic ladder, and I accepted it. These Lords and Ladies of the Villas were our royalty, and I didn't question their right to be. The wives, in their regal finery, were on display for us lower echelon folk. I would eventually discover that they only dressed to impress and slightly "one up" each other. Regardless, they were stunning in their aura of bright lipstick, artfully-applied makeup, sculpted hairdos, distinctively provocative perfumes, clever repartee and, perhaps every other year, a charming remark tossed in your direction.

Holly and I had only attended one "Villas Christmas Festival" together. The event made her "nauseous." It was, in her eyes, "an obnoxious display of wealth." She told me stories which tarnished the halos of several of the majestic ladies, but their sins seemed pardonable, except for the woman who insisted the community remain "all white." She was overruled, although there was no sudden flood of minority applicants. When I returned from college, there was an African American widow living in the Villas and a handsome Latino couple with a non-Latino name. The Villas Ownership Committee probably would have admitted a Kennedy relative, but you never know. There might have been security issues.

So the "Aces" were four of the seven votes on the Ownership Committee. They were all early forties then—in the prime of their financial lives and still riding high in the region's "over 40" competitive tennis hierarchy. As I mentioned, they "owned" singles and doubles at Wampum CC. They were so far superior to the competitors in their age group that they switched doubles partners annually. One year it would be Chase and Hawk beating Kestrel and Shrike in the championship match. The next year it would be Kestrel and Chase beating Hawk and Shrike.

They made their mark elsewhere, as well. Chase's "Bull Market" became the largest yacht in the harbor, and rumors abounded that the Aces took "loose women" for wild boat rides when "the Queens" (their wives) were out of town together. There was a long wharf on Rocky Point and apparently several folks had seen skiffs leaving the dock with loud, provocatively dressed and presumably well-lubricated young females, accompanied by one of the Aces, heading out to Chase's floating den of iniquity.

Chase and Company also frequented the Wampum Hunt Club, a formerly ramshackle cabin that had fallen into disrepair and which they paid to refurbish. They then applied for nonprofit status for the club and defined its mission as "educating gun owners in the South Shore community about the safe usage and storage of their firearms." They were granted tax exempt status and proceeded to deduct all the cabin renovation expenses, for what was really their own lounge, pool hall and land-based party club.

These escapades allegedly began in the early Seventies. Can't confirm at this point in the narrative, but because the witnesses are sober and reliable citizens I'll consider their testimony.

Later, the Aces would recommend to the Ownership Committee the purchase of a tract of land between the Villas and the Atlantic. Because the land was on a steep downward grade, they decided to build a modest one-story structure which would serve as the headquarters of the "Upper Dickinson Environmental Center" and wouldn't block anyone's ocean view. The mission of UDEC would be "to educate current and future generations about the importance of preserving oceanfront property from residential overdevelopment." This too was deemed worthy of nonprofit status by the proper authorities and a board was established to determine how best to achieve the mission. The nine board members included five "dedicated environmentalists" from the Villas and four others from the region whose commitment to the environment (and ties to the Villas) was never

119

questioned. (I referenced UDEC near the end of "Run One.") Stan Kestrel chaired the group, an assignment he would later regret.

This is all I knew about the "Finagling Foursome" of Chase, Hawk, Kestrel and Shrike as I launched the Totem in 1972. I would have known much more if Holly had returned to home base, but she was helping the poor on the West Coast and her mother Laura was poised to escape Wampum on a moonless night.

I came to view Chase and his cohorts as a dangerous bacterial strain injected into our community bloodstream. Most townspeople were oblivious to them, tucked as they were into a remote corner of the town. Some who had crossed swords with them were concerned about their potential to wreak havoc if they didn't get their way. Some who socialized with them coveted their friendship, while others retreated to the other side of the room when they appeared.

I will admit that I had a degree of fascination with the Aces. Chase's yacht aside, they weren't flashy or overt with their money. Except for Hawk, who had to drive expensive cars for business reasons, the others preferred pickup trucks or Jeeps to a Mercedes or BMW. Kestrel was a stylish dresser because his patients were upper crust women, but the others not so much. And to complete the quartet, Shrike's home was "museum quality" — raved about in newspapers and magazines — but that too was to promote his business. None of them was especially loud or assertive in public except Shrike when he'd had too much to drink, and then his three amigos would humor him into silence. This could all have been a clever act of "reverse snobbery" on their part, to make them seem like regular Joes. They had my mother convinced they were upstanding citizens, but not Hat, of course. She called them "the Brats." Her advice: "If you want to win a Pulitzer Prize for journalism, keep your eye on the Brats."

By now, a great writer of fiction like John Updike would have painted lavish word portraits of all four Brats for you. You'd have exquisite details from a craftsman who wasn't only a summa cum laude Harvard grad but also studied drawing and fine art abroad. I lack those lofty credentials, and will only offer this poor defense for the absence of physical data: I want you to imagine how these characters look to you. I'll give you just one detail for each, and your imagination can fill in the rest.

Other than the authoritative voice I mentioned earlier, Chase has a ruddy complexion that can turn crimson when he's antagonized. It's an early warning signal, because otherwise he always seems composed.

Hawk has a verbal range of several octaves, to help him "tune in" and connect with customers and others he's trying to charm and persuade.

Kestrel has the hands of a concert pianist and they are in constant motion, except when he's smoking and trying to relax.

Shrike is the tallest and most imposing of the group, although his occasional bravado masks a deep insecurity caused by the absence of paternal affection. He has trouble maintaining eye contact, which makes him seem aloof and suspicious.

The spouses have bought into their roles as the wives of successful men, although in two cases the masks are starting to slip. What filtered back to me from Holly: Trudy Hawk, the prettiest, is also the happiest, for now. Bunny Kestrel is proud of her husband's acclaimed surgical status, but is still learning to cope with her possessive in-laws. Muffy Shrike is occasionally the victim of domestic abuse, and doesn't know how to stop it.

In my view, Laura Chase is the most troubled of all, having lost her son in an accident she still can't accept and which causes her constant migraines and nightmares. She no longer trusts David. He is now in love with power and control, and she is merely a mantelpiece figurine.

These may not seem like uncommon portraits of wealthy suburban couples. I would agree. But as time passes , the Four Aces will engage in a series of increasingly disruptive behaviors. (As I mention in the Preface: Think Wild West gang in pinstripes.) For those impacted, the Aces will become the stench of a low tide that won't go away. As the Wampum newspaper editor, I'm trying to separate facts from feelings and maintain journalistic integrity.

Be assured there are also wonderful little Wampum stories we *Totem*-ites will harvest for your enjoyment. Wampum is, and I believe will always be, a community that makes the right course corrections and steers toward what it firmly believes is true north.

Chapter 15
Common Discord (1972)

Earlier, I described Wampum Common as a picture postcard of upscale New England suburbia. Three historic Protestant churches and town buildings surrounding a perfectly manicured green mini-park and a fountain large enough for a regatta of toy boats. On Sunday afternoons in late spring through early fall, carillon concerts ring out for residents and visitors. A location so pristine and iconic that it would soon be discovered by Hollywood as a backdrop for feature films.

But in the early 70's the Common has become an ideological battleground. It is the first story of real consequence covered by our *Wampum Totem* and the first instance of confrontational discord anyone could remember.

The point of contention is the Vietnam War. Like the rest of the country, Wampum has taken sides on the war. The "pro" faction, united behind the families of the Wampum soldiers killed in battle, labels the "anti" faction as "flag burners," "draft dodgers," "radicals" and "Commie sympathizers." The anti-war protesters view the Defense Department as a propaganda machine, and the people who believe the propaganda—labeled "The Silent Majority" by Nixon-- as flag-waving dupes.

The *Totem* has weekly statements "From The Prosecution" (anti-war voices) and "From The Defense." In the Peirce household, my mother—the class poet—is proud to be associated with the Silent Majority, while my father—the World War II vet—is against the war because "it's unwinnable." He views the conflict as "the Viet Cong fighting a civil war, the Communists supporting it without committing any of their troops and the US getting ambushed in the jungle while propping up the corrupt regime in Saigon. It's a 'no win' situation."

One Friday night a month on the Common there's a Protest/Counter Protest faceoff, often between next-door neighbors and high school classmates. The "anti" group is mostly young people, often accompanied by the Unitarian or Episcopal minister or a local college professor. The Congregationalists and Roman Catholics tend to be more "blue collar" and "pro."

For a few minutes there are protest songs, impassioned speeches or the reading of names of soldiers killed in battle. Then, as if on signal, a platoon of cars with horns blaring encircle the Common and drown out what one honker called "the pacifist propaganda." This continues for ten or fifteen minutes, with both sides exchanging highly derogatory remarks, and then the cars disperse.

On several occasions, drivers have emerged from their cars to get "up close and hostile" with protesters. A few punches were thrown and a little blood shed. The Wampum police are always notified about protest dates and invited to attend and prevent violence. They never show up. The chief of police, Sean Burns—nicknamed "Chief Thunderthug" by a sarcastic Baby Boomer—has nothing but contempt for the "coward candyasses who won't defend our country from Communism" and he won't lift a finger to protect them. A small town John Wayne "wannabe," he flunked out of the State Police Academy and only became chief because an uncle was a Wampum town council member.

Civic antagonism peaked at "Wampum Supports Our Troops Day" on Veterans Day of '72 at the Town Hall. It was promoted as an opportunity to honor South Shore veterans who had served in Vietnam—especially those like our eight soldiers who had "paid the ultimate price." But no one on either side of the Vietnam debate was prepared for the bitterness that would boil over on this occasion. Quite simply, it overwhelmed us.

Buses began to arrive in mid-morning for the 2pm event, and very soon the parking lot was full and overflowing onto the narrow streets of the Common. At first it seemed like a scheduling error—as if two very different theatrical productions had been "double booked," like *Hair* and a musical version of *Patton*. After all, the Town Hall is a favorite venue for community theatre.

As time passed, it became obvious that if this were theater, it would be "combat theater." The "Support Our Troops" cast sat or stood in the hall while the War Protesters gathered in the parking lot. The protesters included Vietnam Veterans Against The War, clergy, ordinary civilians, sign carriers, students, guitarists and, yes, people who looked like cast members from *Hair*. The troop supporters were current and former veterans, clergy, ordinary civilians, sign carriers, military band members, politicians and people with crew cuts who could have served with Patton. My father was a "tweener": there to support the troops but not the war.

There were also more members of the media than Wampum had ever hosted. Every Boston network station was there to cover this "showdown in the suburbs," "conflict on the Common," "pacifists against patriots" or whatever label they used to entice viewers. The event organizers—VFWs from the Shore communities—would confess later that they expected "a couple of hundred people, at most." *The Boston Chronicle* estimated attendance at over 5,000 and no one questioned the number.

Rev. Brad Tweed, the Episcopal minister at St. Matthews, had secretly planned an anti-war carillon concert that day, which included popular cotemporary protest songs like Country Joe and the Fish's "Feel Like I'm Fixin' to Die," Barry McGuire's "Eve of Destruction," Phil Ochs' "What are You Fighting For" and "I Ain't Marching Anymore," Pete Seeger's "Bring 'Em Home," Nina Simone's "Backlash Blues," based on a civil rights poem by Langston Hughes and, very appropriately for Wampum, Creedence Clearwater's "Fortunate Son." (All eight of our Vietnam casualties were middle class public school grads; there were no "preppies" in the group.) The concert concluded with "Taps" and "We Shall Overcome." The "carillonist," Hope Stevens, was a musical prodigy who performed that day without a single sheet of music.

Over at the Town Hall, the protesters expressed their disdain for local legislators and civic leaders whom they felt were there for a photo op and a chance to wrap themselves in the flag. They chanted: "Stop the killing, stop the lying / We're not winning, only dying!." They sang: "Where have all the soldiers gone? Gone to graveyards every one. When will we ever learn? When will we ever learn?" They read the names of Massachusetts war casualties, followed by: "Gave him a gun and a metal tag, Sent him home in a plastic bag." (Two beats) "Could have been a loving daddy, But he got blown up in a paddy."

Inside the hall, Vietnam vets with a different perspective talked about the support they received from Vietnamese villagers and the contempt they felt from anti-war protesters. Fighting the Nazis was a much more popular conflict, they said, but defeating the Communists was just as important. If we don't stop them, who will? One or two suggested it was time to drop The Big One on Hanoi and flush Ho Chi Minh

126

and his "poisonous snakes" out into the open. One Marine who had lost both legs in combat said he'd rather be a free man in a wheelchair than a prisoner to Communism. The "pro" clergy offered prayers of thanks to those who had sacrificed so bravely to preserve freedom and protect the defenseless. The politicians tried to cover both bases by praising the warriors for their courage and the protesters for assembling peacefully to express their views.

There were some signs of mutual respect. A few of the soldiers from both sides casually saluted each other. The older vets in attendance, like my dad, made a point of thanking all the soldiers for their service and urging everyone to "keep it peaceful." But it seemed like the "fringe elements" on both sides had their fingers on the trigger. From one side: "HOW COULD YOU betray our country?" From the other: "How COULD YOU defend a government that's lying?" Moderation and restraint almost carried the day, but in the end an unfortunate mishap ignited an ugly incident.

As people were leaving the event, the traffic became badly snarled. There should have been police and volunteers available to steer people in the right direction. Unfortunately, those arrangements hadn't been confirmed, and cars were trapped in a maze of confusion.

Chief of Police Burns had decided that he and his officers would conceal their identity by "plainclothing it." If the protesters committed any criminal acts, "Thunderthug" and his men would swoop in and make arrests. He had arranged to have a bus parked behind the Town Hall so that protesters could be transported to a "detention facility" (the elementary school gym, it being a Sunday) and processed. He was very proud of this plan, and looked forward to describing it to the Boston media. As it turned out, he became the "Village Idiot" in the process.

With no guidance from the police, drivers defaulted to the famous Massachusetts "Me First" vehicular mentality. A few fenders were scraped and obscenities were exchanged. Not good, but not tragic. Eventually, though, a truck with a rear view "blind spot" backed into a soldier in a wheelchair and all hell broke loose. People dragged the truck driver out of the cab, only to discover it was an older woman. Out of frustration, and because they were transportationally immobilized, the fringe folks started to ram into people they thought were ideological adversaries. A series of brawls ensued, equal to anything you've seen in a TV western.

Meanwhile, there were others who were panicked by the sudden eruption of violence, and who deserted their vehicles rather than getting caught up in the melee. They headed back to the Town Hall, which became a temporary peace sanctuary.

Thanks to remarkably fast action by the State Police, who got a call from a legislator in attendance, order was restored before anyone was seriously injured. Several days later, the *Totem* would publish "aftermath photos" of the Wampum Town Hall parking lot, which looked like an auto dealership after a tornado. Thankfully, the wheelchair soldier wasn't badly hurt in the collision that started the fracas. Thunderthug's bus came in handy as a "holding pen" for the vehicular assailants, most of whom were out-of-towners.

Perhaps the best example of karma I ever experienced was the post-event press conference, attended by every news media that could find its way to Wampum. Thunderthug tried unsuccessfully to explain his misbegotten strategy for preparing for what the media labeled "Vietnam Comes To Wampum." Then, an articulate state trooper—a representative of the agency that had flunked out the Chief—made mincemeat out of his explanation. Burns had so wanted to arrest "Commie protesters," but instead humiliated himself and the town by failing at the most basic requirements of competent policing.

My *Totem* editorial on "Vietnam Comes To Wampum" concluded with the following: "I spent the afternoon shuttling back and forth between the two ideologically entrenched camps. I heard well-articulated arguments and feelings from people on both sides. They are all good Americans exercising rights that people in other countries, including Vietnam, can only dream about.

"There is, by now, a clear line in the sand over this war. I'm on the 'Get out now' side because I believe there is nothing to be won and no way to win it. The North Vietnamese are more driven by the desire to govern themselves than the need to embrace Communism, and their hatred for western intervention will keep them battling as long as it takes.

"But if you're on the other side of the line, I don't view you as my enemy. We have different points of view, and as a nation we need to find the point between your thesis and my antithesis that will resolve this bloody crisis, as quickly as we can. That's how democracies work.

Life is returning to normal here in picture postcard Wampum. But there's a wide chasm of contempt between us that needs to be bridged."

***

"Vietnam Comes To Wampum" was the talk of the town for weeks in all the places people congregate, especially church. Trevor Bright, the Unitarian Universalist minister, saw the event as "a microcosm of the discord in our society. We tend to gravitate toward a single point of view and never budge," he said. "Last Sunday was a perfect example. We should have invited representatives from both sides to explain their

129

positions, and concluded with a prayer of thanks to the soldiers and a prayer for a just and lasting peace. Then we should have told the police to ditch their disguises and help us get out of the parking lot alive."

The Congregationalists were less than a hundred yards down the Common from the Unitarians. Their pastor, Ethan Bates, came late "to the calling," having spent his early career in sales. His sales talents, it turned out, were a perfect fit with his new profession. He was skilled at convincing parishioners that they were the "working class Christians" who didn't require the "fancy frills" of other Protestant denominations. (That was an obvious dig at the Episcopalians.) Rev. Bates' take on the rally was that "the wars get fought by kids whose parents don't have the money and contacts to keep them out of battle. And it's probably just as well. They follow orders and fight bravely." Pastor Bates was considered "salt of the earth" by townspeople, and they felt badly that his notoriously "loose" daughter Rachel must be a terrible embarrassment to him.

Father Frank O'Malley from St. Paul's was irate that the rally had "ruined the opportunity to honor the memory of the eight brave young men who made the ultimate sacrifice in Vietnam—six of whom belonged to St. Paul's." (There is more about Wampum's Vietnam "Honor Roll" in the next chapter.) He had spoken at the Town Hall rally and accused the peace protesters of "intentionally subverting" an event that "was intended to give supporters of our troops a voice not often heard around here. But the protesters couldn't tolerate giving others a forum for views different from theirs. That's not the America our soldiers are fighting and dying for."

As for St. Matthews, Rev. Tweed became a temporary media star following his decision to endorse the carillon concert of war protest songs. He had to be careful, however.

130

His "flock" of worshipers wasn't exactly a leftist brigade. We were a mix of conservative businesspeople and seniors and a smattering of moderates and liberals. So Tweed had to find a middle ground, and his post-rally sermon about "Christian Voices of Dissent in the New Testament" was delivered in a nonpartisan manner that pleased all factions.

There was no synagogue in Wampum, so no chance to hear a local rabbi's perspective.

Chief Thunderthug kept a low profile for weeks, but was reported as "seething with anger" about being the community scapegoat for the Town Hall "bumper car blowup." Hearing this, the Four Aces invited the Chief to lunch at the Wampum Country Club and, according to community grapevine John Wheeler, thanked him for his efforts to preserve law and order and prevent a riot on the Common. The Chief never forgot this gesture of respect from the Aces, at a time when everyone else seemed to be ridiculing him behind his back. From that point on, he became deaf to any complaints about them. They were "untouchable" within his domain.

It was, I had to admit, a brilliantly manipulative move. For the price of lunch, they had bought a perpetual "Crime Free" card. No speeding tickets. No indecent behavior charges. No questions asked.

Chapter 16
Hat's Off (1978)

America in the Seventies. I see it now as one of those quick-cut videos : American troops in Vietnam, agonized faces at Kent State, the first Earth Day, Nixon eating sushi with Mao in Peking, the opening of Disney World, poor George McGovern trounced by Nixon: 520 to 17 electoral votes, Secretariat winning the Belmont Stakes by 31 lengths, VP Agnew resigning over tax evasion, long gas lines during the Arab Oil Embargo, heiress Patty ("Tania") Hearst arrested for bank robbery with her SLA kidnappers, Viking 1 landing on Mars, Microsoft becoming a registered trademark, *Star Wars* breaking box office records, disco dynamo John Travolta rocking America in his white suit; Carter, Sadat and Begin celebrating the Camp David Peace Accord. And still no World Series championship for the Red Sox.

Vietnam didn't come to Wampum in 1972, as the news reports of our confrontational war and peace rally suggested. It arrived in 1969, while I was graduating from college and looking for work. During that one savage year of the Vietnam War, death snatched the lives of five young soldiers from our community—a shockingly large sacrifice for a little town in the well-to-do suburbs.

On April 18th, 1969, Captain John Lyman—a career Army officer, voted the Most Talented by his Wampum High classmates—was killed while on a search-and-destroy mission when his helicopter landed on a buried mine. At 25, he was the oldest of our casualties that year.

On May 30th, Army PFC Craig Signorelli, age 21, was killed during an ambush while attempting to rescue wounded comrades.

On July 11th, Navy Boiler Technician FCR Eddie Dupree, who had served two tours of duty in Vietnam, was killed in an accident at the Navy Yard in Norfolk, Virginia. He was 20.

On October 19th, Army SFC Allen Keenan, age 21, was ambushed while leading his squad and its armored personnel carrier. He was cited for conspicuous valor and awarded the Silver Star and two Purple Hearts. He had just recently married his high school sweetheart while on leave in Hawaii. Allen and I had been camp counselors together at the Wampum Community Center day camp, and he had gone on to be captain of the Wampum High baseball team and active in numerous school and community organizations.

The final casualty of the year was First Lt. Dennis Ryan, killed on November 29th at age 24. Dennis had been co-captain of the football team, was named to the All Scholastic Team, and went on to graduate from Boston College. He chose to volunteer for service as a Marine and became a Naval aviator and commander of a helicopter squadron in Vietnam. While on a mission to evaluate combat casualties, Denis' helicopter exploded in flight.

There were eight Vietnam casualties in all, including Corporal William Lawler (age 22), PFC Peter Cahill (20) and Sergeant Peter Alborelli, Jr (21). It was a terrible tragedy for our town, about which I'll have more to say later as part of the Wampum Bicentennial in 1994. Despite these untimely and shattering deaths, there is one remarkable war story that lifted our spirits.

In chapter four I profiled Carson Trueblood as an "Uber WASP" and John Wheeler, my landlord, as a "mud WASP." I mentioned that John was a "quiet war hero," who had won a

133

Silver Star at the legendary battle of Iwo Jima, and that his son Rick was widely admired by the boys my age as the most convincing "play soldier" in town. It was no surprise, then, that Rick enlisted in the Marines after graduation. He was an average student but under his father's tutelage had become an Eagle Scout and an experienced outdoorsman.

I knew less about Spencer Trueblood, Carson's son, because he had gone to prep school, but he too had enlisted in the Marines after dropping out of college. He apparently found his classmates spoiled and self-indulgent and had no interest in spending four years with them. While Rick Wheeler's motivation was to follow in his dad's footsteps and prove his superiority over the enemy, Spencer seemed more motivated by rejecting his WASP lifestyle and doing something for others—in this case the beleaguered South Vietnamese.

By coincidence, both Rick and Spencer were assigned to the 4th Marine Regiment, stationed just south of the DMZ in Quang Tri Province. Word got around there were two soldiers from a little town south of Boston, and the two met and became buddies. Quang Tri was a very dangerous place, with fierce ongoing combat between the Marines and Viet Cong. In March of '70, PFC Spencer was on a night patrol that was ambushed in a godforsaken swamp area not far from the Laotian border. Spencer appeared to be a casualty, having been among a small group that was hit by mortar fire. But while two bodies were retrieved, Spencer couldn't be located, and the platoon was forced to retreat under heavy attack.

When Rick Wheeler (also a PFC) learned that his friend was MIA, he convinced his CO to let him conduct a "solo search" of the battle site before sunrise. The reluctant CO agreed, but only on orders that Rick return "at the crack of dawn" if he couldn't locate Spencer. When dawn arrived, Rick hadn't come back, but requests by other volunteers were flatly refused. It seemed likely that the enemy had waited around to see if any Marines would return.

Two nights later, Rick crawled back into camp with Spencer strapped to his back--alive but badly injured from a shrapnel wound and loss of blood. The two had been "bitten by every insect in the jungle and a couple of snakes to boot" but Rick had provided what a medic called "first aid as good as a doctor could have done" and food that Spencer called "stuff I chewed but couldn't look at." For his heroism, Rick was awarded the Silver Star.

Both men survived Vietnam and returned to Wampum, where Rick eventually took over Wheeler Hardware, became a town council member and in his "spare time" volunteered for every youth organization that needed help. Spencer earned a law degree at Boston University, and focused on representing those with a good case but a limited income. Every year, the two went camping and fishing together in northern New York's salmon country, and would reminisce about their dangerous adventure—thanking God again for sparing them and their buddies who came back. Spencer cooked the salmon they caught—always reminding Rick how much better it tasted than the menu of "dead insects and poison plants" Rick had served him on their Vietnam "picnic outing."

This became one of Wampum's favorite Boy Scout "campfire stories"—the theme being that you should be thankful for that burned marshmallow at the end of your stick because things could be a whole lot worse.

With the fall of Saigon in '75, the acrimony over the war faded and Wampum folks began to look forward to America's Bicentennial. But we were not without town conflict. It was as if the 200th had awakened a spirit of resistance, and birthday party or not, we were going to raise some Cain before cutting the cake.

Wampum High School was the site for one prolonged skirmish. A new school superintendent, with impeccable credentials but an aloof and condescending personality, crossed swords with the teachers union over annual appraisals. Then the school board declined to offer the principal—highly popular with students—a contract that would have ensured him tenure. Students walked out of school in protest. Parents stormed the school gym at a "community feedback" meeting demanding the principal be retained. The school board went "thumbs down" again on the principal. Both sides dug in and dragged each other through the poison ivy for eighteen months. School property was vandalized and the superintendent's office was ransacked and spray painted.

The *Totem* tried to play the conflict "down the middle" by including interviews with all the "combatants": school administrators, school board members, teachers, students and townspeople. We eventually ran a front page story with the headline "WHAMP'EM!," but our intention was to shame the community into civilized dialogue, not incite a riot. Eventually the "pro principal" faction had its way, the school board cut ties with the superintendent and a well-respected regional candidate—John Monaghan--was brought in. "They did the only thing they could do," my father smirked. "They hired an Irishman."

This and the "surf and turf" controversy helped double the *Totem*'s circulation during the mid-Seventies. Our "Surf and Turf" series won a Bay State "Gold Medallion" for community news reporting. In my humble but biased opinion it captured the contempt of the Old Boy (and Girl) Network for anyone outside the WASP nest.

Howard Rosen, owner of Wampum's regionally famous restaurant Starfish, had purchased property at the harborfront and wanted to build a hotel where out-of-towners could stay after a meal or a night at the Music Tent. When Rosen presented his plan to what he thought would be a grateful Wampum Rotary Club, he assumed the town merchants would be overjoyed at the thought of additional tourism business. But when the news spread it was viewed suspiciously by townspeople, who came to see Rosen as "a conniving Jew" who was "defiling the harbor area to make a quick buck."

As the anti-Rosen sentiment intensified, a community icon stepped forward to lead the charge against the ill-conceived project. Her name was Rosalind ("Roz" to friends) Sterling, and her family was as close to royalty as it gets in Wampum. Rosalind's father, Luther, was a Titan of Finance on Wall Street who had maintained a summer residence in Wampum so his family could enjoy "a life outside the mayhem of the city." Rosalind, his favorite child, was a socialite, expert horsewoman and passionate philanthropist. She served on a half dozen prominent nonprofit boards in the Boston area and had gifted millions to education and the arts, including Saint Matthews' carillon and Wampum's new Sterling Fine Arts Center, in memory of her father.

Roz and her husband Milton, a Harvard law professor, lived in a magnificent brick mansion, a stone's throw from the yacht club. Visitors to Wampum would drive by and gawk at the splendid gardens and grounds. We townspeople were somewhat surprised that an esteemed personage like Rosalind would get into a "street fight" with Rosen, but she was up to the challenge. Her attorney got a court order to halt construction on the hotel, and she organized a fierce resistance to what she called "the desecration of our harbor." She spoke at several harborside protest events, surrounded by signs like

"Rosen's Project Smells Like Dead Fish" and "Our Message to Howard's Hotel Guests: No Vacancy."

Roz offered Rosen a half million dollars for his property but the restauranteur was determined to move ahead with his hotel, despite the uproar from the group he called "Roz's Reactionaries." He told the *Totem*: "Wampum needs income-producing properties that create jobs and provide revenue. This is one of the most beautiful towns in Massachusetts, but we don't seem to want the aliens from the outside spending more than a few hours here. All we have are a few 'Mom and Pop' bed and breakfasts. My hotel will generate revenues for local merchants and, if my guests enjoy their stay, those dollars will keep coming back." In her *Totem* rebuttal, Ros reminded readers that "our allegedly civic-minded Mr. Rosen" had been accused by a local environmental group of polluting local waterways and killing shellfish.

Rosen had fought his way out of a poor neighborhood to achieve business success, and we discovered, in researching his career, that he had been generous in helping the underprivileged. During the holidays he brought up to twenty busloads of poor people from the Boston area to the Starfish for a free meal and presents. Catholic Charities and the United Jewish Appeal helped him organize these events and he supported both. The recipients of Rosen's largesse were quite different sociologically from the beneficiaries of Roz Sterling's charitable acts. In the end, I think that mattered.

The case went to Norfolk Superior Court and became the South Shore's favorite topic of discussion for several months. Both sides argued their rights and trotted out impressive lineups of business, political, academic and civic VIPs. Roz and Milton called on Harvard law professors, Boston business executives who lived in Wampum and local legislators. Rosen countered with a senior chamber of commerce executive, a

Tufts economist and a surprise visitation from Cardinal O'Connor. On one side of the coin it was a fascinating debate about property owner rights versus the rights of impacted community members; on the darker side, it was provincialism versus progressivism and Jew versus Gentile.

In the end, the judge ruled that the Wampum Board of Appeals had violated town by-laws by misrepresenting the scope and impact of the hotel project. Rosen called the verdict "a victory for privilege over progress." He held on to his property until the recession blew over and sold it five years later to a local developer for three times its original worth. Being sure to dot i's, cross t's and play politics, the developer built and opened the once maligned hotel in less than two years.

***

Early in 1978, our beloved Hat was hospitalized for lung disease, which had been assaulting her system for years. Except for child birth, she had never spent a night in a hospital, and was miserable and embarrassed—wrongly assuming that her "incarceration" (her word, of course) would bankrupt my parents. She did not linger long, due largely to her refusal to eat or succumb to the mind-numbing monotony of being a patient. She was 88 years "well done," and had no interest in, as she put it, "hacking and coughing my lungs out while my family has to sit around and get showered with cooties."

We took Hat to South Coast Hospital on a Wednesday. Saturday morning we received a call from her doctor that her condition had deteriorated badly and we all rushed to her bedside. She asked to talk to my parents first, then Frankie joined them briefly and she asked to speak to me alone.

"Hi Hat."

"Hi, Hon. How's this for an ugly sight?"

"Don't worry. I didn't bring the camera."

"I'm so ready to shed this dried up husk of a body and start a new life somewhere else. "

"Hat, I know you don't want me to get all weepy and sentimental. I just want you to know how much I love you. I don't know what our poor family would have done without you. You held us together like super glue. You made us laugh. You never gave up on Frankie."

"Hang in there with your parents, Jack. They are so proud of you. You're everything that's good in their lives. Most families can pass a Frankie around and share the struggle but they can't."

"While I was sitting outside, I was thinking off all the great talks we had...about make-believe illnesses and wacky people. I remember telling you about pooping my pants during a cross country race because I was too embarrassed to tell mom and dad." (This made her laugh but also triggered an extended series of racking coughs.)

"If I have another fit like that I'm likely to croak. Before that happens, I want to share something I wrote for you. (She pointed to a drawer. I reached in and pulled out an envelope.) *Don't read it now. I'll get embarrassed. Just a few final thoughts from an old bag."* (She was laboring to speak and could only get a few words out at a time.)

"Hat, should I get your doctor?"

"No, I'm fine. Just give me a minute."

"(I took her hand.) I want you to know that you're one of the major reasons I started the newspaper. You and mom got me interested in language and writing and creativity. Without that, I'd still be back in the classroom...We just got our five thousandth subscriber last week."

"(Hat smiled weakly.) *That's wonderful, Jack. Good for you. Just watch out for those Bad Guys. You know who...you know...*"

Another series of deep coughs. Hat squeezed my hand and her eyes rolled up. She tried to continue but had literally run out of oxygen. She took two final, labored breaths, farted and passed away.

We buried Hat the following Wednesday. Several days later, Massachusetts was buried by the famous Blizzard of '78. Over a thousand houses were destroyed and over five thousand damaged. There was enough wind to carry Hattie beyond the clouds and into the Kingdom of Heaven, where I am certain she watches over us with great pride and amusement.

Here's what she wrote to me before she passed:

"Dear Jack,

I want you to know what a wonderful grandson you have been. I'm a proud and lucky grandmother!

Time has gone by so quickly. Yesterday I was flying you around your baby bedroom and today you're running a successful newspaper. You landed in the perfect place for someone who loves to read and write and talk to people. One of your greatest assets is your sense of humor. I have so enjoyed sharing the funny side of life with you. Keep on laughing! Laugh for both of us, because when I try these days I gag. And keep on being the bright spirit who celebrates the good guys and exposes the hypocrites.

Thanks for listening patiently to this old bag.

Love,

Hattie"

***

For me, the sound of the seventies wasn't rock music. It was the cacophony of helicopter blades: the copter whisking Nixon away from his scandal-stained White House in '74; the desperate exits from rooftops during the Fall of Saigon in '75; and (in early '80) the chaotic crash of US military helicopters that aborted the Iran hostage mission and doomed the Carter administration. Clearly a decade of deeply flawed strategies.

Chapter 17
Shot in Wampum (1980)

It was only a matter of time until Wampum got discovered as the perfect locale for a film set in suburbia. The iconically New England Commons area; the palatial mansions on Dickinson Drive overlooking an ocean dappled with sailboats and lobster buoys; our charming little harbor with its assortment of barnacled fishing boats alongside handsomely-furnished yachts and sailboats; the venerable city of Boston in full view across the Bay. A cinematographer's dream.

In early 1980, a film crew was dispatched to find a locale for author John Updike's best-selling novel *Couples,* set in the small New England town of Tarbox--a seacoast community with a demographic remarkably similar to Wampum. When the crew started asking for advice on a Tarboxy-type place to shoot, all fingers pointed down the coast to us. Following visits by the director and production crew, the vote for Wampum was unanimous.

Having read *Couples* in college, I wasn't the least bit surprised to hear it would be filmed in my hometown. Updike was an Ipswich resident (Boston's North Shore), but his characters were demographically comparable to our Wampumites, who also went to reputable colleges, commuted to Boston and grappled with the temptations of adultery in a post-pill world. Updike's core group of ten couples engage in a frenetic series of extramarital affairs, with the narrator commenting at one point that "what they did with each other's bodies became as trivial as defecation."

The film was to feature Burt Reynolds and Sally Field, who starred in *Smokey and the Bandit* and had become Hollywood's "hot couple." Their arrival was keenly anticipated, and rumors abounded about when and where they would be "on locale." As the local newspaper, we were "low man on the *Totem* pole" for news about filming dates. It turned out that the cast spent only three well-protected and deliberately "low profile" days in Wampum. The director got enough footage of our town landmarks to convince audiences they were viewing a well-to-do New England town. The rest was filmed elsewhere, to everyone's chagrin. There were a few Burt and Sally sightings, but none very noteworthy.

Months later, we found out the film would not be released. Apparently, there were conflicts between the director and the studio, and preview audiences—who were expecting a sex comedy—exited the theater muttering about a "waste of good talent." Little is known about Updike's reaction, but the 1987 film version of his book *The Witches of Eastwick*— also shot in this region, with an all-star cast and crew—got a far better audience reception.

What interested me as the local newspaper editor was the continuing buzz created by the decision to locate *Couples* in Wampum. "Why here?" "Do they think we're adulterers?" The general assumption, and mine, was that we were selected for cinematic reasons, but "Why Wampum?" was the hot topic at cocktail parties for most of the year. And why not? Those libidinous couples up the coast in Ipswich, Updike's hometown, can't be that much different from us, can they?

I recalled the "erection section" in my dad's underwear drawer, and how it was really my first introduction to adult sexuality. But that was Mike Hammer, private eye, who consorted with a bevy of loose women. This was no drugstore pulp fiction. This was an acclaimed, award-winning author, a summa cum laude from Harvard, for god's sake. He knows what's going on. In fact, I heard one college professor remark that "*Couples* is more sociology than fiction."

As an English major, I'm always suspicious about how many people actually read the books they talk about. My edition of *Couples* was over 450 pages, and you had to navigate through a lot of conversations, descriptions of household items and narrative asides to find the sexy parts. And they weren't Mike Hammer sexy, by a long shot. But nonetheless, Updike had struck a communal nerve in Wampum. He had made our couples contemplate the prospect of marital infidelity, past, present and future. And if not theirs, then certainly their neighbors'. Could nice young Richard and Joan next door actually be deviant, covetous sexual predators? Apparently they could.

I had a feeling that our Episcopal priest, Brad Tweed, would seize upon the opportunity to address adultery in one of his sermons, and my hunch was correct. He got invited to quite a few cocktail parties and seldom declined, so I knew he had picked up on the concerns of local married women about a possible outbreak of concupiscence. It was his role to communally examine these concerns and suggest "a path of enlightenment and resolution." Talking with him, you understood why he was a priest and you weren't.

Rev. Tweed delivered his sermon in mid-summer, while most of the kids were away at camp. I remember St. Matt's being unusually full for an August Sunday, so the Episcopal ladies' network must have been busy recruiting at the yacht and country clubs.

Intrigued by how my pastor would address the volatile subject of adultery, I took a few notes. Here's what I wrote: "Thousands of references to temptation in the Bible. Eve tempted by the serpent, who was satan. P'ment for adulterers was death or stoning (if a virgin). Key quote: <u>each 1 is tried by being drawn out and enticed by his own desire</u> (James), 2 overcome temptation, know where you're vulnerable. Couples has religious motif: priest/parish/scapegoat. Adultery like a powerful elixir. Pleasure in the moment but destructiv long term. Best course: confide in trusted people, reflect on state of marij, don't blame self, put relshp back together w. trust, honesty, c'ment to fidelity, <u>work w. licensed marriage counselor</u>"

I hope that clears everything up for you, should you ever need it.

One smartass academic in the congregation called it "Tweed's Sermon on 'The Mount'," and I believe that smartass was later discovered mounting one of his students.

I was inspired enough by the sermon to do a little research on adultery. At the time, it remained a criminal case in half the states, and a felony in a few, with a possible prison sentence of up to four years. In the US military, it was potentially a court martial offense. Conversely, the Greco-Romans didn't consider adultery as a crime against the wife if the husband had sex with a slave or an unmarried woman. The punishment was likely an expensive item of jewelry and six months of marital fidelity.

I was reminded of poor Abigail Cooper (see chapter two), who was sentenced to two weeks in the stocks on Wampum Commons for conceiving a child out of wedlock and then suffocating it. The father was a married Congregational minister who was allowed to leave town. Real Massachusetts *Scarlet Letter* stuff, except that Hawthorne's Hester Prynne kept her child (Pearl) and the adulterous minister (Dimmesdale) guilted himself to death. I mention this to emphasize that adultery has been and continues to be "serious stuff" in these parts. In fact, I believe we've become the fictional "hotbed" of adultery—a pun that arguably deserves its own prison sentence.

***

So you may be wondering: Is Wampum actually "Tarbox South"? Are we as adulterous as Updike's fictional village? As editor of the town paper, and so likely "in the know" more than most, it would be ethically sleazy of me to divulge names and occupations of marital transgressors. But I'll make an exception for the Four Aces, who—as I write this—can no longer be victimized by local gossip.

Actually it was only three of the Four Aces. Oliver Hawk wasn't inclined to adulterize because his wife Trudy was unmatchable in charm and sex appeal. When the Aces "entertained" at the Wampum Hunt Club or cruised on Chase's "Bull Market" with sexually available women, "Ollie" would bartend and charm the guests. (My reliable source for whatever precedes or follows about the Aces was an "insider.")

The Hunt Club was Party Central for the Aces. It was the sexual bookend to the "Bull Market"—ideally located off Hawthorne Hollow (see "Run One") and tucked back in the woods where only the partiers could find the entrance. The Aces' wives knew that Fridays were "Boys Night Out," but at least initially thought they gathered in some bar close to the city. In fact, the boys weren't much more than a mile away. They brought "the city" to Wampum, in all its alluring flavors and fragrances.

My original assumption was that they were importing women of disrepute, but I was quite mistaken. Their female companions were a highly diverse population, ranging in ages from eighteen (some say younger) to fifty and including every

147

ethnic and racial grouping. They were bored housewives and college students, secretaries and exotic dancers, real estate agents and marine biologists (no kidding!)

Membership requirements? They had to be "sponsored" by one of the Aces; they had to live in or close to Boston; they had to be unmarried, "congenial and non judgmental"; "at least an 8" on the attractiveness scale; and god knows what else. There was apparently no problem for the Aces to find these women; the problem was keeping the weekly participants to a manageable number (no more than 10).

This shocked me, keeping in mind there were no computer dating services in those days. Also, what was the incentive for the party girls, since there was no financial remuneration for sexual favors? The answers to this question, I was told, were: "it's an adventure"; "it's a fun place to visit"; "the guys are classy, not like in a bar"; "you only do what you want to do; there's no pressure"; "I met some girls who've since become friends"; "I got a job interview out of it."

The Aces themselves tossed a few "baubles and beads" into the mix, like free "off the books" weekend car rentals from Ollie, unclaimed import items from Morgan, high end cosmetics from Stan and insider stock tips from David.

But…but…How do you get away with this for an extended length of time? All the practical, Protestant, middle class, moralistic questions come to mind and suggest that this movie ends badly for everybody. Somebody gets pregnant. One of the bored housewives' outraged husbands sets fire to the Hunt Club with all the partiers inside. One of the Aces' wives gets wind of the scandalous behavior and calls the cops.

Relax, I'm told. How does the outraged husband find the place? And if he does show up, he's told it's a private party for customers of the owners, "which includes your wife." And the cops? The cops are Sean Burns—"Chief Thunderthug"--

148

and his boys. (The Aces, as mentioned, are "tight" with the Chief).

Now if these capers were conducted by mud WASPs, the Worst Case Scenarios would all come crashing down on their heads. They'd be shot dead in Wampum by a jealous husband or a pregnant marine biologist. But the Aces of the world seem to thrive on risk and living outside the lines of conventional behavior. When the knock comes at the door, they have multiple verbal and physical escape routes, while a middle class adulterer would end up as a deer in the flashlights. The Aces have *connections* when times get tough; mud WASPs have relatives, who are out of town at the beach.

Actually, the Hunt Club crowd were the "B listers"; the "Bull Market" beauties were the "A team." Think about it. If you were a 10, with credentials, would you rather get drunk in the woods or ride the waves on a forty-foot yacht? So the invitations to climb aboard Chase's pleasure craft were even tougher to procure. You had to be both smart and stunning: a college graduate, a white collar professional, able to converse intelligently and "cocktail" (first ever use of the word as a verb?) with corporate executives, and an adventurous "anything goes" personality. If the "10" played her cards right, she could cash in handsomely: jewelry, a rent free apartment, vacations in the tropics, even occasionally a junior executive position. Not bad for "adulterizing" in a well-appointed cabin below deck.

These "love boat" excursions were a key to how David Chase built his empire at Monarch Financial. He procured beautiful women for customers and young execs on the rise within his company. The beautiful women were the essence of discretion, and were carefully instructed not to invade the personal "domain" of their escorts. (Only one woman ignored this order and Chase was heard to say "She paid a terrible price for her betrayal.")

In return for Chase's matchmaking, the customers rewarded him with their business and his young colleagues with their undying loyalty. It was a powerful *quid pro quo*, which Chase managed with great finesse. He kept a private file on all his "clients" and "worked the data" constantly through phone calls and personal notes. The messages were always discriminating, never incriminating.

But Chase didn't just "pimp his way to the top." He was an abundantly talented senior executive, with excellent credentials. As mentioned earlier, he was a Dartmouth grad and went on to finish at the top of his class at the prestigious Wharton School. He became a model of corporate leadership: visionary, brilliantly strategic and dedicated to developing and mentoring young talent within the company ("cruisers" or not).

Chase had the "executive presence" aura that seems to dazzle Corporate America. It's all of the above, plus assertiveness and interpersonal charm. He was not, as I was learning incrementally, a man to be taken lightly.

At one point a few years earlier I had asked Hat to invent one of our sarcastic maladies (like "water on the butt") for Chase. She had to think about it for a bit. "At first I thought of monomaniac, but that already exists. So here it is: he's an *egoholic*. He has voices in his head that are saying 'You're the king and they need to bow down to you.'" Brilliantly insightful, Hat.

***

So the "Bull Market" surged ahead, with its cargo of aspiring and alluring young women. Anyone less gifted in the seductive arts would end up running aground or losing a customer overboard. But not Captain Chase. He'd always make it to shore with his crew safe and satiated.

Meanwhile, back on shore, a covert cabal of adulterers were indulging their sexual appetites, while others merely fantasized. Not me, of course. Or you either.

***

A few years ago, I was moved to devote a *Renegade WASP* column to a spoof of the erectile dysfunction commercials that are bombarding us, even during the evening news when the kids are watching. Enough already! Can you imagine these ads being broadcast during *Father Knows Best* or *Ozzie and Harriet* while we were growing up? Or *Gunsmoke*? The network execs would have been hauled up in front of Congress.

So I wrote an imaginary ad for a new product that decreases, rather than enhances, male sex drive, and made it an antidote to adultery. The first few paragraphs as follows:

Feeling an Adulterous Impulse? Try Niagra

If in fact you *are* feeling such an impulse, you may have tried cold showers, the Bible or self gratification, to no avail. Your libido is urging the pleasures of the flesh, while your conscience is reminding you of the consequences.

Good news, men. There's a new drug on the market that can spare you the extramarital misery of an expensive divorce, a broken home and the eternal resentment of your in-laws. It's called Niagra, and it's guaranteed to suppress sexual desire. That's because Niagra contains a suppressant called nobonatal (pronounced "no-bone-at-all"). It works so effectively that within sixty seconds your brain's pleasure center becomes completely dysfunctional and your erotic thoughts are re-channeled to the *Home Shopping Network*.

Like all strong medications, Niagra should be used with caution. It should not be confused with medicines which treat erectile dysfunction (ED). To the contrary, Niagra is an "erectile disinterest" drug. It's a sexual preventative. And while it protects against arousal in potentially incriminating situations, the user may also be rendered incapable of bladder control, muscle coordination and polite conversation.

(My readers made "no bones about it"; they hated the subject matter. Fine. I hate the 24/7 ED commercials.)

Chapter 18
Run Two (1985)

By 1985 it had been thirteen years since I had seen Holly. My connection was her mother Laura Chase, who had loaned me the $10,000 to start the *Totem* and had become our biggest supporter. I had asked her to be part of a small advisory group, and her efforts on our behalf were exceptional. She personally sold at least 500 subscriptions and solicited dozens of business advertisers. I tried on several occasions to pay back her loan, but she would only allow me to take her to lunch. So we met quarterly at the Chowder Bowl to discuss Holly and the current status of the paper.

Holly had left the West Coast in the late seventies and moved with a fellow social worker to the Chicago suburb of Oak Park. The former home of Frank Lloyd Wright and Ernest Hemingway, Oak Park had developed a reputation as a proponent of fair and equal access to housing. Disillusioned with "California hedonism," Holly and her friend Sylvia, a Chicago native, decided that Oak Park would be a community more compatible with their values. Based on their job experience, they were both offered positions with the Oak Park Housing Center and joined the effort to prevent "white flight" and promote racial diversity.

Laura spent as much time visiting Holly and helping her adjust to Chicago life as her allowance from David would allow. She was the most effective relocation assistant a daughter could have. In every conceivable area—housing, doctors, social connections, retail "best buy" stores, even a

153

mooring for "Pegasus"--Laura was there with recommendations from well-informed sources.

And so, with Laura's help, Holly's adjustment to her new Midwestern home was remarkably successful. She developed an eclectic network of city and suburban friends. She took graduate courses in business and eventually earned an MBA at Northwestern's prestigious Kellogg School of Management. She sailed on Lake Michigan. She began to paint landscapes.

And now, Laura informs me, Holly is pregnant.

"I didn't see this coming. I guess it's her biological clock. She's two years away from forty and it must have seemed like now or never."

"Who's the lucky father?"

"Not you, darn it...His name is Ryan. He's a lawyer. They've been dating for about two years. Met through a sailing club." (My stomach tightens at "sailing club.")

"She'll be a wonderful mother. And you'll be a spectacular grandmother. I'm really happy for both of you."

"Thank you. I'm incredibly excited and happy for Holly. She has spent a lot of time in a very dark place, and I'm hoping this will give her the joy she deserves. (After a long pause...) *I will always regret, Jack, that you and Holly weren't allowed the chance to be a couple."*

"My loss is that I didn't get you as a mother-in-law. But it just wasn't in the script. I had to come back and start a newspaper and she needed to stay away and find happiness."

"Well, you've done a hell of a job with the newspaper. Forgive an aging romantic for hoping the story could have had two happy endings."

We never discussed David Chase. She knew what was happening behind her back but never complained in my company.

***

At the time, I was renting a house on White Horse Lane near the harbor-- about a twenty minute walk to work. It's Sunday, and a perfect low humidity day for a run, so I'll take you through a different part of town from Run One.

I start on Salt Mill Lane, which takes me over a tiny bridge that's a favorite "jumping off" spot for teenagers, then past a boat repair yard and the Starfish Restaurant—still owned by Howard Rosen—and a beautiful panoramic view of the harbor. The view is my start-the-day sensory stimulant. The smell combines salt air, a hint of fish and whatever other aromas the wind blows my way. On past the wonderfully eclectic mix of sailboats, inboards, yachts and the commercial fleet I described earlier but which changes from day to day.

Bearing right, I pass the Drop Anchor Hotel (the townfolk insisted that it not be called a motel), which you'll remember got the thumbs down while Rosen was trying to build it but was resurrected under new ownership. Even then the Drop Anchor wasn't initially embraced by the locals, but its clientele weren't the "hoi polloi" originally feared, the harborfront "aesthetic" was quite acceptable and the positive economic impact was undeniable. Just as a rising tide lifts all boats, a rising occupancy rate was lifting local merchants.

I'm now on Beech Street, a connector to Wampum Center. On both sides are beautifully-maintained clapboards and Cape Cods—many owned by families who planted their trees before World War Two. There's room for grandma and grandpa if needed and the kids are happy with bunk beds. Parents attend every PTA Night and town meeting, and there's probably a Wampum town worker in the household, or next door.

At the end of Beech, on the right, are the usually sedate police and fire companies, and a new addition: "Sea Colony" public housing. Wampum resisted public housing until the state threatened sanctions and then agreed to a 28-unit facility which seemed from the outside like an upscale retirement home. My parents viewed it as the godsend they had been waiting for, and were able through contacts to get Frankie admitted as a resident. It wasn't long, however, until Frankie's behavioral issues made him an unwelcome neighbor to the sedate older women who were most of the resident population. And his proximity to the police station made him a sitting duck for the eccentrically—averse cops. I'll give you an update a little later. For now, he's OK and living nearby in a community where he's not notorious.

I take a right off Beech onto Mayflower Passage, which you may remember from "Run One" is the odd name for Main Street in Wampum. I'll jog you through the two main blocks of our downtown. On the left is the Chowder Bowl and an about-to-retire tire store. On the right, a series of shops, including French pastries ("Vive Le Pain!"), a pet boutique ("Paws For Us"), a barely-clinging-to-life antiques shop and Wheeler's Hardware, now managed by John's son Rick while John "supervises the town."

The next block (left side) has a "realtors row" of offices which rode the wave of population growth in the fifties and sixties (an impressive 87%) and are now making commissions on expensive home sales and income from rental-generating condos. The obligatory downtown pharmacy and liquor store were sold and closed during the "flight to the highway" in the seventies, when the brand names moved nearby and "malled" the downtown. (The "highway," Route 4, is the newly paved, formerly potholed commercial road connecting most of the little South Shore communities.) My friends Bob and Carol

156

Bernard bought the old pharmacy and opened a wonderful home décor store, "Fits Right In." They started the Wampum Downtown Merchants Association and recruited a new restaurant ("Fried Clams Forever") and gift shop ("Seaglass and Driftwood") to join the block. Things are looking up.

Across the street and atop its granite throne is the imperious "St. Matt's," which has the market cornered for wealthy WASPs and won't be going out of business anytime soon. If I were to run straight, we'd be back at the Commons, where we've already been, so I'm taking a left at the community center, where I spent many wonderful days as a day camper, a candlepin bowler and an avid consumer of serial movies, including my favorite, *Dr. Fu Manchu*.

Just down the street is the Sterling Arts Center—a civic jewel which the *Totem* has often championed, and which owes its existence to the fundraising efforts of Winslow Parker and (once again) the largesse of Roz Sterling, and many generous "supporting players." The center has galleries, performance space and classrooms for the performing and visual arts and will inspire this and future generations to explore their talents. Bravo to all involved.

I have a couple of minutes until I reach Calvary Hill, and no major landmarks to point out, so as we're passing the arts center let me tell you a little about our local artists. We have regionally and nationally acclaimed painters, sculptors, photographers, filmmakers and performers. If we devoted a month to each of our visual artists at the arts center, it would take years to showcase all their talents. We have a prima ballerina with the Boston Ballet, a RADA-trained actor who has toured a dozen one-man shows to rave reviews, musicians with the Boston Symphony and Boston Pops and that's just the performers I know about.

It has been an enormous pleasure and cultural awakening for me to interview these remarkable people for the *Totem*. Growing up, I was oblivious to their existence. Good example: the farmer down the road—Prentice Greene—owned a 200-acre farm, harvested timber and built pots for the lobster fishermen. He was also a renowned sculptor of small bronze horses. Who knew? Among our other claims to fame, we're an arts colony. Hopefully the center will make us more aware of our region's creative talents.

I now have a big challenge looming ahead. I've reached Calvary Road, known to Wampum's cross country runners as just "Calvary," and it's the steepest hill in town. This is about the halfway point of the course, so when you reach the top you still have a mile and a half to go and your legs feel like they're dragging an elephant. I make it to the top only by taking little bitty steps, and remind myself that it has been twenty years since I ran the course competitively. Pelican Field, where the Wampum Chiefs (to be renamed "Captains" in a few years) play football and run track, is on the right and I soon turn off down a dirt path that leads to the high school.

Wampum High, my alma mater, was "prep school equivalent," thanks to great teachers and smart classmates. Our "Class of '65" was an academically gifted group, with National Merit Scholars and students achieving over 1400 combined scores in math and English. The top scholars—and there were quite a few who topped me—attended the best large and small colleges in the country. As editor of the *Totem*, I now need to maintain some objectivity about the Wampum School District and speak up when high quality education seems to be getting compromised. But I will always be grateful to the Ernie Gardiners and other teachers who added their wisdom to my slim volume of adolescent knowledge.

Past the high school, I take a right on Discovery Drive. This was one of Byron Bentley's early developments, as he was working his way up to Atlantic Villas. The homes were built for returning GIs and middle class families taking the next step up the ladder, thanks to a promotion or family inheritance. At one time, this was considered a prosperous part of town. Now "The Money" has moved out to the ocean or to the exclusive little communities being built around town. Discovery Drive now looks a little dingy—in need of a fresh coat of paint. The road peaks at a point where I remember my legs "tieing up" and my lungs burning, and you asked your body for just one more quarter mile. We finished on a rocky path that ended at the track, and then a final desperate hundred yards to the finish.

Since it's Sunday, there's no one around. I sit on one of the rusty old benches and take a few minutes to reflect on the twenty years since the last cross country race. Holly and I were hoping to start our freshman years in close proximity. We were excited about being together, perhaps for the rest of our lives. Now she's in Chicago, I'm in Wampum and she's pregnant by another man. Twenty years, twenty laps around the track. Professionally, a wonderful adventure. Personally, I have no one to share it with. I continue to suck on a blade of grass until a sea gull swoops down and reminds me it's time to move on.

***

Laura Chase must have mentioned our lunch meeting to Holly, and about a week later I received a letter.

"Dear Jack,

So terribly sorry to be out of touch for so long! The winds of change have been blowing at hurricane force out here and hopefully are sweeping me in the right direction.

I've been making some progress with my career plans, which I think I shared briefly with you last time. One of my classmates at Kellogg, Lindsay Hollister, is starting a financial and estate planning business and wants me to be a partner. She's incredibly connected in the well-to-do Chicago suburbs and thinks there's a market for her idea. Her father is a corporate hotshot and feels he can steer business her way, and her mother is from a prominent family. I've been studying on my own for a CFP (Certified Financial Planner), so that's what I'd bring to the party.

I like Lindsay. She has real entrepreneurial zeal and doesn't want to settle for being the one woman in an all-white-male law firm. We both know the pitfalls of starting a new business. Kellogg taught us all about the downsides. But I feel like I'm ready to jump off the high board and see if I can avoid doing a belly flop. Hey…What's the worst that can happen? I end up teaching sailing and living in the boathouse.

Speaking of sailing, I've had Peg out almost every weekend and she takes the best Lake Michigan can throw at her. What a wonderful old gal. She has a few more dents and scratches since you and I were racing her around Wampum, but she still loves a challenge. Like me, I guess.

I know you and mom are still getting together to talk about the newspaper, and what an expensive little sponge I've been (just kidding, mom), so I assume she has shared the news that I'm pregnant (and due in four months). Why?? I just decided that whoever I do or don't become professionally, I want to become a mother…and the biological ticking was keeping me up at night. The father, Ryan, is a tax attorney with a great sense of humor. Not your typical lawyer, so don't worry. Like

160

me, he's excited about having a child but isn't putting any pressure on about marriage, a home in the suburbs, or anything else. I will try to do better about communicating given this major upcoming Life Event.

Just two more things. My mom is panicked that I'm drinking during my pregnancy. Please reassure her that everything is under control and I just have one glass of wine a week to toast the baby.

Also, I know that mom will never talk with you about her husband ("my dead father" to those who ask me). Just please let me know if he does anything that would endanger or impact her in a negative way. We are working on a plan to extricate her from that creep, but it's complicated.

Please keep those copies of the *Totem* coming. <u>So proud of you</u>! Wampum couldn't possibly have a better paper or a more talented editor.

Love,

Holly

p.s. Can't wait to show you my paintings. I think I'm channeling Benjy. At least I hope so.

***

During the run, I mentioned that Frankie was living in a nearby community, following a series of behavioral problems that led to his banishment from Wampum's only public housing facility. When dad and I met with Chief "Thunderthug" I was shocked to see the long list of Frankie complaints recorded in just two years. Most of them involved his acting out anger and frustration in socially unacceptable ways. He had a particular problem with the supermarket, which was about a three mile walk for him in all kinds of fickle Massachusetts weather. So he arrived frustrated, and it only got worse.

At first, they refused to accept some of the bottles and cans he tried to redeem for cash, and this led to angry exchanges with the staff, which were shared with the police. Then, Frankie became annoyed that the market wasn't stocking items he had requested. Finally, when he couldn't find the pickles that were never in stock—or that the market decided they wouldn't stock because Frankie continually demanded them—he pulled some other pickles off the shelf and smashed them on the floor. That brought the police, and Frankie was hauled off to the station in handcuffs. The chief made my mother take Frankie back to Bayberry Road for a few days "because word will get around Sea Colony about this and the older women will be frightened."

In a small town like ours, there was no tolerance for public acts of hostility by anyone except the wealthy. If you had a "RE-tard" in the family you either sent them away to an institution or kept them locked in the basement. My poor beleaguered parents were summoned to the station on several other occasions and finally decided to apply for housing in a neighboring town, where Frankie would be less conspicuous. He has been assigned a counselor and there have been no serious issues in his first year of new residency.

But if you're the parent of a Frankie, you never know when the phone will ring. Trust me: it takes a terrible toll, and there's no running away from it. It's a Life Sentence.

Chapter 19
All Heart (1987)

The Heart Ball of 1987 was Trudy Hawk's "coming out party" as a Big League Hostess of charitable events on the South Shore. It was held in June at Wampum's premiere location for high end social activities, the Faulkner estate. The Faulkners had moved to Wampum in the early 1950s and bought one of the town's "summer cottages" built by wealthy Bostonians in the twenties. It's a breathtaking 15-acre expanse on lower Bayberry Road, with a massive front lawn where my buddies and I once played touch football and were never chased away. We'd occasionally see Ed Faulkner practicing his fly fishing up near the house, while nearby his wife Natalie pruned her legions of rose bushes.

The Faulkners were what Hat used to call "Rich-tocrats." Almost from the moment they arrived, their home became the town's social community center. Like all Mega Properties it had its own name—"The Gardens"—and if you wanted the perfect spot for a wedding, a benefit or a flower show you started with the Faulkners, and unless it was a Democratic Party fundraiser they would try hard to accommodate you. On any given weekend, you could drive by and see hot air balloons, brides and grooms, croquet and Frisbee tournaments, antique car shows and once even the Cardinal of Boston arriving in a helicopter for a statewide fundraiser.

This year, the Heart Association had secured permission from the Faulkners for their "Bottom of Our Hearts" Ball in June, to include benefactors from all over the South Shore. It seemed like a perfect fit for Hawk Luxury Motors, and Oliver

Hawk was quite willing to be the Principal Sponsor if his wife Trudy could chair the affair. This created some consternation because the organization had already approached the wife of a famed Boston cardiologist to host the event. A co-chair arrangement was quickly negotiated and Trudy was elevated to the top of the invitation, along with Margaret (Mrs. Eliot) Pearl. Margaret would soon be swept aside by, as one insider put it, the "tornadic force of Trudy's ambition." This was the role Trudy had dreamed about, and she would command center stage from the outset.

Keeping in mind that this was long before the advent of social media, Trudy's recruitment effort was phenomenal. Her Heart Ball "marketing quiver" included heart-shaped self mailers, ads in regional medical magazines, phone-a-friend scripts, clever broadcast and print materials produced and placed at no charge, testimonials from heart patients, and much more. She got husband Oliver to contribute a Mercedes as a door prize and asked Mercedes marketing execs how to get maximum promotional mileage.

Then, just when she had started to get peoples' attention, she dropped her Bombshell: the Special Guest would be Bob Hope. (The Faulkners had met him in the Fifties and volunteered to be high level Republican contributors whenever the GOP needed support. A few million donor dollars later, he was happy to return the favors.) Ticket sales went through the roof at that point, and everyone involved with "Bottom of Our Hearts" was a hero. What had been just another "ho hum" disease-related annual ask became a Slam Bang Sellout three months in advance. The previous Heart Ball ticket sales record, with a lot of arm twisting, had been 275. This year, following a huddle with the Faulkners and the now jubilant event organizers, the sellout number was increased from 500 to 1,000. No one—including the

Faulkners—was quite sure how that number of people could be accommodated without absolute chaos, but everyone—especially the Faulkners—knew this was a "once in a lifetime" fundraising opportunity for the Heart Association, so full speed ahead.

Trudy became even more entrepreneurial at this point. As ticket sales continued to pour in, and reached 900, she announced a sellout and put the last 100 in a dresser drawer. When wealthy latecomers begged to be included, Trudy made them agree to purchase or provide a thousand dollar auction item. She sold the last 100 two by two and raised an additional $50,000. By doing so, she became a local legend, and the leading candidate to propel your fundraiser to the Promised Land. (Hey, I'm a newspaper guy. I pay attention to this stuff.)

The silent and live auction items made those of previous events seem "minor league." Along with the Mercedes ($50. per ticket for the drawing), she lined up an autographed photo (actually several) with Hope, luncheon with Nancy Reagan at the White House, weeks at posh cottages from Nantucket to Hawaii, and from the other Aces: expensive jewelry (Shrike), a Mystery Cruise aboard "Bull Market" (Chase) and the plastic surgery of your choice (nose job, anyone?) from Kestrel. These would have been welcome items at a Kennedy Center fundraiser.

I purchased my tickets early: two for my parents (my mother was over the moon!) and two for me, which included my escort for the evening, arranged by Trudy. Several of the single women doctors, who didn't want to attend unescorted, were "placed" with unmarried men. I agreed to be one of the recruits in return for "media access privileges." We were to meet our dates at Trudy's house, have a cocktail and depart in time to beat the masses to "The Gardens."

165

Since Trudy also chaired the Weather Committee, the Big Day was flawless: bright sunshine, low humidity and a gorgeous view that seemed to reach all the way to England, the WASP Homeland. I was stopped at the Villas guard house, checked off the guard's typewritten list, and waved ahead to Trudy and Oliver's little palace. I was wearing cranberry pants, which seemed right for the occasion, but also felt like a costume piece beyond my means and social status. (If you have these thoughts, you're a mud WASP.)

My date was Kardya Pericardi, a lovely Indian cardiologist. Trudy introduced us and, on a day when her social status and reputation were on the line, was incredibly gracious and cooler than a cucumber. I let myself be immersed in feminine beauty for several minutes while Trudy recited our personal and professional credentials. There were five other couples. Had she written and rehearsed these intros in addition to everything else on her list? Kardya was wearing a pink full length dress with a slit, while Trudy was advertising cleavage in a scarlet mini dress. (I'm not an astute observer of fashion, despite coaching.) Both women were perfectly "accessorized" and dappled in fragrances that I hope will anoint us all in the Kingdom of Heaven, if we're lucky enough to make the cut.

In the short drive from The Villas to the Gardens, Kardya shared a few of the pluses and minuses of being a female physician. Her father "Ravi" was a proctologist, so medicine was in the family DNA, but making money was a new experience, since her grandfather had been a laborer in India. It had taken remarkable effort and some good fortune to get the Pericardis to Boston, where Ravi was able to work for the US Navy. He became Kardya's patron and mentor, and steered her through the world of medical politics and egos.

The pluses for Kardya were her patients, who frequently communicated their gratitude, and her hospital, Boston's St.

Agnes, which accepted patients without medical insurance. The minuses included the inevitable gender discrimination by (mostly older) male physicians and the hospital bureaucracy, which reduced her patient time. Despite the negatives, she felt incredibly fortunate to be a doctor and thanked me repeatedly for being her escort. I told her it was my pleasure, while thinking that if I had chest pains during the Heart Ball, I would be in the company of the best-looking cardiologist in America. I think her perfume was making me delirious.

The Gardens had never looked more festive, or more populated by guests. Everything was decorated in a red motif, including Eleanor Faulkner, who as hostess was the Queen of Hearts. There was a red hot air balloon tethered on the front lawn, croquet with heart-shaped wickets and a hundred foot putting green with prizes for closest to the heart-shaped hole. The outdoor activities were so elaborate and visually engaging that traffic on Bayberry Lane backed up for a half mile and had to be rerouted.

Inside, in the "Operations Rooms," were dozens of "high end" auction items surrounded by gourmet delicacies in quantities sufficient to feed a third world nation. Trudy and her committee had solicited culinary items from every popular restaurant and food vendor in the region and staged "Recipes That Win Hearts" demos with popular chefs in the Faulkners' airplane hangar-sized kitchen.

I could give you three more paragraphs of heart-designed items, but that would be heartless of me. I finally spotted my parents in the throng and I will brag that my mother was the epitome of grace and good taste. She and dad didn't attend major events like this, and she later told me it was the most exciting evening she could remember, except for her wedding in Coronado, California during the war. She was pleased to see I had a date and wasn't just jotting notes for the *Totem* and

167

pretending not to miss Holly. (I'm forty now and to my mother I'm an "agonizingly confirmed bachelor" with little prospect of producing grandchildren in her lifetime.)

Kardya urged me to "do what newspaper editors do" while she connected with fellow doctors and friends. I knew about a quarter of the attendees, the others being high rollers from various medical communities and star gazers eager to see Bob Hope, whatever the charity. As the group became excited and increasingly lubricated, its collective voice rose to a Grand Central Station on steroids level.

So many of the women were stunning, and I realized for the first time how many components are required to achieve beauty, or its reasonable facsimile: tiaras and other *objets de tete*; incredible earrings which if all joined together at this event would stretch to San Francisco; mascara enough, in total, to construct eyelashes large enough to fly you out of the room; triple-anti-aging, quadruple-anti-wrinkle, and pre-pubescent skin creams; lipsticks of all colors and textures — enough to create a rainbow from Wampum to Boston; and enough hairspray to reinflate the Hindenburg and fly it back to Germany. And that's just from the neck up. Forget about the career advice from *The Graduate* ("Plastics!"); how about "Cosmetics"?

Laura Chase was in Chicago, but it appeared David Chase wouldn't be lacking female companionship for the evening. I had heard from the Villa grapevine ("Villavines" was an always reputable source) that Chase had purchased a dozen extra Heart Ball tickets "to help the cause." Some were his work colleagues and the remainder were the "A list" from his pleasure cruise rolodex. He invited the best from his "stable" and they alone were worth the price of admission. The goal of the event was to promote heart health, and certainly Chase's bevy of beauties quickened pulses and sent blood rushing to

168

all parts of the male anatomy. There were rumors for weeks after about hanky panky in the rose bushes and all around the Faulkner estate, including the discovery of a used condom in a guest bedroom. No confirmation on this from the Faulkners, however, who would have been mortified by any rumors they had hosted a "charitable orgy."

Just at the moment it seemed we couldn't force another cocktail or canape down our gullets, the lights dimmed a few times, we were hushed from all directions, and Trudy Hawk stepped to the microphone. Without the help of even an index card, she thanked a long list of Heart Ball beneficiaries and led sustained applause for the Faulkners. She then announced that, while the final results weren't in, the old record for revenues raised by the Heart Ball--$350,000—had not only been surpassed, but shattered. Revenues would be over $600,000. "Just like the theme of our event, you gave from the bottom of your hearts, and made this a night to remember! And it's just beginning. It's now my extraordinary honor to introduce a good friend of our hosts, and America's greatest entertainer: Mr. Bob Hope!" (I'm paraphrasing here. There was a lengthy intro, probably written by Hope's PR people, but Trudy delivered it flawlessly.)

Hope—all 82 years of him—descended the staircase in green pants and a madras jacket to a thunderous ovation. He kidded the Faulkners, whom he claimed had told him they were just having a few friends over for cocktails. He thanked the doctors, whose colleagues were constantly giving him advice he ignored, and then dying on him. Jokes about President Reagan's golf game and his congratulations to Nancy for being America's first woman president. A winning remark: that he never thought the "Road to Wampum" would end with so many beautiful women. And his special thanks to Trudy, who had auctioned off photos with him for outrageous prices. He said they would be delivered after considerable retouching. Wampum was starstruck and Trudy, from this point on, was socially a "Made Woman."

The Heart Ball took its rightful place in the Wampum Social Hall of Fame, along with the other memorable galas from years past. We produced a special insert for the *Totem*, and had to reprint an extra thousand for the scrapbookers. Kardya sent a lovely note, and we had dinner a couple of times before mutually agreeing our schedules were incompatible. I attended two other "heartraisers" with her until one of her fellow physicians was smart enough to step up and remove her from the Waiting Room.

***

That summer, my dad was diagnosed with an inoperable brain tumor. We didn't tell him because we were afraid he might announce he was going fishing on his boat, the *Side Boy*, and never come back. He wouldn't want to burden anyone with his disability. Fortunately, the final stage was swift, and dad didn't suffer. He died in mid-November, just before his seventy-second birthday, and told me that if "whatever I have kills me, I've lived a long and satisfying life."

Being a war veteran, my dad felt that his post-war "survival years" were a bonus. He could have been killed in combat, like many others who didn't come home. Instead, he was able to raise and support a family and move to a beautiful community. So seventy-two years was to him a long life.

And there were certainly many "satisfying" moments with his Wampum friends and family, his youth volunteer work and all the joys of proximity to the ocean. But not quite a "happy" life. His boss at Golden Sportswear was sarcastic and manipulative, and there was no escaping him because of

170

company politics. Hat was in many ways a godsend, but her presence at times seemed to diminish his authority. Frankie absolutely drained him of energy, humor and ultimately, hope. Dad never complained about Frankie, at least to me. He actually believed his son's mental illness had come from his side of the family.

My dad had retired at age 70, still feeling uneasy that his savings weren't adequate to provide for Frankie after his death. He and my mom never got to do the traveling they talked about for so long. They just didn't feel comfortable leaving town, despite my assurances that Frankie would be under my close scrutiny and "you both deserve a vacation...Go!" It didn't happen and then, with the cancer, it couldn't happen.

My final conversation with my father was so typically focused on his concern for others.

"Jack, I feel like things are taking a turn for the worse, so I want to share a few thoughts with you...Keep an eye on your mother. Her lung disease is really taking its toll. Not much we can do, but stop in and say hello. She's crazy about you and you're the best medicine of all...Let's not give up on Frankie. I think something's going to come along that will help him keep his anger in check and balance things out." (He was right.) "How's Charlie Burke doing these days? I heard they were opening a new office in Norwell. Give him some good PR if you can. What a great success story." (My dad had "surrogate fathered" Charlie after Burke the father left town with a whiskey bottle. Thanks to mother Rosemary and son Charlie and their 24/7 efforts, Burke Real Estate had really prospered during the population boom.) "Thank everybody who's been showing up and bringing me real food. Some of them look worse than I do."

St. Matthews was packed for his funeral service. Grown-up "alums" of his Little League teams, Cub Scouts, Boy Scouts, and acolytes...his work colleagues, who car-pooled from Dorchester and brought the largest floral arrangement I'd ever seen...his old family friends, most of whom shared his competitive passion for bridge...his fishing buddies and the "Wampum harbor crew"...Charlie Burke and others he'd mentored, who in turn would give back to other young men...and the Wampum town leaders, who knew how much Dick Peirce had meant to the community.

I served as crucifer for the service. Frankie and my former teacher Ernie Gardiner were torch bearers. My mother watched proudly and tearfully.

Earlier that day, I wrote my father a note and put it in a side pocket of his favorite navy blue suit.

"Dad,

I love you as much as any son could love his father. There will be many others here today who love you as well. They remember your gift of caring, and the wonderful things you taught us, like "real teamwork," Morse code and tying a bowline with one hand. Your legacy will be all the lives you touched, and all the lives they touch in your memory. I will take care of mother and Frankie, and you watch over us from where you are, and deserve to be.

Love,

Jack

(When the Red Sox finally win the Series, I'll get drunk for both of us.)"

Charlie Burke came up to me after the service and told me (again) how much my father had meant to him: "The service today was filled with people who realize the impact your dad had on their lives. Like me. He's my role model for being a

172

great father. If he hadn't treated me like a son, I probably would have ended up a delinquent. That's why my son's middle name is Richard."

I didn't know this, but what a beautiful tribute. Especially from an Irish Catholic, Dad.

Chapter 20
Entangled (1988)

By 1988, it seemed that "the reign of the Four Aces" (my expression) was in jeopardy, although not on the tennis court.

They had won all the singles, doubles and mixed doubles championships at the Wampum Country Club for the past five years, but…the wild parties at the Hunt Club continued, and the local police condoned them, claiming it was private property, there was no public disturbance given the remote location, and all the guests were "of age." Apparently not, according to some of Wampum's teenage girls, who claimed they had been admitted to parties and served liquor.

Two local builders complained that the Upper Dickinson Environmental Center didn't deserve nonprofit status and should be put on the real estate market rather than continuing to receive undeserved tax deductions. The Villas attorney had managed so far to fend off a legal challenge.

The Wampum "townies" were upset at the Villas for discontinuing their two annual charitable events: the May Open House and the Christmas celebration, which had provided needed revenues for the Little League and the Historical Society. The Villas responded that the fundraisers were extremely labor intensive and the residents no longer had the time to devote to them, given their other responsibilities. (The Villas did solicit contributions for both nonprofits, but they were less than half the previous amounts.)

Then there was the speeding issue. Villas residents were notoriously oblivious to local speed limits, which they exceeded by 20-30 mph without even a warning from Wampum's finest. Why? Most felt it was the Villas' whopping annual donation to the Policemen's Ball. The Villas folks actually had a "V" on their bumpers to alert the cops to their favored status.

The "favored status" rule became a little confusing for Chief Thunderthug the night Muffy Shrike arrived at the station to report husband Morgan for domestic abuse. She was sobbing, disheveled and had a black eye. While an officer took Muffy's statement, the Chief was on the phone with Morgan getting his account of the incident. He confirmed they had been arguing, but claimed he had opened the bedroom door suddenly as Muffy entered the room and her bruise was an accident.

Lawyers were engaged and six weeks later, much to Thunderthug's relief, the matter was settled out of court without a guilty plea. According to Laura Chase, Muffy got a handsome cash settlement and a month in Hilton Head, without Morgan. Laura consoled her in the days immediately following the assault and confirmed she was traumatized. This was the third time Morgan had punched her while intoxicated.

The Shrikes became a "guest bedroom couple," in Villas parlance, but this time it was a "locked guest bedroom," not a sexual abstinence issue.

At roughly the same time, word got around that Stan Kestrel was being sued by a patient over a rhinoplasty operation that in the young woman's opinion hadn't gone well. If the story were written up in the *National Enquirer*, it would have been titled "Rhinoplasty Gets Nasty." Apparently, one of Stan's wealthiest clients had promised his mistress a nose job, and she assumed she was being sculpted into the next Mrs. Millionaire. Instead, Stan's friend decided that a divorce would be financially devastating and opted to make amends with his wife. Furious, the mistress sued both the husband and Stan as accomplices in a plot to "manipulate her with false promises and alter her appearance against her will."

When I bumped into him at the hardware store, Stan managed to find some humor in the mistress getting "nosed out" by the wife. "But you wouldn't believe the stories some of these patients concoct, mostly to avoid paying the bill. Our malpractice insurance costs are through the roof and up in the stratosphere."

When all was said and done, the mistress prevailed. Despite her ridiculous claim, Stan's lawyers didn't want to risk a sympathetic judge, so Finishing Touches Surgical Associates and the chastened husband split a payment of $100,000. How do they determine these things? God only nose!

Now 41, I began to consider what more I could do as editor of the *Totem* to prod the community conscience. I had overslept the turbulent sixties, stoned and oblivious. Now I might partially atone by exposing how a charming suburban American community can compromise its character. I tried fending off this thought, because I knew it would offend the North Wampum constituency.

Until now, I had been a jovial community cheerleader, singing the praises of artists, educators, small businesspeople, academics and other local luminaries who make us a special place. I had spared the *Totem* from many of the potentially offensive *Renegade WASP* columns I was writing for city weeklies. Now, if I wrote the editorial I had in mind, I would undoubtedly piss off the privileged.

I discussed my concern with Laura Chase, whose instincts I always trusted, but whose points of view were generally far left of the Villas crowd. We were seeing less and less of Laura as her commutes to Oak Park to visit Holly and granddaughter Laurel became more frequent.

"You should write your editorial, Jack. I think you're overestimating the blowback from the Upper Crust. The people who matter know how much you care about Wampum and will respect your point of view."

"Laura, I'm just concerned it will seem like an attack against the wealthy by someone with a middle class chip on his shoulder."

"But you're not attacking financial success...you're exposing an attitude. You're saying that these self-centered newcomers want to put up 'No Trespassing' signs under 'Entering Wampum'. Before, it was about us as a community; now it's about me and the hell with everybody else."

"Wow! How about you write the editorial and I'll just say it was submitted by a Concerned Citizen?"

"Because I can't say it as well as you can. You're the journalist. You need to tell us why we're heading in the wrong direction."

A couple of weeks later, I had a final draft:

Welcome to Wampum, or No Trespassing?

I'm an admirer of the poet Robert Frost. One of my favorites is "The Road Not Taken," in which his narrator pauses at a point where two roads divide and lead in different directions. He decides to take "the one less traveled by/And that has made all the difference."

As a native resident of our lovely village, I believe we have arrived at that fork in the road where we need to decide as a community who we want to be. Frost tells us the roads don't look that different, but once you start on one or the other, you're not likely to turn back.

We will celebrate 200 years as a township in 1994. We've tamed a rugged environment, employed innovative trades and skills to support ourselves, agreed to govern democratically and worship freely and we've managed to create a communal bond, despite our different ethnicities.

This bond is a precious thing, as intangible as it may seem. We're lobster fishermen, local business owners, college professors, town employees, commuters to Boston, retirees and all manner of other things that make our little town so diverse and unique. We've generously invested ourselves as Boy and Girl Scout leaders, PTA members, nonprofit volunteers, cultural contributors, coaches, Sunday school teachers and in many other enriching activities.

We can be a combative family at times, but we also have a good heart and an instinct for steering Wampum in the right direction. An example is our standing up to Goring Waste Management, whose liquified trash was leaching into our reservoir, polluting the groundwater and damaging wetlands. We took them to court and won, preventing what would have been a hazardous, long-term environmental problem for the town.

I believe there's another pollution problem we need to confront: attitudinal pollution. A small segment of our population views itself as deserving special status, based on its economic impact: high property tax payments, higher than average local purchases and a few politically strategic civic contributions.

This is New Money—not the Old Money that has invested so generously in Wampum over the years, with no expectation of special treatment. The New Money wants to make and play by its own rules. One coastal enclave in particular makes residents sign a binding contract before being admitted. They have also created two nonprofit organizations: the Wampum Hunt Club and the Upper Dickinson Environmental Center.

The mission of the Hunt Club is to educate gun owners on the safe usage and storage of firearms. Our community should be aware of its existence and the fact that all improvements made to the club are tax deductible. Not being a gun owner, I haven't visited, but am told it has become a "social center" for mostly out-of-town females. I hope they're getting well trained. The club is somewhere in the woods off Hawthorne Hollow, on a "Road Not Taken" by most of us.

Even less is known about the Upper Dickinson Environmental Center, whose mission is to preserve oceanfront property from residential overdevelopment. It's conveniently located directly across the street from the Villas—presumably to prevent residential overdevelopment from obscuring the Villas' highly valued ocean views. I know where UDEC is, but can't recommend a visit, since its tiny headquarters has been under repair since UDEC's inception. They could have had a voice in the Goring pollution hearings, but didn't utter a peep.

This affluent area of town seems to be thinly patrolled based on the Wampum Police Department's records of speeding tickets over the last five years. Of the roughly five thousand tickets written, only five were written to speeders in the Upper Dickinson area, and three of those were "thrown out." For those of us who've been frontally assaulted by a variety of expensive autos whipping around curves on "Upper Dic," I find the ticket number hard to believe. And yet Chief Burns assures me that the neighborhood in question is "a regular part of our beat." Two tickets in five years on the "UD Expressway"? Beats me!

Don't get me wrong. This isn't an indictment of wealth, without which we wouldn't be the Wampum everyone wants to visit. It's an indictment of the Arrogance of Privilege, which prefers to be exclusive, private and indifferent to being part of

179

any community outside its castle walls. I don't see the Arrogance of Privilege folks at town meetings, or Little League games or Memorial Day parades or in volunteer positions. This is how we "Enter Wampum" and confirm our affiliation with fellow citizens.

So to return to Frost for a moment, when the road forks, take the one with the "Welcome to Wampum: Join Our Community" sign, not the one with the BMW heading straight at you, trying to drive you into a ditch. For Wampum, it will make "all the difference."

(Note: The *Totem* will print responses to this editorial in the weeks to come.)"

***

There were many notes of approval for my editorial and not a single note of dissent. I was amused that several people from surrounding communities also had their "Arrogance of Privilege" types who preferred to stay aloof from the general community. I even got a nice note from Cap Campbell, my model for the civicly committed WASP who expects nothing in return except the pleasure of helping others.

I wasn't at all surprised, several weeks later, to receive a phone message from David Chase, who asked if "we might get together to discuss the Arrogance of Privilege editorial." We arranged a meeting date and when I arrived at the Villas clubhouse, I was met by the entire quartet of Aces. After shaking hands, the group got right down to business, with Chase taking the lead. I asked if I could tape our conversation, but Chase declined, claiming it "might constrain participation," so I took notes. I have recreated (and condensed) the dialogue as accurately as I can.

180

Chase: As members of the Villas Ownership Group, we'd like to share the concerns of our residents that we were singled out and — we feel — unjustly accused in your editorial.

Hawk: The Villas has been a generous contributor to the Historical Society and the town Little League for quite a few years, but you didn't mention this. Instead, you refer to (and here he reads from the paper) 'strategically political civic contributions'. So are you saying our support is based on political considerations?

Peirce (That's me): I've heard comments from trusted sources that your contributions have declined considerably in recent years. Is there a reason for that?

Shrike: We have a right to contribute to whoever we want! That's up to our members. We didn't sign any contracts with anybody.

Peirce: I don't want to speak for the nonprofits, but usually if support gets reduced dramatically there's an alert from the donor it's going to happen, so the nonprofit doesn't budget at the same level.

Hawk: My wife chaired the Heart Ball fundraiser two years ago, which included a helluva lot of work by the Villas, but I didn't see any mention of that.

Peirce: I'm sure you remember the extensive coverage we gave that event, including several photos of Trudy and her committee members.

Chase: I think we should focus on the "Arrogance of Privilege" references, in which you clearly indict the Villas. Yes, we do have a member agreement, which is standard for communities like ours, and which the residents request. We've also created two nonprofits, which reflect our commitment to gun safety and environmental preservation. That's well within our rights as citizens.

Kestrel: I'm on the board of UDEC, and we're trying to prevent overdevelopment in this area. I'm sure that's something the townspeople can support.

Peirce: If you'd like to send me your most recent nonprofit filing and the minutes from your last three board meetings, I'd be happy to

181

consider an update article. (This didn't happen, and there was no mention of the Hunt Club during our discussion.)

Shrike: What's your point about the traffic tickets? You make it sound like Chief Burns is 'on the take'. I see him all the time around here. He's the best thing this town has going for it.

Peirce: I reported the real numbers, and left it to our readers to reach their own conclusions.

Chase: Actually, I think you reached their conclusions for them. Listen, you probably need to sit down with a good lawyer and talk about where you may be vulnerable in this editorial. We'll be doing the same thing. In the meantime, the residents wish to cancel their subscriptions to your paper, and there may be some business ads canceled as well. We'll keep on reading the New York Times and The Wall Street Journal...the 'Arrogance of Privilege' publications. We're done. Thanks for listening.

That's my summary, with all the "BS" eliminated. It went as I expected, and I left feeling confident I wouldn't be hearing from their attorney.

***

Two other significant events from 1988:
The editorial got townspeople talking about the Villas' two nonprofits, and I was eventually contacted by a representative from the Massachusetts Attorney General's office. (Wampum residents know people who know People in High Places.) We had a lengthy conversation about UDEC and the Hunt Club, and I was pleased to provide him with David Chase's phone number and address. Very soon afterward, I was visited by two impressively-credentialed investigators with notebooks open. I had a warm feeling that the red light at the Hunt Club was about to be extinguished.

The other event concerns a David Chase holiday party at the Villas that got out of control. The Aces gave their spouses tickets to *The Nutcracker* in Boston and a weekend at a swanky hotel. While they were away, the boys invited the cream of Group A (the Yacht Club lovelies) and Group B (The Hunt Club girls) to a lavishly catered "client banquet," that included strippers and a Boom Boom Room. Several rooms in the Chase mansion were trashed, the frame for one of Benjy's paintings was smashed and a drunken departing visitor crashed into the entry gate. Despite all this, Chase would have gotten off scott free with the help of an expert cleaning crew he had hired for the following morning.

His mistake came at the end of the night. When his attempt to negotiate a threesome was unsuccessful, he turned his attention to a lovely young dark-haired bartender. When she too spurned his advances, he groped her and tried to carry her into the bedroom. Fortunately, one of her work colleagues came to her rescue and the two fled immediately. Unfortunately for Chase, the bartender filed sexual assault charges. Her name was Sylvia Oliveiros, and she was the niece of Freddy Fernandes, the lobster fisherman.

By the end of the year, I was feeling like a Renegade WASP again.

Chapter 21
Entraped (1990)

It seemed inconceivable to us Wampum HS '65 grads, but 1990 was our 25th reunion year. Many of us saw each other on a regular basis, but there were the expatriates (about 70% of us) who believed the Road to Happiness and Prosperity could only lead out of town. For a few years, I was one of them.

There were 115 of us, and about 75 reunited during a highly congenial August weekend. As with all reuniongoers, nature had favored some and ravaged others. At first, it's all about appearances, but it gets much less uptight for everybody after a glass of wine or two.

Several of those who remained in Wampum had done very well thanks to the dramatically appreciating real estate market and the demand among the newly-arrived upscalers for personal and landscaping services. One of our class wits commented "Most of us don't have Wampum enough to live here. Once you leave town you can't afford to come back except for reunions." And he was right. After dad's death, my mother had moved to a modest apartment in a less expensive nearby suburb.

Our reunion included a New England clambake, harborside cocktails, boat rides and many old memories recalled and exaggerated. Most of us had remained in the Northeast, and we were highly diversified careerwise: teachers, nurses, engineers, craftspeople, finance folks, writers, a few lobster fishermen and a surplus of lawyers. An even split between surviving marriages and divorces. A few early deaths, the first three being AIDS, a suicide and a murder by a deranged husband—the victim being my first girlfriend.

The weekend included the dedication of a new all-weather track at the high school in honor of coach Dave Charles, a cancer victim, and his three-year ('62-'65) unbeaten track team. Current and former track members participated by running continuous laps for 100 hundred miles, which took from noon on Friday to midnight. Class members, former faculty and even townspeople contributed a total of $10,000-- $100 dollars a mile—to raise money for new uniforms, track equipment and a fund for future needs. The *Totem* ran photos and brief bios of the runners. My track buddy Brian Farrell and I both ran twenty of the four hundred laps, while my teacher and bridge buddy Ernie Gardiner and many others cheered us on. It remains a cherished memory.

I invited Frankie to join me for one of the reunion events and several of my classmates came up to say hello. Others kept their distance, which I understood because of his notoriety for unpredictable behavior. He enjoyed himself and ate enough for three people. Many folks had kind comments about the *Totem* and our coverage of community activities. A few asked about the "Entering Wampum" editorial and its repercussions. I replied that I hadn't been invited to any parties at the Villas and assumed I'd been "Villa"-fied, which always got chuckles, but I realized had gotten stale. Our class only had a couple of Villas residents and they didn't show up, but I had a complete dossier of feedback from Laura Chase. Her advice: "Don't go riding your bike on any of the main roads." I laughed, but thereafter did all my long bike rides outside of town.

From everything I could tell, and everything Laura told me, the Aces were keeping a low profile as they tried to manage the messes they'd created. Oliver Hawk was being aggressively investigated by the IRS for business-related tax fraud. Most of the problem was his overly ambitious treasurer, who wanted everything Oliver had but didn't want to earn it honestly. So he created a virtually foolproof system of skimming profits from the dealership's leasing operations. But apparently it was only "virtually" foolproof, and someone auditing the Hawk dealership's finances was more vigilant than anticipated. Desperate to exonerate himself, the treasurer claimed that Hawk had "created an atmosphere of corruption" by providing free auto leases to preferred customers and offering "dramatically under book" buyback deals when the leases expired. It seemed they were both working illegally at cross purposes, but the financial data would determine degree of guilt. In the auto industry, this falls into the category of "asset misappropriation" and apparently is quite common.

Meanwhile, the investigation into the two "home grown" nonprofits was gathering steam. Neither UDEC nor the Hunt Club had submitted required annual paperwork, and responsibility for that rested with Stan Kestrel, who was listed as president of both. Stan had articles of incorporation, drawn up by a Villas attorney, but no meeting minutes or financial records existed, and the attorney had moved away.

The IRS sent two investigative agents to town and they had filled several notebooks with mostly incriminating commentary from community interviewees. The IRS prohibits nonprofits from engaging in activities outside their statement of purpose and can revoke their nonprofit status. If that happens, any donations to the ex-nonprofit become taxable income.

Then there was Chase's alleged sexual assault of Sylvia Oliveiros. Sylvia's work colleague had testified Chase dragged her into his bedroom with the intention of having sex with her, and Sylvia had strenuously resisted. Chase was able to coerce two friends who had been elsewhere in the house to testify they saw the couple kissing. After considering the conflicting testimonies, listening to character witnesses on both sides, and citing Chase's "clean record," a judge dismissed the sexual assault charge, with a warning to Chase about the implications of any future misconduct. Freddy Fernandes was furious about the verdict and vowed in court to "make sure justice is done" for his niece. It was rumored that Chase secretly paid a substantial amount to Sylvia for lost compensation and "mental anguish."

That leaves Morgan Shrike, who had been a spouse in exile at the Villas, and finally decided to move out and into the Hunt Club. Never very sociable, even inside the Villas, he kept a low profile around town, which naturally made him an object of suspicion. Laura Chase loathed him.

"Morgan Shrike is a dangerous individual. The spousal abuse is just the tip of the iceberg with that guy. His anger issues go all the way back to his boyhood, when his father ordered him around like a Marine trainee. Apparently, his mother never spoke up on his behalf, so he has a deep resentment of women. Dangerous guy. A big screw loose up there."

Shrike was one of the "eyewitnesses" Chase had recruited to testify on his behalf. According to Laura, Shrike was now dating a divorced woman from the Hunt Club group, whom he had instructed to report to the IRS investigator about the "gun safety instruction" she was receiving. Unbelievable. Laura also claimed that Shrike had "very suspicious business associates who drive around in dark cars with tinted glass."

187

I got some additional perspectives on the Aces at a Friday night bridge game with Ernie Gardiner (my ex-English teacher if you missed him earlier), Ed the history teacher and Bob the science teacher. Ernie and Ed had retired from teaching but Bob was still "in the detention center," as they called it.

The three enjoyed trying to pry confidential information out of me, which they felt entitled to since I had been fortunate enough to be their student. Ever since my "Entering Wampum" editorial, which Ernie liked because of the Robert Frost reference, they viewed me as their "inside source" on the Aces, who by now had become notorious in most Wampum social circles.

Ed (my bridge partner): *So Jack, what's happening with the IRS investigations? I hear they've interviewed about half the town.*

Me: No decision yet, but they have plenty of evidence that neither of the nonprofits is legit. Pass.

Ernie (Bob's bridge partner): *If they don't lose their status, I think we declare this bridge group a nonprofit and deduct all our expenses for the last five years. One heart.*

Ed: That means Bob, Jack and I can deduct a few thousand each and you can deduct maybe ten bucks for the Saltines. Pass.

Bob: I think we ask Hawk's wife to be president and SHE can bring the snacks. Two hearts.

Me: Trudy Hawk has my vote. We can make her the Queen of Hearts. Pass.

Ernie: Three votes for Trudy, as long as she wears a tight red dress. And three hearts from me.

Ed: As long as it's low cut, four votes. And a pass.

Bob: I'm passing also. So Jack, you can invite her and her low cut red dress to my house next Friday and I'll make sure to give Patty

188

(his wife) movie money. Tell her we're waiting for IRS certification but that shouldn't be a problem.

Me: Your bid for three hearts. (Ed leads and Ernie begins to play the hand. Bob is the dummy.) OK, I'll tell Trudy she only needs to bring dessert, and not to worry about the calories.

Ernie: We should assign a suit to each of the four Aces. Somebody start, cuz I can't play and be creative at the same time.

Ed: I'll go first because I don't know them that well, but I've heard that Shrike beats up his wife. So he should be the ace of clubs.

Bob: I'll take diamonds. When you have a trophy wife like Trudy you have to buy her diamonds, so Hawk is the ace of diamonds.

Me: Good one, Bob. That leaves hearts and spades. I'm going to make Chase the ace of hearts, because Ernie taught me the meaning of irony.

Ernie: I knew you'd pick Chase. So that leaves spades, and who is the ace of spades?

Me: Stan Kestrel, the plastic surgeon.

Ernie: He's the least notorious of the bunch, but let me think...He can be the ace of spades because he digs things out of people that they don't want to be attached to anymore.

Bob: Only you could come up with that one, maestro.

Ed: Sure, but he's the English major. He HAS to be Mister Metaphor because he can't remember important things like dates and events.

Me: Hey, don't be demeaning my English mentor.

Ernie: Thank you, Jack. You made a wise choice in choosing English. We're the creative force in the universe. Ed's people wear tweed jackets and live in the past.

Me: Despite our brotherhood, Ernie, I have to play this card. You're down one.

Ernie: Damn it, Jack. You just trumped my ace!

Chapter 22:
Trumping Aces (1992)

In 1992, my mentor Elliott "Cap" (short for Captain) Campbell and his wife Kitty sold their Wampum summer home and returned to Annapolis. "Cap" was now 80, had retired as a professor and coach from the Naval Academy, and the Campbells wanted to settle in one spot and not have to maintain two properties. I introduced "Cap" to you in chapter four, and I'll remind you of one earlier line: "He was a Boston 'blue blood' with a ton of humanity and not an ounce of pretension."

I wrote a tribute to "Cap" for the *Totem*, helped greatly by an article in *Sports Illustrated* I had clipped and saved. I wanted the town to know what an illustrious person had been part of our community for such a long time. To me, he is the epitome of the WASP gentleman, who always found time for an inquisitive little baseball fan and later, a young track athlete. Here's what I wrote:

A Hearty Salute to "Cap" Campbell and Wife Kitty As They Leave Wampum for Annapolis

I always enjoyed *The Reader's Digest* series called "The Most Unforgettable Person I've Ever Met." This week, the person I'd put in that category is leaving Wampum after many years of "summer commuting" from the Naval Academy in Annapolis. He is Captain Elliott "Cap" Campbell, and he and his wife Kitty have graced us with their presence since the early fifties.

The Campbells have been our family's next door neighbors since we moved to Wampum. Upon hearing I was a young baseball fan, "Cap" invited me to come over and see his Red Sox memorabilia. That began a friendship that has continued for almost forty years. I had an open invitation to visit the Campbells at any convenient time during the summer. For my twelfth birthday, in 1959, "Cap" gave me a spring training practice bat used by Ted Williams. An incredible thrill.

Here's what I didn't know at the time, but want to share with you. "Cap" Campbell is *Mr. Red Sox*. He has written three "Cap"tivating books about the Sox: *Red Sox Fever*, *Red Sox Forever* and a 75th anniversary edition (1901-1975). He corresponds with players and scouts and has over a thousand cards, pictures, paintings and letters. Babe Ruth pitched for Boston in the first game "Cap" attended, in 1918, and he has been a passionate fan and historian in the nine decades since that time.

Having the foremost authority on one of America's most famous teams living next door was amazing good fortune. But there's more. As I grew into my teens, I was encouraged by my friend Brian Farrell to try cross country and then track and field. It turned out to be the best sport for me, given my lower than average hand-eye coordination skills but my higher-than-average tolerance for pain. Turns out, "Cap" was coach of the Naval Academy track and cross country teams. How's that for double serendipity?

"Cap" would become *the most successful coach in the history of the Academy*. (One of his runners was a plebe named Jimmy Carter). So he made the seamless transition from "my friend the Red Sox authority" to "my friend the track consultant." While I ended up being just a pretty good small town runner, "Cap" gave me excellent advice about training, conditioning and race strategy. I sent him detailed descriptions of every 880 race I ran in my senior year, and he always responded encouragingly.

In college, I drifted away from track and into frat house social life. But in recent years, Cap has remained a treasured mentor and sage advisor on all matters of life and business. His talented wife Kitty couldn't be a more compatible partner for him, and I am grateful for her generosity, support and good humor. When I walk past the Campbell house, I can still envision the "back porch ballerinas," with Kitty playing the piano and urging them to "lift on point."

Please join me in wishing "Cap" and Kitty a healthy and happy retirement in Annapolis after many years as one of Wampum's most delightful couples.

***

On the other end of the spectrum, the Aces were approaching the final stage of their four-decade ego trip of professional prominence, tennis supremacy and scandalous behavior. The storm clouds were moving in quickly.

Oliver Hawk had begun an eighteen-month sentence for IRS tax violations at a Connecticut "white collar prison." The timing had been bad for him. The IRS was cracking down on high level tax violators and everything Hawk said in his defense seemed self-incriminating. It didn't help that his treasurer testified aggressively against him in an effort to get his own sentence reduced. (That strategy backfired. The treasurer was sentenced to three years for embezzling funds. Same white collar prison, but hopefully not the same cell.)

To me, Hawk was a victim of his own need to be liked. He went way overboard in providing favors to a core of wealthy customers who didn't need, but were happy to accept, free or highly discounted auto leases for their girlfriends or laughably low-priced lease buyback vehicles. Like BMWs and Benzes with 5,000 miles for five or six grand. Why, Oliver? I can understand your cutting a deal for the other Aces, but why go so far over the line and risk everything?

One of those everythings was Trudy, who had risen to prominence for her organizational talents, extensive network and personal charm. (Was that part of the problem?) After Oliver's sentencing, Trudy filed for divorce and immediately signaled that she was available. Her friends eventually connected her with a recently-widowed state senator. He instantly recognized her potential as a political asset—beauty, brains, charisma—and she vaulted into the lead over the other marital candidates.

Two years later they were married and she moved to Wellesley (west of Boston) to begin a new life. Long story short: five years after their wedding, Senator Harrington became Governor Harrington and Trudy became First Lady of Massachusetts. Because of her high profile involvement, Trudy was acclaimed by one newspaper as "the governor's honorary campaign manager." Believe me, there was nothing "honorary" about it.

I wrote a feature about Trudy at the time of her wedding, knowing that Wampum would remember her and her local charitable successes. Turns out she was a mud WASP. She was Trudy Jones, the daughter of a plumber from Quincy, and had met Oliver while auditioning for a commercial promoting Hawk Luxury Motors. At one point during our interview for the *Totem*, she made an interesting remark about her life at the Villas: "From Day One, I felt like I had to fight the image of the gold-digging Blond Bimbo. But instead of being intimidated by that, it became my inspiration. I was driven to prove that I had a brain and the organizational skills to take charge when I was given the opportunity."

After leaving prison, Oliver Hawk sold his home in the Villas and moved down to Plymouth, where a friend in the auto business gave him a job in sales. Deeply embarrassed about his tarnished reputation, he changed his professional surname from "Hawk" to "Martin" and kept a low profile. His only passions were his little sailboat and the local tavern, where he met daily with drinking buddies and began a slow downward spiral into belly fat and oblivion. He never again picked up a tennis racquet.

Stan Kestrel, meanwhile, was getting his knuckles rapped by the IRS for the Villas' non-functioning nonprofits. Unfortunately for Stan, it was his name on the documents of incorporation. Testimony from many Wampum residents confirmed that neither the Hunt Club nor the Environmental Center had provided any legitimate services to justify their not-for-profit status. Furthermore, there were numerous complaints that the Hunt Club had been a corrupting influence on the underage female population.

As an interviewee, I got the impression that the two IRS investigative agents were determined to make a high profile example of the transgressors. Our proximity to the abundant print and broadcast media outlets in the Greater Boston area made this an ideal location for a showdown in which the IRS would actually be viewed as the "good guys." Positive PR for the IRS? Priceless!

Given the extent of the community outcry, the IRS was able to schedule a rare public hearing so all grievances could be aired. The Wampum town hall was packed to the rafters with outraged citizenry of all ages and genders as well as multiple media sources. (It recalled "Vietnam Comes to Wampum," but this time opinions were unanimous as to the guilty parties.)

We heard from angry parents whose teenage daughters had been hustled by "high profile businessmen who should be prosecuted for corrupting minors"; from gun lobbyists who claimed that the Hunt Club's violation of its mission "endangered our Second Amendment rights"; from environmentalists who complained that UDEC "did absolutely nothing to address the serious concerns of the pro-environment community"; and, with the IRS representatives grinning from ear to ear, that "a few wealthy individuals were given tax deductions to entertain themselves at the expense of honest taxpayers like us."

Only Stan Kestrel was made to endure the verbal onslaught from the audience, and it was a tidal wave of animosity.

The headline in a prominent Boston newspaper the next day was "Villa-in Gate Nonprofit Scandal Rocks Quaint South Shore Community," and it was "off to the races" for the media. If punishment had been determined after the town hall meeting, Stan Kestrel—probably the least disreputable of the Four Aces—would have been placed in the stocks on the Common so locals could heap abuse on him.

Public sentiment was unmoved by the testimony of the Aces' friends, who served as character witnesses, and in a few cases even claimed to be the beneficiaries of Hunt Club or UDEC services. These were submitted in writing or during private meetings, since no one wanted to face the wrath of fellow townspeople at the hearing. Chief Thunderthug, not surprisingly, had no records to confirm underage corruption charges.

Two weeks later, the IRS slapped a fine of $250,000 on the boards of the two nonprofits, both of which had the same members. The media jumped on this, since it was the largest fine of its kind ever levied against local nonprofits in the New England region. UDEC and the Hunt Club were ordered to pay back any contributions and reimbursements plus penalties for tax deductions claimed. Plus IRS overhead expenses. A death blow to the Aces, right? Not quite. They were covered by "D&O" (Directors and Officers) insurance, which anted up an agreed upon $125,000, and their own personal liability policies covered the rest. They didn't pay a dime out of pocket.

Stan and Bunny Kestrel knew they were "burnt toast" in Wampum, and decided to pull up stakes and move south to Hilton Head. They had vacationed there often and knew it would provide a fresh start. Bunny and Laura Chase were good friends, and Laura later passed along very positive reports from the Kestrels. Stan dropped his WASPy disguise and actually started attending a synagogue along with Bunny, who converted. Stan had invested wisely and they could cavort to all corners of the world and not have to return to New England winters. Their daughter Kristin was working as a community outreach director for the Boston Ballet. She had been one of Kitty Campbell's summer ballerinas and was able to channel her passion for dance into a fulfilling career.

Except for Laura, the Kestrels never again spoke to the other Aces. They continued to play tennis, but eventually opted for golf. I was happy to hear, a few years later, that both Stan and Bunny had taken leadership positions with the United Jewish Appeal. They were terribly embarrassed by the Wampum nonprofit scandal and I'm sure appreciated the chance to "give back" in a meaningful way to their new community.

***

Now, for David Chase.

Chase's acquittal on charges of assaulting Sylvia Oliveiros angered the Wampum community. The townspeople viewed it as a privileged rich man being allowed to "have his way with a townie," and the judge of "sparing the rod" to protect

Chase from the embarrassment of an assault conviction. Once again, Thunderthug appeared to be protecting the rich folks. He couldn't produce a breathalyzer test for Chase on the night of the incident, and claimed Chase "showed no signs of being intoxicated, and apologized to Miss Oliveiros for upsetting her."

I can attest that following the acquittal, there were rumors about retribution against Chase for his sexually predatory behaviors. Had a vigilante strike force been recruited, it would have included representatives from every neighborhood in Wampum.

Laura Chase reported to me that her husband had taken a leave of absence after the Oliveiros hearing. Predictable behavior for an almost-convicted corporate executive. But he hadn't left for the tropics to play golf, as she expected. Instead, he was undergoing medical tests and being evasive about the details. She had noticed dramatic changes in his appearance and behavior, especially nausea, weight loss and a yellowing of his skin and pupils. Then, suddenly, he was hospitalized.

The diagnosis was late stage liver cancer. Chase had apparently ignored all the danger signs, just as Laura said his father had done before dying from stomach cancer. David's cancer had devolved from cirrhosis, a scarring of liver tissue, often—and in this case definitely—caused by alcohol abuse.

***

I was able to get Chase's hospital address from Monarch Financial by pretending to be a former Monarch colleague. (I didn't want to ask Laura.) When I asked the hospital about visitation hours they said he wasn't seeing visitors but "friends like me have been dropping by in the late afternoon when he reads on the third floor patio."

On my second visit, Chase was alone on the patio.

"Hello, David. I wondered if you had any thoughts to share with our 'Totem' readers about the Oliveiros trial?"

"I'm not accepting visitors except close friends, and you certainly don't qualify."

"As you sit here contemplating your life, do you have any regrets as a husband or father?"

"Not anything I'd share with you. So why don't you get the hell out of here."

"What really happened to your son Benjy?"

"(Chase picked up his phone.) I'm dialing Security, so you have about two minutes to leave or be thrown out."

"So here's my two minutes…You ordered the murder of your son because his mental illness embarrassed you, and then bought people off to cover it up. You should have gone to prison, but all it cost you was your wife and daughter.

"Then you started pimping around to build up your power base. You played sexual godfather to your young recruits so they'd kiss your ass and you'd have dirt on them if you ever needed it.

"But you went over the line. And this time I think—I pray in fact—that it's going to cost you.

"Right now, they're talking about you over at Monarch Financial. 'Did you hear David Chase got charged with groping a bartender? They say he throws wild parties on his yacht, for customers and even our employees.'

"You're starting to smell bad over at Monarch, Ace. Some pretty well-connected folks are calling your CEO and your board members and telling them to sack you. It's not a summer camp murder this time. It's corporate politics. The vultures are circling and they can smell your reputation rotting. And you're not around to defend yourself. The word inside is that you're not sick, you're suspended...until they fire you.

"(I looked at my watch.) That's my two minutes. Looks like no Security for you. You'll just have to sit here and drown out the memories."

***

Laura kept her little family (Holly, Laura's sister and me, her honorary-son-in-law) well updated during the four months it took for the cancer to terminate Chase. The "royal physicians," as Laura called them, tried everything inside and then outside the treatment manual, ending with radiation oncology. But it was too late. The tumors prevailed. In addition to the other systemic damage caused by the cancer, Laura wanted me to know that it shrank his testicles.

The funeral was held in Boston, where Chase worked. A wise decision, since except for a few Villas friends of Laura's—whom she "limousined" to the viewing and service—there would have been no grievers from the Wampum community.

Laura said the turnout from Monarch Financial was considerable but "his senior colleagues offered perfunctory condolences and were gone in a heartbeat...and the CEO was conveniently out of town." As I anticipated, the news about his assault hearing had spread quickly through the company. There were fewer than a dozen "mourners" at the Chase family grave site in Brookline, and no family member would ever visit again.

Holly flew in to support her mother, and I drove to Boston to say a quick hello because she was flying back to Chicago that evening. We met for coffee and an English muffin, which was all she wanted. I asked how she felt, and if the occasion had been difficult for her.

"I wasn't going to come, because you know how I feel. But there's no way I could let my mother face this alone. She's been my strength all these years and I hope I gave a little back today."

"You did. Absolutely. Your mother is an incredible woman. She's one of my closest friends, and I don't know where the paper would be without her. In fact, it probably <u>wouldn't</u> be."

"The Totem was her gift to you, Jack. She knew you'd make it a success. I also think it was her apology for the rotten way my father treated you...and both of us."

"Your father became an object of scorn to the entire town. I'm sure your mother has shared it all with you. If it hadn't been for the cancer he might have been lynched."

"My father <u>was</u> a cancer. A malignant cancer. He injected himself into people and poisoned them. My mother and I...and you...we're Chase cancer survivors."

And in that moment I thought: That's the eulogy you deserve, you evil bastard. Delivered by your own daughter. It should be inscribed on your tombstone.

***

On the ride home, I did a mental replay of our meeting. I was happy I could help Holly articulate the anger she deserved to feel. Still, she seemed evasive about her current life. Her daughter Laurel, now seven, was excelling at school—<u>public</u> school, Holly emphasized—riding horses fearlessly and swinging a mean tennis racquet.

When I asked about Laurel's father Ryan, she told me they had decided not to marry but have remained friends and that he "adores Laurel and never misses any of her activities."

When I raised an eyebrow, she commented, "It's me, Jack. I just can't commit to marriage after everything that's happened."

Work was going OK, but she felt that social work had given her much more satisfaction. "My boss Lindsay is a little too driven. She should have hired my mother. We're better friends than we are work partners."

Pegasus was still afloat but "gathering barnacles, because I don't have time to keep her ship shape. I'm thinking of selling her and using the money for Laurel's riding lessons."

She had looked tired and drained of the energy that had always animated her. She wasn't aging well, and wasn't trying to hide it. I should confess that on the way home I pulled the car off the road and started crying. I probably cried for five minutes, letting small spurts of pent-up frustration leak out of me. I may be a Chase cancer survivor, but I'll never be in remission from him.

***

In November, *The Wampum Totem* was named *Community Newspaper of the Year* by the Massachusetts Press Association. This was our 20th year of publication, and we were all thrilled by the recognition. I invited Laura Chase to join me and the entire staff at the awards banquet, and she accepted. She had been busy managing the final affairs of the Chase estate and preparing to join Holly in Chicago. It was a richly deserved "bon voyage" acknowledgment for the person who had done so much to counter the corrosive influence of her spouse.

The *Totem* was honored for "promoting the rich history and culture of the town of Wampum and the South Shore region. While supporting education and business development, you also provide incisive and balanced coverage of the local issues important to your readership. We also applaud your recognition of civic volunteer efforts, especially those which engage young people. And finally, we appreciate your judicious use of humor in reporting the news."

I accepted the award "with great appreciation for a staff that fully embraces the importance of the community newspaper as both a civic cheerleader and a respected, unbiased voice of truth." I pointed out that we had grown "from a staff of five, all of whom worked for free for the first three months, to a staff of twenty five, who do the work of about a hundred."

I asked Laura Chase to come forward to join me, and the entire staff gave her a standing ovation. "Laura is the angel of opportunity who invested in us when we were just a one page outline on the kitchen table," I remarked. "But we didn't get a hands off investor. We got a woman who not only wrote the check to create *The Wampum Totem*, but then went out and sold subscriptions to it. I'm still trying to pay back her loan and she's still refusing. Laura, on behalf of all of us, thank you for bringing the news to Wampum!"

Then a wonderful thing happened. The entire audience stood up and cheered Laura Chase, led by the sizeable Wampum contingent who had driven all the way to Framingham to celebrate with us.

Driving home that night, I savored a few of the memories that Laura's patronage had made possible for me and the paper. This led me to consider how profound the influence of the Chase family had been on my life. Holly: A lifelong romance. Chase: An amoral antagonist and self-serving manipulator. Laura: Absolute and uncompromising loyalty to Holly and me.

Before I "wrap" 2002, some very good news on the law and order front: The Wampum Board of Selectmen decided not to renew the contract of police chief Sean ("Thunderthug") Burns, and have appointed a search committee to recruit his successor. As we reported in the *Totem*, there had been numerous complaints about the "favorable treatment" Burns extended to certain individuals in the community.

Chapter 23
Wampum 200th (1994)

The Wampum bicentennial made us temporarily step outside our over-scheduled lives and stop to appreciate the uniqueness of our community's history and heritage. The tribute--"Come   Onboard Wampum 200: 1794-1994"-- was a 5-year effort that involved literally hundreds of townspeople, who contributed their funds, volunteer labors and family histories. It was in every way a tribute to the adaptability and ingenuity that have made us a favorite "port of call" for two centuries.

The year began with a carillon concert on New Year's Day, which most of us listened to inside our heated cars. It included an eclectic choice of classical, patriotic, pop and seasonal music, concluding with the Wampum High fight song, "Auld Lang Syne" and "God Bless America." We were enticed outdoors by young volunteers who passed out Wampum 200 candles and asked us to stand in a circle and sing the national anthem with the high school chorus. We were then invited to the Congregational Church for hot chocolate, gingerbread cookies and a few remarks from Charlie Wordsworth, chair of "Onboard 200." Charlie asked us all to pick up "Come Onboard" postcards with key celebration dates and mail them to our out-of-town friends.

Because our cold winter weather discourages outdoor activities except for hockey and occasional sledding, the first quarter segment of "Onboard Wampum 200" was scheduled indoors. The Wampum Historical Society (never "Hysterical" in my experience) took the winter lead with a bicentennial exhibit featuring artifacts from every major chapter of town history, many contributed by local families. The local Indian artifacts, "crime deterrent implements" (stocks, thumb screws) and shipbuilding blueprints and tools were big favorites. The Society also organized weekend tours of 25 "historically significant" Wampum homes (5 per weekend over 5 weeks), but not a single residence from The Villas.

The fourth quarter of 1994 also favored indoor activities, including a Halloween party at an actual haunted house once owned by ship captain Silas Bates. The ghostly ambiance was accentuated by creative sound effects and strategically concealed crew members and mermaids, who popped out unexpectedly. All who came in costume were invited to help themselves from a huge treasure trunk of treats.

In November, the Historical Society hired an event organizer to stage an elaborate Thanksgiving Feast of Fellowship on the Common. The goal—which was achieved-- was to get at least one Wampum citizen from every year since 1901 to attend, and then to take a photo of the entire group of 94 ('94 being the anniversary date) in Thanksgiving attire. The photo appeared on national print and broadcast media. Attendees brought food and clothes for charitable organizations and signed a Pact of Fellowship with their name and country of origin, which was later posted in the Town Hall.

The event concluded with a pageant recreating the first Thanksgiving (about 90 minutes south of us in Plymouth), complete with live turkeys from a local farm. "The Feast" was beautifully planned and executed, enhanced by unusually mild weather and celebrated as one of our bicentennial's "shining moments." The *Totem* added a four-page supplement—barely enough for all the engaging photos and comments.

The April-September months were the "outdoor season" for Wampum 200, and they were booked to the hilt. In late April, we invited athletes to our first "Wampum Run to the Beach" five miler. We lucked out with the weather, which remained glorious for almost all our outdoor events. In subsequent years—given the unpredictability of April weather around here—the race would become "The Jog through the Fog" or "The Strain through the Rain." But the inaugural run was dry and balmy, and a hundred people gave it a try, including me. The winner, a college junior from Randolph, sprinted to the finish line in a time of 24 minutes. I did it in 32, and have never improved on that time. Since I chaired the first event, I'm proud it has continued and now attracts over four hundred athletes who compete for the Beach Pail Trophy and, along with sponsors, help us raise about $15,000 annually for town beautification efforts.

Memorial Day '94 was another indelible memory of Wampum 200. It had always been a day to honor our veterans and celebrate our young peoples' involvement in the community. This year, our parade included Navy, Army and Air Force military bands. It was special recognition for the Wampum soldiers who made the "ultimate sacrifice" in Vietnam—8 casualties from a town of 5,000, including 5 in 1969 alone, as I mentioned in chapter 16.

The Memorial Day organizing committee, together with the VFW, arranged to have plaques created and installed in the neighborhoods of the fallen soldiers. A shuttle bus took us to each of the locations so we could pay our respects. Two school buses had been scheduled; it required ten to accommodate all those who wanted to participate. If you had ever driven a large vehicle, you were "on duty" that day.

The parade from the Little League field to the Common included, for the first time, two floats built by the high school shop classes. The floats featured the peripatetic Captain John Smith, who discovered the region, along with a representative cast of key figures including Indians, Pilgrims, ship captains and crew, Union soldiers, farmers, lobstermen (and women), more soldiers, yachtsmen and our most famous athlete, Rob Feeney, who was an All American college and All Pro football player. Costumes and makeup were courtesy of the Wampum Music Tent.

The paraders and spectators were greeted on the Common by Governor Phillips, who lauded Wampum as "a model for how a great American community evolves: with respect for those who struggled and sacrificed before us, and with a dedication to contribute the best of ourselves to those who will come after us." The governor was joined by senior representatives from all branches of the Armed Forces and a massive contingent of legislators in the dedication of Patriot Park "in honor of every Wampum veteran whose service has preserved and protected our freedoms."

As I left the event, I thought about how proud all the former citizens—all the way back to 1794 – would feel about who we had become, and their role in that "becoming."

***

The bicentennial also included two centennial observances: the 100th birthdays of the Wampum Yacht Club and the Wampum Country Club. The Yacht Club hosted the Tower Cup for the nation's best women sailors, competing in the International 210 class.

The Country Club, one of the oldest in America, hosted a centennial golf tournament, with multiple social events, and announced a $6 million "Drive for Two Hundred" campaign to upgrade the clubhouse and golf course. Champion amateur golfers from around the country played in the tournament and were hosted by club members.

Both anniversary celebrations brought large audiences to Wampum and attracted extensive media coverage. And there was much more "Onboard Wampum" to come.

The bicentennial provided a great opportunity to showcase the history of the Wampum harbor area, and the entire month of August was dedicated to "Harborside Highlights," featuring the "Captain John Smith Walk."

The Walk leads visitors past a grist mill, formerly a boatyard; an old salt house, which provided the salt to pack schools of cod and mackerel; Portuguese Hall, a social organization for seafaring families from the Azores, who have been part of our nautical history since the beginning; the Customs House; several stone wharves, where clipper ships landed and small businesses thrived; and the principal shipyard for large sailing vessels—now a prominent estate— built from 1800 to 1866 during our "Age of Sail." When our supply of oak was totally depleted and steamships appeared, shipbuilding ceased, and when the fishing grounds became overfished, the mackerel schooners disappeared. And yet, we survived and adapted.

**

Our very popular annual Wampum Arts Festival, usually held in June, was moved to the Fourth of July in order to accommodate the Yacht and Country Club centennial activities. The honoree that year was our nationally famous landscape artist Tomas Lukasz, who had moved to the States with his parents during the Czech uprising against Nazi occupation. On the Fourth, Tomas received a special citation from the Boston Museum of Fine Arts, and the museum announced the opening of a Lukasz exhibition in 1995, to be attended by the Czech ambassador and other dignitaries. Tomas was eloquent in connecting the events of the American and Czech revolutions and the liberating effect of freedom on his career as an artist.

The Arts Festival proceeded and the attendees commented on the unusual quality of the crafts and artwork. As with the other "Onboard Wampum" events, Wampum was definitely putting its best foot forward as a tourist destination.

Then, suddenly, the festival became the stage for a remarkable act of Providence. It would connect us to a tragic event thirty-three years earlier and to an ill-fated victim from our distant past.

During the late afternoon, thunder clouds blew in quickly and large raindrops chased us to our cars. For five minutes the Common was battered by thunder, lightning and high winds. The finale was the crash of a large tree limb onto the trunk of a car, directly in front of First Parish Church. Police officer Keith Logan, the nephew of Vietnam vet Rick Wheeler (chapter 16), was the first on the scene and became engaged in an animated discussion with the occupant of the unfortunate auto.

When I arrived with a few other would-be helpers, I noticed that the driver was Morgan Shrike, in a highly agitated state. Then we heard the cries of a young child in the back seat. Shrike was pleading that he needed to get the child, a young girl, back to her mother, his daughter. Keith was trying to calm him down, and urging that Shrike and his "granddaughter" ride with him back to the station—about a half mile away—"where we can make arrangements for a tow, and call your daughter."

Shrike became almost hysterical in his refusal to take the officer's advice, and tried to wrestle the large limb off his car. "It's the Fourth of July! There's no tow service around today! Just help me move the branch and I can make it home. The child is terrified. She just wants her mother!"

"Mr. Shrike...Your front end is caved in. There's no way you can drive this car, even if we could move the branch. And I wouldn't let you try, because you have a young child with you. Please come along with me to the station so we can work things out."

It suddenly dawned on me that Shrike didn't have a daughter, and therefore couldn't have a granddaughter. I pulled Keith aside and told him this. He put a hand on my shoulder and said calmly, "I need to get this guy to the station. If the girl isn't a family member, we'll have him in the right place."

After a tirade of abusive language from Shrike, Keith was forced to handcuff him and march him to the police cruiser, while carrying and comforting the terrified little girl. I followed them, hoping I could provide some perspective.

The girl's parents arrived shortly after us and were overjoyed to see their daughter. They had been distracted by the storm and were panicked when little "Joy" (short for Joyce) suddenly wasn't there. They assumed that Shrike was a "kind stranger" who found her and brought her to the station, and they thanked him profusely. He just nodded, smiled and said nothing. Keith took them into his office, recorded their personal information and, as they were leaving with Joy, assured them he would be in contact the next day to report on the investigation. He then ushered Shrike into his office to take a statement. After about twenty minutes the two emerged and Keith locked him in one of Wampum's two jail cells. He then thanked me for helping out, rolled his eyes and shook his head.

"He never called his wife. He called his lawyer, who told him to say nothing until he gets here tomorrow."

"What about the granddaughter story?"

"All he would say is that he wasn't feeling well, needed a good night's sleep and would explain what happened in the morning. I told him OK, but until then he'd have to remain in custody."

"I wonder how he'll explain the child safety seat in the back."

"That will be interesting...This isn't our first encounter with Mr. Shrike, but it's sure a whole different ballgame."

After leaving home, Shrike had been living in a neighboring town. His business, Shrike Global Imports, was rumored to be "on the rocks," and he had become increasingly indifferent to managing it. Sitting in the jail cell, he looked like a vagabond on the verge of a breakdown.

As it turned out, our fourth Ace was playing out an inconceivably sinister hand.

***

My dad often used the expression "to make a long story short...," and I'll try.

You may remember a reference in chapter two ("Welcome to Wampum") to the kidnapping at a local supermarket of a young girl named Jennifer Quarry, who was never found, and whose mother eventually died in a suspicious head-on collision with a tree, which was presumed to be a suicide. That incident in 1961 turned out to be one of a series of New England kidnappings that *The Boston Chronicle* labeled "The Cinderella Abductions." Little "Joy" would have been the sixty-third Cinderella if not for the tree limb crashing down on Morgan Shrike's car.

In addition to being CEO of Shrike Global Imports, Morgan Shrike was also an exporter, of young girls. He and his fellow abductors (in current parlance, "sex traffickers") snatched and sold the girls to wealthy individuals—mostly Europeans—who purchased them for $250,000 each, and used them for a variety of illicit purposes. In the few instances when inquiries were made, the abductees were described as the adopted orphans of American parents.

The *Chronicle* ended up winning multiple awards for its meticulous reporting and coverage of the "Cinderellas." Shrike was one of the masterminds of the operation. A few of his contacts from the global import business provided connections to a dark circle of disreputables. One of the two "customers" the *Chronicle* was able to interview confessed to using his abductee as a maid and eventually a sex companion before "leasing her" for 6-month periods to wealthy older men and women.

Within forty-eight hours of their abductions, the girls were transported one-by-one out of Boston on a fast boat to the Cape, and then flown from a secret landing strip to one of three European airports, where they could be smuggled out without interference. They were then delivered to their new "parents." Only six people were needed for each abduction, and five of them were paid a total of $30,000 per job, with the rest going to Chase and his cohorts.

Thirty-four years after the first abduction in 1960, the four-person, white-collar "Cinderella ring" had earned millions. Sadly, only a dozen of the sixty-two kidnapped girls were able to be found, and only a handful of those could be successfully rehabbed and reintegrated. While family members of the abductees all eventually came forward, and then prayed for good news, there were no records of where the girls had been delivered. European countries and law enforcement agencies did their best to help through a variety of communications vehicles, but fifty girls (including Jennifer Quarry) were never reunited with their families.

The trial for the kidnappers was postponed several times, and three of the kidnappers eventually "died mysteriously" while in custody, including Morgan Shrike. To those familiar with "prison justice," the only surprise was that the fourth survived. And he ended up hanging himself.

Wampum's Four Aces: two dead; one incarcerated, disgraced and abandoned; one publicly lambasted and forced to leave town. A Dantean Inferno of moral flaws. Act Five of a Shakespearean tragedy. A "fallen from grace" saga that will be long remembered, especially by those of us who were "cast members."

Now, there's one more element to the Cinderella story that I will share with you, and you can decide how much credibility to attach to it. I attach a great deal, but that's because I believe in divine intervention.

We know that a woman named Abigail Cooper (chapter two, "Welcome to Wampum"), who lived in the late 1600s, froze to death on our Common while serving a two-week sentence in the stocks. She had engaged in an adulterous relationship with the town's Congregational minister, and when she gave birth to their child she strangled it out of shame. The minister was eventually allowed to leave the community, while poor Abigail was buried in an unmarked grave.

I believe that Abigail was given a chance to redeem herself the day Morgan Shrike tried to kidnap little Joy, and that it was her act of will which dropped the limb on Shrike's car, to thwart what would have been the tragic loss of another child. If you agree, take a moment to thank Abigail for her intervention. The arts festival and the subsequent thunder storm gave Shrike a perfect opportunity for a "snatch and scram," and in another 30 seconds or less he would have been gone.

In my mind, it had to be Abigail.

***

"Onboard Wampum" marched on to smash all tourism records. Businesses had a banner year and some new tourist-oriented ventures were launched. The fourth quarter included an antique car show, the creation of a commission to inventory Wampum's historical assets and a series of ecumenical services at our town churches during Advent.

As the finale for our extraordinary bicentennial year, I decided to invite everyone involved in the planning and implementation of "Onboard Wampum" to a Midnight Run from the beach to the downtown. That shouldn't surprise you, since we've already done a Run One and Two together.

I knew that only a small number would brave the likely frigidity of New Year's Eve temperatures, so I told the others to meet us at Fits Right In, the Bernards' store, where we'd share champagne and desserts and watch the ball drop (after freezing our own off).

I ended up with twenty hearty souls, and we jogged the two miles to downtown Wampum on a remarkably balmy night in the high forties. We turned onto Penney Road, which had been mostly marshland when my parents moved to town, and was now inhabited by Boston commuters who had "bought low" and were riding high. Penney had the most eclectic mix of traditional and modern homes in town, and future purchasers would pay dearly for the close-to-the-water-back-from-the-road privacy.

My runners were also an "eclectic mix" from around town, and we shared a passionate support for "Onboard Wampum" and our pride in its way-better-than-expected success. As we trotted along, we joked about some of the funnier moments, like the new priest (Father McHugh) falling overboard during the bicentennial "blessing of the fleet." A large man, he made a big splash and bobbed up in his drenched vestments, exclaiming: "I came to bless the fleet but instead I'm baptizing it!" He was immediately embraced and adored by his parish. The Yacht Club and the Country Club had done their best to "one up" each other during their contiguous centennial celebrations. Someone suggested they should have printed a tee shirt saying "I Yacht to Stop Drinking Or I'll Miss Tee Time at the Club."

As we connected with Bayberry Road, I remembered this was the road my parents had traveled when they brought their infant Jack home from the hospital. Born in '47, here I was 47 years later celebrating a 200th town birthday with fellow Wampumeers, some of whom were descendants of early settlers. I believe there were "spirit companions" making the trip with us as well: Indians, farmers, shipbuilders, fishermen, business owners, artists and actors, Abigail Cooper—freed from guilt, Hat and my dad, Irishmen and WASPs jogging side by side, and I hope many others. It was an emotional moment. In fact, it was sort of a Bicentennial Curtain Call. The moon was watching over us, as lemony luminous as I'd ever seen him.

Before we knew it, we'd arrived at the Common, and decided to walk the final two hundred yards past our community's spiritual center. The timing was perfect. It was 11pm and we had an hour to greet the other 60 guests at Fits

Right In, most of whom were dressed in shirts which proclaimed "I survived Onboard Wampum 200!" and in smaller print, "Now please turn out the lights and take me home." There were shirts for all, and we runners wrestled into them and joined the party.

The Bernards had outdone themselves in decorating and setting up delectable dessert stations, catered by every eating establishment in town. Just before midnight, Charlie Wordsworth quieted us down for a toast.

"Folks, I think we've done about everything we could to celebrate the amazing heritage of this community. I'm so proud of everyone who got Onboard our bicentennial and sailed it to success. Let's raise our glasses to Wampum, for 200 years of proud history and another 200 of great accomplishments ahead."

And we all replied, "To Wampum!"

Then it was a New Year, and we began our third century.

Chapter 24
A Renegade WASP Looks Back (2018)

"See that big buoy ova theyuh?"

In 1995, a year after the Wampum 200th, Freddy Fernandes invited me to go flounder fishing on a late spring day, and I was happy to accept. I introduced you to Freddy in chapter 9, when he took Holly and me for a spin around the "hahba" and explained the basics of lobster fishing. He reappeared later at the hearing to investigate David Chase's assault on his niece Sylvia.

I wanted to thank Freddy again for organizing the lobster fishermen as volunteers during the bicentennial. They had discussed "Lobstering 101" with visitors along the Harborside Walk, and were a big hit, especially among the kids. Hundreds, maybe thousands, of photos were taken of youngsters holding big lobsters and hamming it up, while moms warned them not to get bitten by the big claws and the "lobster persons" (there were two women) promised that wouldn't happen because the claws were pegged.

I hadn't noticed the big buoy, and assumed it was just another lobster trap marker, but the colors were vivid and unlike any others in the lobster grounds.

"I got a story to tell ya about that buoy."

In fact, the buoy was the real reason we were there.

***

It's late 2018 now, I'm 71 years young, and I feel invigorated by this long walk we've had together. I hope there are moments that resonated with you and made our time together meaningful.

The actual writing has taken about three years, and has frequently been interrupted by televised sporting events, leisure reading—which I justified as research but mostly wasn't--the daily tasks of maintaining a household, physical exercise to maintain blood flow to the brain—although its impact on creativity hasn't really been established—and efforts to fight off my cat Peaches—to whom nothing is more important than food, especially my writing. And that's just my top five interruptions.

So how does the creative part happen? For me, it's like going up into the attic with a small candle: the attic being the creative cranny of my brain, and the candle being a flickering light source searching among musty artifacts for the right cardboard box. Once I find the box I try to find the right folder, and when I've done that sometimes the candle goes out. But every now and then it flares and I discover something I didn't even know was there. Then, of course, the phone rings.

But I persevered, for the sake of Holly, Benjy, Laura and Laurel (Holly's daughter) whose story needed to be told.

Laura passed away from a stroke in 2002, at the age of 80. She was living with Holly and granddaughter Laurel in Oak Park, and I believe her heart valves just finally collapsed from stress. She was one of my heroes, and I wrote in her epitaph for the *Totem* that "Wampum is the prime beneficiary of Laura Chase's love for truth and beauty. Despite the crushing loss of her son Benjy and the inescapable burden of domestic crises, her strength of character always prevailed, and inspired us." I sent Laurel a copy, along with a note telling her how much I admired her mother and grandmother.

While I still submit "emeritus columns" to the *Totem* (the thought being "let the old fart fill up some space"), I retired ("swallowed the anchor" in Yankee speak) as editor in 2014, and passed the torch to Beth Brady, an ace reporter and wonderful writer. We are now a thirty-two page paper, our readers having told us that was all they could digest given other weekly distractions. We're still located above Wheeler's Hardware, but have made it a much more staff-friendly environment. You can even bring your dog to work as long as he/she doesn't bite anyone.

I love being free from the administrative responsibilities of running the paper, like human resources, building maintenance and balancing the budget. I now have more time for reading, socializing and futile attempts at the gym to keep old age at bay.

The aging process is its own separate book. It's actually a tragicomedy, with our deteriorating bodily functions playing both roles. The ravages of disease are tragic, as are smoking, overeating and inactivity. The increasing amount of time we spend fiddling in the bathroom is comic, as are farting, belching and the application of anti-aging creams.

I'm still not married, but in 2013 met a delightful woman, Heather Scott, who manages the Wampum Music Tent and with whom I share a love of travel, tennis and the performing arts. A few years younger than I, she calls me her "aging preppie," and considers me a work in progress, especially my extensive wardrobe of fading khakis and corduroys. I'm grateful for someone who is informed and conversant on multiple issues, works hard to keep her figure, and tells me when I need a breath mint. I spend a great deal of time daydreaming, trying to remember names and wondering where I left my glasses, so it takes patience to keep me on track now that I've disconnected my "executive functioning system."

Heather has taken the Music Tent in exciting new directions, including an indoor facility for staging new plays during the winter months. She hosts a statewide one-act student playwriting festival every spring and has mentored students who've attended Yale Drama School and are working successfully in New York and regional theatres. Her network is extensive, and we're constantly heading On and Off-Broadway to see favorite actors and plays.

What, you might ask, is Renegade WASPy about all this? I've obviously settled down with a white woman of similar Scottish ancestry. Right? Actually, Heather's father Peter was a history professor who married an accomplished painter. He met her at one of her gallery exhibits, admired her talent, they had dinner and two years later were married in her native Jamaica. So their daughter Heather and I are a biracial couple. It's just the pattern of my life. I hope Olympia, my former literary mentor, is watching and smiling on some celestial Mt. Olympus.

While I wanted to introduce you to Heather, I won't be adding any additional "cast members." I want to reflect on the 47 years described in the previous twenty-three chapters, which concluded twenty-four years ago. Too much math?

I started with 10 "reflective thoughts," and then pared those down to five, so you wouldn't be muttering something like "Who do you think you are, *Socrates*, for God's sake?"

First: *"Technology is advancing much faster than we are."* Consider movies. Look at the special effects advances between the first and the latest episodes of *Star Wars*. Amazing, right? Now how about our values and attitudes? Despite the enlightened themes and messages of the films we've attended all these years, we're still killing each other with increasingly sophisticated weapons. We're destroying the environment and endangering wildlife at an alarming rate. We're increasingly incapable of differentiating between facts and propaganda. We fear diversity and have split into two camps, one of which has forgotten how, through diversity, we became the world's greatest nation. It's 2018, and politically we've actually regressed from the Nixon years. The farce is with us.

Second: *"Gravitate toward positive energy."* Positive energy people radiate warmth, congeniality, empathy, interest in you as a person and how they can help you achieve your goals. Negative energy people are pessimistic, judgmental, manipulative and self-indulgent. Positive energy people I profiled: Hat, Cap, Olympia, Ernie Gardiner, Professor Hollis, Holly and Laura Chase, Trudy Hawk, Freddy Fernandes. I'm grateful for their positive impact on my life. You know who the negative energy people are, in this book and elsewhere.

Third: *"All the world really is a stage."* And each of us in our time plays many parts...in my case: son, brother, friend, student, athlete, boyfriend, teacher, writer, editor, community member, volunteer and daydreamer. Being an English major, I not only want to be on stage; I want to write the script.

Fourth: *"#Time for women!"* Time for women to be elected. Time for women to be promoted and paid equally. Time for women to be believed when they're victims of domestic violence and sexual assault. Time for men to admit we've all been guilty of inappropriate behavior and to be public about it.

Fifth: *"In the end, it's about family and friends."* All the books we've read...All the honors we've received...All the luxuries we've acquired...It's not about them. In the end, it's about the people who will cherish our memory (<u>or not</u>) when we're gone.

***

From a family standpoint, I'm an orphan now. My mother Elizabeth died from lung disease in 1998 at age 82, and Frankie lost his battle with melanoma in 2013, at age 59. Both my parents were only children, and Frankie was my only sibling. Three deaths (including my dad), no births. With no new branches, our family tree is firewood after me. But I firmly believe the Peirces will be "recycled" to a greater purpose.

My mother's legacy to me was her love of language and instinct for how words should be grouped to create the proper rhythms, patterns and messages . "It's like a puzzle, and you can tell when the pieces fit together," she would tell me, as she urged me to try a new draft. "It doesn't always have to be subject/verb. Change it up, or it'll get monotonous." She was an annoyingly relentless editor, but eventually she began to make sense. There's an analogy with the writing of music. A sentence, like a musical stanza, can go "flat" on you, and then you have to try some variations to perk it up. She was also passionate about certain film actors and their ability to move her emotionally. That made me appreciate the power of certain people—and not always people I like—to command an audience and influence opinions.

While we do live many parts in our lifetime, Frankie was forced by mental illness to continually replay the part of the outcast—the one left standing without a chair when the music stopped . He couldn't hold a job. He couldn't drive a car. And yet he managed to struggle along, living a Spartan existence in public housing, supported by a pension he received as the son of a veteran. To me, it was a wretched existence. To Frankie, it was proof he could tough it out on his own. He had a psychiatric social worker who checked on him periodically, and I thank God for her and her devoted care. Among other things, she made sure he took his medicine, without which he was a menace to society and himself. He enjoyed my taking him to dinner, because his menu was depressingly bland, but I always remained part of the Peirce power structure that was over- regimenting his life.

Frankie's melanoma was almost inevitable. He was fair-complected, never used sunscreen and the sun's UV rays followed him everywhere. The cancer was first diagnosed in his groin area, reappeared a year later in his left shoulder (causing the amputation of his left arm), moved insidiously to his right arm and dared the doctors to keep him alive. Since there were no more treatment options, Frankie was moved to hospice care. A small support group of Frankie's former classmates, who had chauffeured him to class reunions and events, helped keep a vigil during his last few months.

I dreaded the funeral because I felt the town had long ago passed judgment on Frankie as a belligerent malcontent. Certainly there would be no more than a few reluctant attendees. So I was deeply moved by the many visitors who came to express their regrets at Frankie's passing, and even more, their admiration for his courage and perseverance. One woman I had never met marveled at how "he'd come striding by our house every day at the same time. At first our dog barked at him, but eventually he would wait for him with his tail wagging." Several of our old neighbors stopped by to share fond memories of Frankie and his outdoor adventures.

The core group of Frankie's "guardian angels" were a revelation. One former classmate asked her children to make lunch for him every year "so they would learn the importance of treating special needs people with kindness." His classmate Paul bought Frankie a sports coat before a reunion (I never

223

knew) and presented him with a new pair of sneakers from the class "to get you around the community for the next thousand miles."

At the time, I thought, "This is what being a Christian is really about," but of course it's about "living your faith or humanity," no matter where, or if, you go to church.

Rest in peace, Frankie. I know you're surrounded by love, wherever you walk.

And my dad can rest in peace for another reason: No more "Wait 'til next year." The Red Sox finally won the World Series, on October 27, 2004. They had one-and-three-quarters feet in the grave during the playoffs before climbing out, beating the Yankees' great reliever Mariano Rivera in game 4 of the ALCS, winning another three straight (never done before) and sweeping their Series nemesis St. Louis Cardinals to win Boston's first championship since 1918, when my dad was three, and oblivious. I visited his grave and clinked a glass of champagne on his tombstone to celebrate the return of the Holy Grail after 86 years, and the exorcism of the Curse of the Babe.

I mentioned that Laura Chase passed away in 2002. Ten years later (April, 2012) I received a note and obituary notice from her Chicago friend Eleanor Mitchell, whom Laura had asked to contact me if Holly needed emergency help or support. I tried unsuccessfully to stay in touch with Holly after Laura's funeral, and finally decided to "leave the ball in her court" about ongoing communications.

The following is Eleanor's note, part of which I know Laura had drafted for her:

Dear Mr. Peirce,

I'm very sorry to tell you that Holly Chase passed away from liver disease on April 20th. As per her wishes, there was no burial service and her friend Lindsay scattered her ashes in Lake Michigan.

Laurel's father Ryan is supervising the distribution of Holly's estate.

Holly wanted you to know how much she treasured your friendship and how proud she was of your successes as editor of the Wampum newspaper. She regrets that her deteriorating health prevented her from keeping in touch with friends like you.

I'm terribly sorry to share this sad news with you.

With deep regrets,

Eleanor Mitchell

I have had six years to recover from that note, but it still causes a wave of nausea.

Both Eleanor and Laurel were generous in sharing the details of Holly's last years. She contracted a genetic liver disease called hemochromatosis, caused by mutated genes passed along by both parents. Laura didn't know this before she passed, but I'm sure would have found it further proof her marriage was cursed.

The "hemo" usually isn't fatal, but in Holly's case was protracted and lethal. It gets more serious for a woman after menopause, and is greatly aggravated by alcohol abuse—an addiction Holly continually battled, and lost. Her medical team were "all in" to save her life, but the disease would not be repelled. Iron overload led to cirrhosis, then to liver cancer, congestive heart failure and a deathly gray skin pallor. Holly didn't want me or anyone else to witness her decline from a healthy, attractive woman to a human cadaver.

The more I thought about this grim final act, the more it seemed fated to happen. Holly and Chase were joined in a lethal embrace. Chase passed a deadly gene to his daughter, eliminated her brother, tormented her mother, banished her boyfriend, and humiliated her family. Then, instead of suffering his just desserts, he died in a hospital bed. His daughter was left with agonizing memories and no chance for retribution.

In the days and weeks that followed, I kept wondering how I might have prevented Holly's tragic death.

There must have been a point at which I could have asserted myself and resisted Chase's autocratic plans. Something like the last scene of *The Graduate*, when the Dustin Hoffman character rescues his girlfriend from a certain-to-fail marriage blessed by her parents.

Where was the "Renegade WASP" when Holly needed me...to help investigate the crime of Benjy's death, to join her in Chicago and begin a new life, to be a supportive partner if she began to lean on the bottle. Her death by cancer wasn't inevitable; it was a worst case scenario. It was preventable.

And then I'd temporarily console myself. I didn't have the money back then. Didn't have a career track record. Didn't know a soul in the Chicago area. We would have floundered, and our relationship would have gone to hell. Chase would have cut off financial support to Holly, and if necessary, Laura. It wouldn't have been a Hollywood ending; it would have been a real life *Titanic*.

I finally had to take sedatives to release me from the prison of my thoughts. As I drifted off one night, a memory popped into my mind: Freddy Fernandes. The buoy.

***

It's the morning of New Year's Day, 2018, and I'm once again at Wampum Beach, looking through my binoculars. I come every year since my fishing trip with Freddy Fernandes, back in 1995. It puts my life in perspective.

Thankfully, the buoy is still there, nodding gently on this calm day. I remember once again how overwhelmed I was by the story Freddy told me. He's gone now, but wherever he sleeps, he sleeps with a smile.

One last look at the buoy's bright blue and orange--Benjy's colors of choice. A grave reminder.

Then I trudge back through the sand to my car, ready to begin another year, but never to forget the past.

***

My Five Favorite *Renegade WASP* Columns

(*Renegade WASP* selection 1, published in February, 2016)
Black Lives Matter, and Black Fathers Too

In the wake of a racial crisis in America, black and white political leaders often decry the absence of "candid racial dialogue."

President Obama has encouraged such an exchange, in an effort to bridge the racial divide and promote an honest exchange of opinions on race-related issues. If this is happening, I'm not subscribing to the journal that's publishing the results.

For the record, I'm a two-time Obama voter who grew up in a white conservative Republican household. I've attended black churches, served on a UNCF board and mentored a black student, but I'm not pretending to be a civil rights champion. I just want to participate in the "candid racial dialogue" that we're being urged to engage in. So here goes...

Do Black Lives Matter? Absolutely. Positively. Emphatically. And when deadly force is used against presumed perpetrators who are unarmed, we need to insist that the results are investigated thoroughly and impartially. It's happening far too often, and the victims are almost exclusively people of color. We should be deeply disturbed by this, and should voice our concerns to law enforcement officials and our legislators through all the tools available, including public protest.

The "Black Lives Matter" movement is calling us out, and rightly so. We fought this fight in the Sixties and Seventies. We should be way beyond it now. Law enforcement must filter out potential "bad cops with bad attitudes" and the justice system should at all levels prosecute acts of violence and discrimination, especially when police appear to be violating civil rights.

So here's my "candid racial comment": Other than its absolutely essential role in protesting the many civil rights abuses, the African American community needs to talk about what it can do, and is doing, to keep black fathers at home with their children.

Every study I have read confirms the critical role the father plays in a child's development. Two-parent homes are a major factor in determining if a low-income child can break out of the cycle of poverty and disadvantage. Children who grow up without a father score lower on IQ tests; get held back a grade in school; and are more likely to suffer physical and mental health impairment and drug addiction. This, in turn, has dire consequences for employment and economic mobility. The data is all there; check it out.

Today, about 70% of black children are born out of wedlock. If the mother is a teenager, she has only a 50% chance of earning a high school diploma by age 22, compared with nearly 90% for non-teen moms. If you finish high school, get a job and get married before having children, statistics say you have a 98% chance of breaking out of poverty.

In weeks to come, I'll report on efforts by the African American community to break the poverty cycle, like "My Brother's Keeper," which through mentoring is helping young men of color make better choices.

My challenge to black fathers is to step up and parent your children. Provide the love and personal support that will probably be the most important influence in their lives. Reject the old "One Mother, One Parent" household model and create a new Father/Mother Partnership where every family member has a better chance for growth and opportunity.

Black fathers: <u>You matter</u>. Big time.

We Can't Afford Financial Illiteracy

I keep reading about how we Americans haven't saved enough money for retirement, and so will need to keep working until we collapse.

As you might expect, the retirement savings gap between minorities and whites is considerable, fueling our other fiscal concern: income inequality. In 2013, 3 of 4 African American and 4 of 5 Latino working-age households had less than $10,000 in retirement savings, according to the National Institute on Retirement Security (Rana Foroohar in *Time*: 5/18/15). Half of comparable white households had at least $10,000, but any amount less than six figures is insufficient given longer life spans.

Data too old? I'll bet you my next Social Security payment that those numbers haven't improved in the last five years. We've gone from the mortgage crisis (where lenders got bailed out and minority homeowners got busted) to stagnant or falling wages caused by a decline in consumer demand (which is 70% of the US economy). I keep a thick file of articles related to financial literacy, and the same savings horror stories keep resurfacing like the awful sequels to slasher movies.

Another article (Adam Shell in *USA Today*: 4/19/18) discussed the reasons why even financially stable Americans delay important financial decisions such as saving for retirement. Apparently, only 35% of us feel comfortable planning for retirement, and I'd argue some of them are kidding themselves. Only 23% said they're equipped to make a new investment and a similar 22% are concerned they lack the knowledge to make a change to their investments.

Every bad news financial article includes a solution or two for solving the problem, such as seeking a financial advisor, consulting the internet and developing a financial plan. Good suggestions, but by the time we adults implement them many of the horses and dollars have escaped through the barn door.

I agree with *USA Today*'s Pete the Planner (4/22/18), who advises/warns us: "You have 45 years to figure out your financial life, but you can do most of the dirty work on Day 1. That's because to understand money is to understand time. If you understand time, then your financial life will be relatively smooth."

The time value of money was a core concept of a 10-unit financial literacy program called *Money$mart*, sponsored by Meridian Bancorp and developed by the Pennsylvania Council on Economic Education. Students learned how to write a check, balance a checkbook, develop a financial plan, understand payroll deductions and make informed financial decisions.

I reviewed the materials and remember one example of "the magic of compounding," which showed the difference between investing $100 a month at a 9% annual rate, starting at age 25 (over $500,000 after 41 years) and investing the same amount at the same rate starting at age 55 ($19,566 after 11 years). That's what happens when you start investing for retirement too late.

The years between ages 21 and 35, when earnings haven't yet peaked, are the wealth-building years. In no other period do savings have as much potential for growth. But because few young people give any serious thought to financial planning, they fail to capitalize on this opportunity.

So here's my suggestion: **Make financial literacy part of the school curriculum.**

Download some of the excellent online financial literacy materials. Give students from all socioeconomic levels the knowledge they need to grow up "money smart" and add a few zeros to their nest eggs. It's an investment we can't afford not to make.

(*Renegade WASP* selection 3, published in November, 2017)

Second Amendment Wrongs

Here's the Second Amendment to the Constitution in its entirety: "A well regulated Militia, being necessary to the security of a free State, the right of the people to keep and bear Arms, shall not be infringed."

According to former Supreme Court justice John Paul Stevens, federal judges uniformly understood for over 200 years that the amendment "applied only to keeping and bearing arms for military purposes" and "while it limited the power of the federal government, it did not impose any limit whatsoever on the power of states or local governments to regulate the use or ownership of firearms."

In 2008, a conservative Supreme Court, by a 5 to 4 vote, ruled in Heller v. District of Columbia that the Second Amendment protects a civilian's right to keep a handgun in his home for purposes of self defense. The majority opinion was written by Justice Antonin Scalia. Two years later, in another 5-4 vote, the Court decided in McDonald v. Chicago that the Due Process Clause of the 14th Amendment limited the power of Chicago to outlaw the possession of handguns by private citizens, and it affirmed the right of individuals in every state to keep and bear arms.

Following another Court ruling in 2016, Caetano v. Massachusetts, the Second Amendment now extends "to all forms of bearable arms." That means Adam Lanza's mother (27 dead at Sandy Hook Elementary), Omar Mateen (killed 49 in an Orlando nightclub), Stephen Paddock (killed 58 at a Las Vegas outdoor concert) and all future mass murderers are/were within their rights to own guns of mass destruction. It's why, according to *USA Today*, "we lead the world in gun-related homicides at a rate 4 to 16 times higher than any other advanced nation." *Pediatrics* magazine reported in 2014 that "Almost one child or teen an hour is injured by a firearm seriously enough to require hospitalization...and 6% result in death."

Words like "unthinkable" and "unspeakable" are uttered after gun violence tragedies. I would apply these words to the legislators who "cave" to political backlash from the NRA and an extremist minority of their electorate. It's cowardly.

I agree with William Vizzard, a former ATF official and now a criminal justice professor, when he describes the NRA as "a populist lobby. They're not interested in fixing things. They want to stir things up, and the more they stir things up, the more members they get and the more money they make."

As for the gun extremists, I urge you to read Jill Filipovic's essay "It's Always Men" in the "After The Massacre" article in *Time* (10/16/17 issue) about the Las Vegas murders. She describes a group of American gun "super owners... who make up just 3% of the adult population but own an average of 17 guns apiece...a subculture of mostly white, mostly male, mostly conservative gun obsessives." She concludes: "It is undeniable that more guns mean more gun deaths. But we choose to let this ecosystem thrive, while we bleed out."

Justice Douglas, in his book *Six Amendments*, argues that "public policies concerning gun control should be decided by the voters' elected representatives, not by federal judges." *USA Today* mentions two state gun initiatives in its editorial "Don't wait for Congress to act on gun control." Massachusetts requires an ID card to purchase rifles or shotguns, and a license to buy handguns (including private sales). Applicants pay a $100 fee, are photographed, fingerprinted and interviewed, and must take a gun safety course. Delaware passed a "red flag" law which allows families to obtain a temporary court order to seize the firearm of a relative who may be dangerous or suicidal, until the crisis passes.

I think it's time for some political leaders to step up and be JFK's "Profiles in Courage" on the gun violence issue. Hopefully before another "unthinkable" (but preventable) mass murder. Send me your thoughts.

(*Renegade WASP* selection 4, published in December, 2013)
I Am Your Polar Bear, On Thin Ice

I am a polar bear and I need your help.

I live in the Arctic north, and our home—our habitat—has been changing in a way that is dangerous to all of us. Every year there is less ice.

Less ice means I can't walk as far out as before to find food, and must swim the rest of the way, which is very tiring. I can lose 20% of my body fat on one long swim.

Less ice also means I have trouble building a maternity den for my baby cub.

I usually give birth to two cubs, but this year only one, and he is underweight.

My cub and I need seal meat, because it is rich in blubber, and important for our diet. I wait for hours at seal breathing holes to catch them when they come up for air.

Only about 2% of my hunts are successful.

If I can't catch a seal, I need to search for other food, like small mammals or bird eggs. If I can't find enough food on land my cub and I must eat seaweed or human garbage.

Something else is different. The water has become dirtier because of pollution. There are oil spills, which damage my hair. Without enough hair to keep me warm, I can die from hypothermia.

The pollution also poisons the food I eat and feed my cub.

I want you to understand…It is a wonderful thing to be a polar bear. I love my cubs and teaching them to hunt. We are the largest marine mammals and we fear no natural enemies.

But we fear our new enemies: climate change and pollution.

If the ice keeps melting, we may lose half our population, or worse.

When the sea ice melts early, we must go ashore and wait until it freezes before we can hunt again. We must fast during that time, and our fasts are becoming longer, from 4 months to 6 months.

When it is time to hunt again, my body is weaker and I am not able to hunt as well.

I am your polar bear, and I need your help to survive.

We are not the happy cartoon characters you see drinking Coca Cola in the cartoon. We are on very thin ice, and only you can save us.

Please be our voice. We need you to speak on our behalf.

(*The World Wildlife Federation* and *The National Wildlife Federation* have polar bear adoption sites, and will welcome your contribution and active engagement. Please help preserve the habitat, and the continued existence, of these magnificent animals.)

(*Renegade WASP* selection 5, published in March, 1990)

My Grandmother Hat's Advice:
Prepare For Your Afterlife

This is a tribute to my grandmother Hat, who passed away at age 90 last month and was the most impactful of all the role models in my life.

Just before she died, Hat whispered to me that we would meet again someday and continue the good-humored exchanges we enjoyed for our forty-plus years together. This includes her final self-deprecating remark: "When you see me, please try not to scream. I'll be the ugliest ghost in the room."

My mother, father and I would often ask Hat where she kept her Funny Pills. She had the most creative and engaging sense of humor of anyone we knew, and when it wasn't self-deprecating it was either directed at one of us or at a community "celebrity" who, in Hat's opinion "deserves a statue so the pigeons can poop on it."

I could fill pages more with what we called "Hatechisms," but today I'm remembering a more private passion of Hat's. Hat not only believed with great certainty in life after death, but often shared very specific details about the afterlife she anticipated. Shakespeare called death the "undiscovered country," but Hat seemed to have most of it mapped out.

"Jackie (her name for me until I left for college), I don't understand why people are afraid of death. It's just the next step; it's not the final curtain. Nobody even talks about death. It's more secretive than sex or your life savings." I remember my mother's embarrassment when Hat asked our minister about his view on the afterlife. When he told her she was too young to think about it, she replied "Heck no. I'm looking forward to it. I've even asked God for my favorite furniture and drapes."

There was a Victorian side to Hat's view of the afterlife as a reward for a life well lived. But there was something much more to it than a well-appointed room in God's mansion. There was some Protestant Work Ethic, too. She wanted another chance to be of service—to contribute her knowledge and skills to a Divine Cause that would fully engage her and all of us afterlifers. Emphasis on *all*. No one gets left behind in the dumpster. You and a few others, together with a spiritual advisor, examine your lives, share insights and eventually are recycled to a new dimension, where your positive energies can be invested. Her afterlife was/is equal opportunity. No extra credit for Christians, or others of a "higher faith."

This led to a lot of questions on my part, being a teenager:

No Hell? "No hell. If you were a monster, you spend more time purging your negative energies."

What do you look like? "You look like yourself on your best day."

Are you reunited with family members? "Yes, eventually. But not right away."

Hat and I had some great discussions about life after death. My parents were tolerant because Hat was holding the family together during a very tough time. But my dad was a "by the Book (St. James version)" guy and my mother felt we should each reach our own conclusions.

Looking back, what I admire is that Hat created her very own metaphor for life after death, regardless of how the real experience turns out. And she got me thinking about death as a passage, not a tombstone. She wanted me to look at life as the first stage in an ongoing process of positive activity.

If Hat's metaphor holds up, I hope you get her as a spiritual advisor. You will have a wonderful, empathetic companion and you'll laugh your ass off, if you have one.

About the author

Jeff Gordon graduated from Trinity College, CT (BA, English) and The University of North Carolina at Chapel Hill (MA, English). During his career he was a high school English teacher, Director of Education and Community Services for the Hartford Stage Company, and a communications and corporate relations officer for two Fortune 100 companies (Wachovia Bank and Exelon Energy). *Renegade WASP* is his first work of fiction.

Author's Afterword

It wouldn't be difficult to determine the real identity of my fictional hometown of Wampum. There are numerous references to well-known locations, especially for those who have driven through on a summer or fall day, looking for a lobster roll or a stunning view of the ocean.

My hometown was and still is a wonderful place to grow up. As noted throughout the narrative, it has a remarkable history and a distinguished citizenry, and is considered one of Massachusetts' most charming locales. Every word written in its praise is richly deserved.

I am especially grateful to Jacqueline Dormitzer for her detailed account of the town's history from 1950 to 2000, which served as the framework for the fact-based parts of the narrative. I include her information about the eight brave young soldiers who were casualties of the Vietnam War because their story is an essential part of the fabric of our community. Only their last names are changed.

Otherwise, Renegade WASP is a work of fiction. Wampum is meant to be a seacoast village southeast of Boston, featuring fictional people doing fictional things not unlike the things real people do.

I encourage readers to share your thoughts about the book (my first) with me at author.jeffgordon@gmail.com. Your comments will help guide my future efforts.

Renegade WASP Bibliography and References

Baltzell, E. Digby. **The Protestant Establishment: Aristocracy and Caste in America**. New York: Random House, 1964.

Bigelow, E. Victor. **A Narrative History of the Town of Cohasset, Massachusetts**. Cohasset, Massachusetts: Committee on Town History, 1898

Dormitzer, Jacqueline M. **A Narrative History of the Town of Cohasset, Massachusetts, Volume III.** Published by the Town of Cohasset, Massachusetts, 2002.

Wadsworth, David H., Morse, Paula and DeGiacomo, Lynne. **Images of America: Cohasset.** Great Britain: Arcadia Publishing, 2004.

Bartlett, John and O'Brien, Geoffrey eds. **Bartlett's Familiar Quotations.** New York: Little, Brown and Company, 2012.

Hendrickson, Robert. **Yankee Talk: A Dictionary of New England Expressions.** New York: Facts on File, 1996.

. . . .

Prologue: The final line is the first line of T.S. Eliot's poem *"The Love Song of J. Alfred Prufrock."*

Chapter 6: (p. 27) The song lyrics are from "Wonderful World" by Sam Cooke, Lou Adler and Herb Alpert.

Chapter 8: (p. 36) The street name "Rabbit Run" is the title of a John Updike novel.

Chapter 15: (p.73) The lyrics "Where have all the soldiers gone?" are inspired by Pete Seeger's "Where Have All the Flowers Gone?."

Chapter 16: The Wampum Vietnam war casualties are reported on pp.134-139 in Jacqueline Dormitzer's *History of Cohasset* volume 3, cited above. Only the names are changed.

Chapter 17: (p. 83) The quote is from John Updike's *Couples* (New York, Alfred A. Knopf, 1968) p.83.

Chapter 20: (p. 103) The quote is from Robert Frost's poem "The Road Not Taken."

Chapter 22: (pp. 111-112) The accomplishments attributed to "Cap" Campbell were those of my "real life" neighbor Captain Ellery Clark, "Mr. Red Sox" and a truly extraordinary individual and mentor.

Renegade WASP essay 1: Sources are "Baltimore's riots are a reflection of family disintegration" by Francis Barry in the *Wilmington News Journal* (5/9/15) and "Parent engagement matters most for student success" by Yvonne Johnson and Chandra Pitts in the *Wilmington News Journal* (12/19/15).

Renegade WASP essay 2: Sources are "America's Broken Ladder" by Rana Foroohar in *Time* (5/18/15), "Having right mind set can boost your finances" by Adam Shell in *USA Today* (4/19/18) and "Early discipline can lead to long-term financial success" by Peter Dunn in *USA Today* (4/22/18).

Renegade WASP essay 3: Sources are John P. Stevens *Six Amendments* (New York: Little Brown and Company, 2014), "After The Massacre" by Elliott, Sweetland, Edwards and Alter in *Time* (10/16/17), "It's Always Men" by Jill Filipovic in *Time* (10/16/17), "From marksmanship group into mighty gun lobby" by Achenbach, Higham and Horwitz in *The Washington Post* (1/13/13) and "20 young people a day go to hospital for gun injuries" by Michelle Healy in *USA Today* (1/27/14).

Renegade WASP essay 4: Sources are World Wildlife Federation and National Wildlife Federation websites about polar bears.

Sincerest thanks to Bill Oliva for his rigorous proofreading.